MW01241705

DESPERATE REFLECTIONS

FURY FALLS INN · BOOK 3

BETTY BOLTÉ

This is a work of fiction. Names, characters, places, and incidents are a product of the author's imagination. Locales and public names are sometimes used for atmospheric purposes. Any resemblance to actual people, living or dead, or to businesses, companies, events, institutions, or locales is completely coincidental.

www.MysticOwlPublishing.com

Copyright © 2021 by Betty Bolté
www.bettybolte.com
Digital ISBN: 978-1-7354669-2-7
Paperback ISBN: 978-1-7354669-3-4

Also by Betty Bolté

Becoming Lady Washington: A Novel
Notes of Love and War

FURY FALLS INN
The Haunting of Fury Falls Inn
Under Lock and Key
Desperate Reflections

SECRETS OF ROSEVILLE
Undying Love
Haunted Melody
The Touchstone of Raven Hollow
Veiled Visions of Love
Charmed Against All Odds

A MORE PERFECT UNION
Elizabeth's Hope
Emily's Vow
Amy's Choice
Samantha's Secret
Evelyn's Promise

*Dedicated in loving memory to fellow author,
chapter mate, critique partner, and dear friend,
Anne Parent*

Dear Reader,

This story continues the series of six supernatural historical fiction stories set in 1821 northern Alabama. With each of these, I fully expect I'll discover more about the history of this state I call home.

I'd like to thank my beta readers—Sue, Alicia, Danielle, and Chris—who read a prepublication version of *Desperate Reflections* and provided invaluable feedback. I appreciate your time, observations, and suggestions for improving the story!

I'd also like to thank readers like you who continue to inspire me to write stories with joy and passion. I always enjoy hearing from my readers, so please drop me a line at betty@bettybolte.com any time.

If you enjoy this book, please subscribe to my newsletter via www.bettybolte.com to be informed of the release of the rest of the books in the series. You can also learn more about me, my other books, and read excerpts of each book at my website. You may also enjoy learning more about the behind the scenes research and recipes included in this story at www.bettybolte.net.

Again, thanks for reading! I hope you enjoy *Desperate Reflections*.

Betty

Chapter One

Northern Alabama, August 1821

*T*he time had come for a change. If they were meant to impress, then they would need to improve more than the furniture of the inn.

Cassie Fairhope paused at the doorway to the noisy dining room, quickly scanning the twenty cloth-covered tables, each surrounded by low-backed wooden chairs. Many of the chairs were occupied by working and business men, a tankard or mug in hand as they gestured while they conversed. Each table featured a candlestick and a small vase of flowers from her garden behind the inn. An immense fireplace centered on the left wall with vases of wilting flowers on the mantel. Ones she'd need to replace soon. The square piano she used to entertain guests graced the front corner, its fine wood workmanship evident in its gloss and detailing. Her fingers itched to dance over the ivories and sing some songs but she had more urgent business at the moment. She glanced to the right where the huge carved wood bar claimed dominance and a loving smile eased onto her lips at the scene before her.

Flint Hamilton rubbed a red rag over the new mahogany counter, his muscles flexing beneath the white sleeves of his dress shirt. His tan vest and black string tie made him look competent as well. As always, he was clean shaven and neatly turned out. He made a fine innkeeper for the Fury Falls Inn and an even finer suitor. Especially when he aimed smiling green eyes her way.

Despite her initial surprise at his presence a month ago, she now recognized her father's sound judgement in hiring him to take care of the place during his absence. Her ma had never forgiven Pa for leaving on an extended trip to Savannah to obtain new furniture for the inn while she and Cassie were in Nashville shopping for dresses and hats and other irrelevant bits and baubles. Leaving Flint in charge instead of Mercy. Since her ma's murder and subsequent haunting of the inn, Cassie doubted she'd ever forgive him. But then, Cassie doubted she'd ever forgive herself for her role in her mother's death either.

Cassie's heart lifted as Flint continued smiling at her, drawing her to him with a wink. She hurried toward him, forming her arguments as she stopped to rest her hands on the edge of the gleaming bar.

"Flint, I have an idea." She tapped a finger on the bar. "About our serving attire."

He carefully folded the towel and set it aside. "Such as?"

"A cleaner and more flattering appearance." A clank drew Cassie's attention to the door. Mandy Crawford hurried into the room carrying a tray loaded down with steaming plates. Mandy's plain gray dress and rumpled white apron appeared as bad as Cassie's own. Indeed, the petite woman needed some color about her instead of wearing gray with her brown hair. She turned back to Flint. "What if I were to make Mandy and I some new matching outfits?"

"Is that necessary?" He stopped polishing the shiny surface. "Really?"

"Don't you want to make a grand impression on Senator Graham when he comes in a couple of months?"

"Of course." Flint pressed his palms onto the bar. "That's why I replaced the scarred pine wood with this mahogany top."

"Well, so do I. For my pa's sake and yours. He's coming all the way here because he's heard of the benefits of the hot mineral springs. He'll discover we offer much more than just the springs like so many others already have. Which is why people come here so frequently and repeatedly. But wearing these old rags won't impress anyone." She motioned to her dress with a grimace on her face. A tear split the cuff of her blouse. The dark green skirt had faded to lime in places and the hem was beginning to fray. "All I need is the material and to purchase some dressy collars and cuffs and buttons. I'm sure we could find what I need in Huntsville."

Mandy strode over, tapping the empty tray against her leg as she halted. "What do you need in town?"

Flint picked up the towel, draping it over his arm. "Cassie wants to make you both some uniforms to wear while serving. What do you think?"

Cassie peered at the other woman, noting her brown hair pulled into a loose bun on top of her head. She wasn't a beauty by any means but she was pretty and her quiet demeanor and simple goodness shone from light brown eyes. Perhaps a dark blue skirt and white blouse would best emphasize her features.

"I don't know why it's necessary." Mandy rested the tray against her leg. "Am I not dressed decently enough for you?"

Guilt swept through Cassie when she sensed the unease emanating from the other waitress. "It's more that I think it's important to present a neat and clean appearance for our guests." She hadn't intended to hurt the other woman's feelings by suggesting anything amiss but the other woman didn't know that. "It's not anything you've done wrong, I promise."

Mandy pursed her lips for a brief moment. "Fine with me. Can you manage or do you need help with making whatever you're making?"

"I'd welcome your assistance if you'd like." Mandy didn't linger after her shift ended, instead immediately heading for wherever she lived. "I won't have time to work on them until after the evening rush, though. Do you mind staying?"

"I'd prefer to go home before it gets dark." Mandy shrugged and hefted the tray, preparing to go back to the kitchen. "But if you need help, I can do so once in a while."

"Then thank you. Perhaps you'd consider staying overnight when you do. You can share with me."

"Sounds like a fine idea." Mandy tapped the tray against her leg again. "Right now, I've got to get fresh linens for the tables."

"Go on, then." She gave Mandy a brief hug and then addressed Flint. "When might we go into town for supplies?"

The sooner she could begin the better she'd like it. She had become self-conscious of her attire and longed to freshen her wardrobe. At least when serving meals and drinks in the dining room. Or when she entertained the guests at the square piano.

Flint opened his mouth to reply and then glanced at the doorway. Cassie followed his astonished gaze. A young man sporting sideburns and slicked hair hesitated in the door, dressed in the most elaborate outfit she'd ever seen. Obviously he'd hired a tailor to make the bright blue frock coat with wide collars. His light-colored trousers included straps that wrapped under his square-toed shoes. He held a tall silk top hat in one hand and a saddle bag in the other as he paced toward them.

Flint reacted first. He crossed the room to greet the stranger. "Welcome to the Fury Falls Inn, sir. How may I be of service?"

"I have come on business." The stranger stopped, glancing around the room and then meeting Flint's carefully arranged countenance.

Mandy smiled shyly at him as she hurried out of the dining room to finish preparing for the next rush of customers. He didn't appear to notice her, continuing to regard Flint with cold disdain.

Flint shrugged and shook his head. "I'm sorry, sir, but I'm not interested in whatever you're selling today."

"You think I'm selling something?" The man pressed his lips together for a moment, annoyance simmering in his eyes. "I'm here on personal business, not sales."

Cassie joined Flint as he addressed the tall stranger. Or was he? His piercing blue-eyed gaze met hers and she blinked. Those eyes seemed very familiar. Tall and broad-shouldered he reminded her of her oldest brother, Giles, in the way he carried himself. He had the same dark hair, too. Then she noticed a thin jagged scar on his strong chin and she squealed with delight.

Flint startled and twisted around. "Cassie?"

She didn't blame him for being confused by her reaction. A wave of joy crashed through her as she smiled at her brother's quizzical expression. He didn't recognize her. She could see it in his wary expression. She'd fix that right away.

"Abram!" Cassie ran to her brother and threw her arms around him, uncaring she might rumple his dandified self. "You came."

He dropped the bag and then gripped her waist with one hand to brace against her impact. "Cassandra, I presume?"

She gave him one last squeeze and then stepped back. "It's been too long. I'm glad you're finally here."

"I am very pleased to see you looking so fine." He

glanced around the room and then back to her. "Not that I will remain in this god-forsaken part of the country, of course."

"Oh, but you must." He acted so pompous and distant she almost didn't recognize the carefree, laughing brother she once played games with. He had to be inside this haughty creature somewhere. "Wait until I tell you what Ma has finally revealed about our family."

Abram stiffened, pulling his shoulders back and lifting his chin to look down his nose at her. "I shall only be here long enough to pay my respects to her grave and then I must return to my employment with Senator Alexander Thompson. He can only spare my efforts for a brief time."

Her brother's attitude irked her but she strove to hide her irritation behind a smile. He'd journeyed all the way from the Territory of Columbia to treat her like she was a pesky child. He had much to learn about her and the rest of the family, but she'd just start with his specific request and see what happened next. "Then I guess you want to follow me out back to where she's buried."

Flint hung the towel on a rail. "I think I shall tag along. You never know who you might find out back."

Abram lifted a brow at Flint's remark. "And you are?"

"My apologies. I should have introduced myself. I'm Flint Hamilton, the interim innkeeper while your father is away on business."

"And he's my beau." Cassie wrapped an arm around Flint's waist.

"I see." Abram tapped his top hat into place. "Shall we go?"

"Do you want me to find Giles?" The surprise flashing in her brother's eyes made her smile. "I know he's been looking forward to seeing you."

"How is my older brother?" Abram glanced around the room as if afraid Giles might pop out and grab him.

"Doing just fine." Cassie took hold of Abram's arm to draw his gaze. "Since you want to see Ma's grave and pay your respects, let's go before I have to get back to work. Ready?"

"I am as prepared for the event as I can ever be." Abram tapped his hat again as his Adam's apple slid up then down. He kicked his bag behind the bar and nodded once. "Lead the way."

The sight greeting Abram as his sister pushed through the door onto a covered porch made him sniff with disdain. The structure, a large dog trot house with two separate buildings connected by a covered passage, must have been built by farm hands since it appeared roughly slapped together to his trained eye. True, the brick and stone structure looked solid and sturdy, but the floor boards of the covered passage were not snugged together properly. Then when she led him through and down the wooden steps into the backyard he barely restrained a weary sigh at the row of clapboard outbuildings. He'd never resided in such a mediocre hostelry. Not since finally achieving his goal of working for the national government.

He heard Flint close the door to the inn, followed by his heavy footsteps as he hurried to catch up to them as they neared the one place he knew he must go but did not want to. He'd only made the trip to satisfy a duty not a desire. After his parents sent him and his brothers away to fend for themselves, he harbored no love toward either of them. Only his sister, if he was being honest. She was the only one who held sway over him.

"The family cemetery is over this way, Abram." Cassie sauntered beside him, obviously in no hurry to cross the grassy expanse toward the picket fenced area.

"We put in the marker a few days ago," Flint said as he fell into step with Cassie's leisurely pace.

"A decidedly appropriate and respectful touch." Abram would rather be anywhere but strolling through the grass toward his mother's grave, so he didn't rush either. "You never said how she died."

Cassie glanced at him and then away. "She was shot in the head in her bedroom."

"What? Why?" Shock ripped through him at his mother's violent death. He had no idea she'd been killed. Thinking instead she'd had some accident or illness. He swallowed the bile rising at the grisly image forming in his mind.

She pulled him to a halt. "Some men thought she was hiding a treasure in her room."

"Cassie, don't." Flint took her free hand and interlocked his fingers with hers. "I'll say it again. It's not your fault."

"What exactly is not your fault?" Abram peered at her as she chewed her lower lip for a second. She'd grown into a beautiful young woman, but her guilt shaded her features. Dimming the light in her eyes and flattening the lines of her mouth.

"I let it slip in the dining room that I'd been helping Ma with her treasures." She met his surprised gaze with tearful eyes. "It's what she called her trinkets and memorabilia."

"But you didn't pull that trigger, so stop beating yourself up about it." Flint tugged her around to face him.

Abram stood silently, giving himself a moment to consider what she'd said. What she blamed herself for.

"I know in my head I didn't kill her but my heart still mourns for her." She accepted Flint's light kiss and then sighed. "Let's go. I have much to tell Abram after he pays his respects."

Flint arched his brows. "That's going to be quite a conversation."

"Why is that?" So many questions and mysteries seemed to simmer around his sister. He'd not anticipated stumbling into such a situation but he would only stay a day or two and then turn his black gelding toward home and the hustle and bustle of government hearings and senate business. He skimmed the area, a foreboding filling his chest as he did.

Cassie gave him a searching look and then started humming a lullaby as they continued toward the metal gate leading into the cemetery.

"Why are you humming?" Abram sucked in a long breath as they drew closer to the grave. He held it for the count of three and let it out slowly.

"I'm told my voice helps calm people." She grinned mischievously at him. "Right, Flint?"

"Indeed." Flint chuckled as he opened the gate to the family cemetery.

"I don't need a lullaby. I'm not a child." Abram inspected the enclosed space before him as tension built in his core. He really didn't want to move any closer but that was one of the reasons he'd come. The other more important reason was to make sure his little sister whom he'd always adored was properly taken care of and in a safe situation. Then he'd feel comfortable going about his life as planned.

Within the surrounding fence, a dark gray marble stone glimmered in the shade of the trees. It wasn't a very big space. What struck him most forcefully was its lone occupant. Only one marker in the cemetery. The only grave, too.

"We had to bury her quickly because of the hot summer days when she died." Cassie stopped in front of the gate. "A simple ceremony led by Sheridan and it was over."

"Who is Sheridan?" Abram stood beside her, reluctant to move closer to his mother's gravesite.

"The inn's esteemed cook and a dear family friend." Flint held the gate while Cassie strode through. "After you, Abram."

"Sheridan is my best friend, truth be told," Cassie said. "I don't know what I'd do without him."

Abram walked past the other man, sensing disapproval

in his eyes. He lifted his chin a touch. Flint's opinion was of no importance. Abram stood beside Cassie, reading the simple inscription carved on the face of the stone. His mother's name and dates of birth and death. Very plain and factual. But then what more would he expect from such a place?

Flint stiffened beside him with a brief intake of air. "Cassie."

She followed his gaze and Abram glanced to where they both looked. Then he peered closer at the woman's figure hovering near the fence. Wearing a light blue dress, her ash-blond hair flowing down her back, and her unique aqua eyes twinkling at him. Slowly he realized the identity of the translucent woman.

"What…how?" He stammered at the image of his mother and fell back several strides.

"I should have warned you." Cassie turned toward him, reaching out with one hand as if to take his hand. "It's okay. Don't be afraid."

He stared at the specter for another second and then shook his head. "No. It's not possible. It's a terrible trick or a horrid joke."

"Welcome, my son. Don't be afraid." Mercy drifted closer to him with a slight smile. "I won't hurt you."

Never would he have imagined he'd encounter a ghost. Definitely not his mother's. He had not prepared himself. He'd had no expectation of seeing his mother, alive or dead. As she closed the distance between them, fear built inside like a volcano preparing to erupt. With a terrified scream, he fell back a step, then another, and then found himself spinning around and racing across the yard.

The image of the ghostly woman in a blue dress—his *dead* mother for goodness sake—hovering above the earth refused to dissipate in his mind's eye. Her gentle smile did nothing to calm the terror clawing inside at the thought of her haunting the inn and its inhabitants. More to the point, haunting him. One comforting thought in relenting and making the journey to the inn was that he'd not need to see or talk to his mother. Ever again. Yet there she stood—or rather floated, welcoming him to her gravesite. Her burial place. His shoulders rocked at the idea of her presence as a specter. Why was she lingering and not going on to the next realm where she belonged?

He'd made an utter fool of himself but his feet wouldn't stop carrying him toward the passage. If he were a horse, he'd gallop away. A strange tingling started in his hands and he glanced down to see black hair on the back of one. Shocked, he blinked and it vanished. Now he was seeing things. Must be the adrenaline flashing through his veins.

A few more strides and he slowed to trot up the steps and inside the first door he came to. Perhaps he'd go back to the dining room where Flint had been working at the bar and get a drink. Anything to remove the taste of terror from his mouth. He was unaccustomed to being anything but in control of the situation. He'd made a career out of being prepared, steady in a crisis, and ready to tackle any problem with calm assurance. Or at least the appearance of calm, adjusting to lightning quick changes with aplomb, despite the turmoil around him. Until that moment when he'd seen his mother's ghost. Whiskey. That's what he needed. He burst into the large entrance hall of the inn and crashed into a woman carrying a stack of cloth.

"Oh!" The girl's hands flew up to protect herself from the impact of his larger frame into her slender form.

He steadied her, but the pile of linens landed in a heap on the floor. Her upper arms quivered in his grasp, alerting him to her shock. "Are you all right, miss?"

The mouse of a girl blinked at him from wide pale

brown eyes, her brown hair mussed and gray dress rumpled. Her gaze sharpened as she took a calming breath. "Pray watch where you are going, sir. Now I've got to find fresh napkins before the dinner rush."

Scanning the unfortunate girl, he noted the dearth of color about her person. She was very plain and simple in every regard. Not worth his time or attention, yet he'd failed in his prime aim of presenting a sterling appearance and making the best first impression possible at all times. If not for the scary incident in the backyard, he'd not be in this position. He owed the woman an apology and then he'd depart and find that drink to calm down before he faced his sister and her suitor. He owed them an apology as well.

"Please forgive my abrupt entrance, miss." He nodded in deference to her. "I had a fright and didn't handle the incident well. My apologies."

She glanced pointedly at his hands still clasping her arms. "If you'd be so kind…"

He grimaced as he released her. "I am sorry." He adjusted his top hat which by some miracle remained on his head even if askew. At least he wasn't in a state of undress during his embarrassment. "If you'll excuse me, I shall leave you in peace."

"A gentleman would assist a lady in putting things to rights before removing himself from the scene of the disorder he created." She propped her hands on her slender hips and glared at him for a moment then shook her head in annoyance. "Never mind. I'll manage."

No girl had ever spoken to him with such vinegar in her tone. Finding women willing to go out on the town with him was a simple task. His most recent female companion had even kissed him goodbye and was sitting at home waiting upon his return. Of average height, she was graceful and sweet, matching her personality to her appearance with perfection. In fact, he thought her perfect in most every way.

Except, perhaps, in her tendency to cling. By contrast the wench staring at him was short and dull, except for her sharp tongue.

The young woman shook her head and then stooped to begin gathering the fallen linens while he lingered, unsure whether to help or flee. He'd botched everything since he'd arrived at the Fury Falls Inn. First, he'd been wrongly accused of being a salesman when he thought his attire entirely appropriate, then insulting his sister by not recognizing her, followed by proving himself a coward. But to have careened into a woman and caused such a disaster proved the worst thing he could have done. He bent over to pick up several of the napkins and add them to the pile she was rebuilding on the floor. She didn't even glance at him but finished folding the last square of cloth, then lifted the pile as she rose to her full height. Her head barely reached his shoulder as she hugged the pile to her chest.

"I suppose now you expect my gratitude?"

He shook his head. "I would prefer your forgiveness."

She inclined her head and then straightened. "Since you did help some, then yes."

He tipped his hat to her, relieved at the gentling of her voice. "Thank you. Now I must go before I embarrass myself again."

She nodded once and then spun on her heel and strode through a swinging door into what proved to be a busy kitchen. He hadn't even learned her name. She obviously worked at the inn, so he'd likely cross paths with her. With good fortune he wouldn't embarrass himself again in her presence. He stood there for another moment until the door closed behind her. Then foregoing the temptation of a drink he reversed direction and went back outside to find his sister to try to make amends for his cowardly actions.

Chapter Two

"Well, that was unexpected." Flint squeezed Cassie's hand as they hurried across the yard after her brother.

"Not entirely, actually. That's why I started humming, but it wasn't enough." Cassie released a long sigh. "I felt his fear building but didn't have a chance to try to explain. To calm him down."

Flint glanced behind him, scanning the area for any sign of Mercy. "She shouldn't have shown up like that. It was unfair to him."

"Let's just find him and fill him in on everything, all right?" Cassie hurried up the steps to the porch.

Flint strode right behind her and then bumped into her when she stopped suddenly. "Sorry. What's wrong?"

She pointed to where Abram leaned against the wall outside the door leading into the inn, his hands covering his eyes. She eased closer to her brother. "Abram, come with me into the residence. We need to talk."

The dandy spread his fingers to peek through them at Cassie. While the man's clothes were finely tailored and spoke of quite an expense, Flint disliked the man's attitude. Acting as if the clothes made him better than anyone else.

Time would tell whether Abram's words and actions supported his apparent claim of superiority. Highly doubtful, though, based on what he'd seen so far.

"You knew?" Abram let his hands fall to his sides as he ambled across the passage to where Cassie and Flint stood. The cravat at his throat trembled, revealing his shaken constitution. "Our mother is a specter?"

"Most folks call them haints around here, but yes." Cassie clasped her brother's arm. "Come into the parlor."

Flint took up his favorite position by the fireplace mantel with its elegant clock and row of framed portraits. While Abram and Cassie settled on two of the four Queen Anne style blue padded chairs with armrests facing the fireplace in a semicircle, he surveyed the room. Small occasional tables stood between the chairs, ready to hold a tea cup and saucer or sewing. The blue and red painted wood floor was scattered with thin floral carpets he'd ordered to give the room an upgrade. After all, bare floors were drafty and plain. Perhaps he should replace the drapes, too. Abram emitted a low grunt as he adjusted his position on the spindly chair. Flint had chosen to stand rather than be on the same level as the foppish young man.

"Since Ma died, she's been lingering," Cassie began. "She comes and goes as she chooses, which is irritating at times. Like when she doesn't want to talk about certain subjects. Poof! She vanishes."

Abram raised his brows and held out a hand as if to stop a runaway horse. "Wait, slow down. You've had conversations with her?"

The poor man obviously was having a difficult time grasping the reality his sister presented. If he had trouble with the idea that the inn was haunted by his mother's ghost, he'd have a really hard time accepting everything else Cassie was about to tell him. Flint wanted to feel sorry for him but he couldn't. He felt sorry for Cassie having such a brother.

"Many. In fact, I need to tell you about our family. See, it turns out that we come from a family of witches. Isn't that exciting?"

"Witches?" Abram stared at her and then jolted back in his chair. "You're a witch?"

Cassie nodded. "I'm an empath and siren, too. That's why I started humming. I'm sorry it wasn't enough to take the edge off your panic. And Giles is our Guardian because he possesses superhuman strength. I seriously wish he were here right now, but he's out patrolling the property."

"You needn't fear any of them." Flint tried to reassure the shocked man. But Cassie's trembling brother simply stared uncomprehendingly at him. "Nobody here wishes you harm. But there is a threat we must all face together, now that you're here."

"What do I have to do with anything?" Abram asked in a voice strained and hesitant.

"Ma says we each have powers. Do you know what yours is?"

"Powers? I have powers?"

"Cassie?" Giles suddenly strode into the room, hesitated when he spotted Abram. He peered at Cassie for a moment before nodding once, and then crossed to stand in front of his brother. The large man filled the room with pulsing energy, his black hair brushing his broad shoulders. "Hello, Abram. And I'd said it's probable that you do. I'm glad you made it."

Flint crossed his arms and tapped his fingers on his elbow. Interesting. Cassie mentioned Giles and he shows up as if summoned. But that couldn't be. Could it?

Abram slowly stood and shook hands with Giles. "It's been a long time, brother."

The difference between the two brothers proved amazing. Giles with his calm confidence versus the airs of Abram. Flint never would have thought them related if it weren't for the similarity in appearance. Both dark haired with piercing gazes, though different eye color. Or perhaps, more the shape of their facial features. Other than the scar on Abram's chin that set him apart. What had he been doing to earn such a mark? Flint would probably never know since he didn't care enough to ask.

"Flint will get you settled into a room and we can catch up on what you've been doing." Giles sat down on an unoccupied chair and crossed his legs. "We need to bring you up to date on what you can do to help with the situation."

Flint narrowed his eyes at the resistance in Abram's expression. "Now that you're here, it's important for you to understand the threat to your sister."

Abram slid his gaze to meet Flint's. "What threat?"

"There are two, actually. One known and one unknown."

"Such as?"

"Your mother is worried her sisters may try to recruit Cassie to create a dark magic trinity." Flint straightened from draping his arm on the mantel to sink onto a vacant chair.

"They won't because I don't want to be part of anything like that." Cassie tapped the armrest of her upholstered chair. "There's no reason for me to. But Ma's very worried about them attempting to convince me to do…something."

Abram relaxed in his chair as he considered the group. "So that's the known. What's the unknown?"

Giles kept his serious regard on his brother. "The deputy is investigating several murders in the region. Mostly women."

"Like our mother?" Abram pressed his palms on his knees. "Shot?"

"That's unknown to us as well. But the men who killed Ma are in jail awaiting trial." Giles studied Abram for several moments. "We need to figure out what your power

17

is so you can learn to use it to defend Cassie, no matter what happens next."

"I don't think I have any powers." Abram rested his hands on his thighs. "I'm just a senator's aide, not a wizard."

"Not wizard, but a warlock." Cassie smiled at him. "We'll just have to see what you can do."

"Other than look pretty." Flint couldn't help himself. The man must have spent an hour between shaving and perfecting his sideburns and greased hair let alone the length of time he likely spent cleaning his gaudy attire. He sure stuck out among the more practical attire worn by the working men.

"Appearances matter in my line of work." Abram pulled himself up straight, brushing invisible lint from the sleeve of his bright blue coat. "I simply try to meet the expectations of my peers."

"I expect—" Cassie shot a stern glance at Abram. "I expect you may have noticed a change in yourself over the last several weeks. Since Ma's death. That would be when her binding spell was broken so we got our powers back."

"Sorry to disappoint but I haven't." Abram glanced between them, his eyes landing on Cassie. "If you're correct that I have powers, how am I to know?"

"Good question. Maybe Ma can help us figure it out."

Abram swallowed hard, the sound punctuating Cassie's sentence. "Must we?"

The fop's discomfiture brought a smile to Flint's lips. The chap didn't realize just what he'd walked into when he arrived at the Fury Falls Inn. "Looks like it."

The very idea of summoning the ghost of his mother sent chills through him, but he needed answers only she could provide. He'd only been at the inn for a few hours but the entire view of his family had been overturned and forever changed. Abram straightened his shoulders and gripped his knees. "Very well, then. Call her."

"You're sure?" Cassie regarded him silently as he wrestled with how to respond.

On one hand, he was curious what new ability he might possess. But on the other, he didn't like the idea of being counted on to stay and fight for his sister against any threats. He most desired to go back to his normal life, to his work and his beautiful sometime lady friend, away from family and any and all secrets they may have. Then again, his dear sister needed him and that meant he couldn't turn his back on her as much as he'd wanted to upon his arrival. After all, hadn't he come all this way to make sure she was safe and provided for? He drew in a deep breath and nodded.

"Here goes. Ma! We need your help." Cassie searched the far reaches of the room with her eyes. "We'll see if that entices her."

"She has her own mind even if not a body." Giles chuckled at Abram's tense posture.

"I don't think it's funny." His brother seemed to be poking fun at him which only made Abram more on edge. "You've had time to become accustomed to the present circumstances."

"My apologies, brother. I couldn't resist." Giles winked and then addressed Cassie. "I hope she comes."

Flint crossed his ankles and rested back in his chair. "We can only wait and see."

"I'm not sure I want to see her." Abram gripped his knees harder to prevent himself from jumping out of the chair and pacing. He skimmed his gaze around the room, noting the fine oak dining table and six cane bottom chairs at the back, the huge incongruous doll's house between the front windows, and the cluster of chairs by the stairs.

"See who?" Mercy shimmered into view between Abram and Cassie's chairs, hovering a few inches above the floor.

"Ma! Don't do that." Cassie frowned at Mercy as she shook her head. "You've frightened Abram."

Abram swallowed the ball of fear in his throat and forced his fingers to release his throbbing knees. No way was he going to demonstrate the depth of anxiety he felt in front of his brother and sister. "Mother."

"Abram." Mercy smiled softly at him. "You've always been such an attractive young man, aside from the scar of course."

She had to mention that to him. Point out his one imperfection to everyone, something he couldn't do anything about. The scar reminded him every single day of his error as a boy. He'd dived into a pond and ended up scraping his chin on a submerged tree. A broken limb had gouged his chin and scratched his face. The small scratches had healed and disappeared but not the gash. No, it became a half-inch-long reminder of his accident and his foolishness.

"I'd appreciate it if you'd not emphasize the imper-fection on my chin." He gazed steadily at his mother's ghost until she shrugged lightly. "Thank you."

"Ma, we were wondering if you know what Abram's ability is. He hasn't noticed any change in himself."

Mercy lowered until her ghostly feet touched the floor. "If I remember correctly, Abram, I believe you are shape-shifter. So you can glam away your scar if it bothers you so much."

A wash of shock flooded his soul. He had the power to make himself perfect? The very idea that he was a warlock with powers surprised him, but he wasn't about to let on as to how much. And if they could be used to his benefit, then he'd accept them. His sister and brother already had, so why not? "Glam it away? What does that mean?"

"If you have a strong enough intent, which I think you do given your recent request of me, you merely need to concentrate on how you'd like to look instead. Visualize the result you desire."

Could it be that easy? He'd worn that badge of failure ever since the accident. The temptation swamped his common sense. His initial reaction of resistance faded away but he was left with the fear of failure. "What if I can't?"

"You must believe in yourself and your ability for it to work." Cassie leaned forward. "It can't hurt to try."

Cassie was right. Swallowing the lingering fear like a spoonful of castor oil, he closed his eyes and imagined himself without the scar. Just smooth skin across his chin. Tried to impress the image on his mind as he frowned in concentration.

"Something is happening…" Flint sounded astonished.

Abram kept his eyes closed and focused harder on the image of perfection. A tepid buzz flowed across his face for a moment and then dissipated.

Cassie gasped and he opened his eyes to see her smiling at him. "It went away but now it's back. You can glam. How amazing that you can change your appearance."

"But it wasn't permanent." He frowned at his mother. "Why didn't it stay the way I envisioned?"

"My dear son, you can change how you appear but not who you are. The scar will always be a part of you whether you glam it or not."

"So when he glams it's only for as long as he concentrates on making the change?" Giles leaned forward to rest his elbows on his knees. "What else can he do with that ability?"

"With practice and intent, he will be able to transform himself into any animal or human shape." Mercy's tone revealed her pride as she folded her arms across her chest and smiled down at Abram. "It's quite a unique and impressive gift."

"I can become anything?" Abram sat back in his chair, aware his voice actually squeaked out the last word. He swallowed again as he glanced at his sister and brother. "What good is that in trying to defend Cassie?"

"A good question." Flint sat up straight and then stood to cross over to Cassie's chair. "I'm sure you'll figure it out when it's necessary. For now, I must get back to work as does Cassie."

Cassie rose from her chair to take Flint's hand. "Yes, I must go but I'm glad we know what your special abilities are. You'll want to practice until you can control how long you can hold the transformation."

Abram visualized his perfect chin again while looking at Cassie, felt the buzz return.

"There. Like that." Cassie applauded his efforts. "See how long you can manage to glam the scar away. Then maybe try something bigger."

Mercy dropped her hands to her sides and shimmered. "Nice job, son."

Abram started to reply but she vanished. He blinked as he searched the room for any trace of his mother. "She does leave quite suddenly."

Giles stood and headed for the door. "You'll get used to it with time."

Abram followed the others as they made their way across the passage and into the inn. He needed to tend to his horse and settle in, but wasn't certain he would ever become accustomed to any of what he'd stumbled upon. His mind whirled from the revelations. Not only was the inn haunted by his mother's ghost, but his family possessed special powers. He didn't know if he could take any more surprises like his ability to shapeshift into another person or animal. A sudden memory of hair on the back of his hand gave him pause. He'd started to change into the horse he'd pictured. He really needed to learn how to control his gift before something—like him—went awry.

Chapter Three

The next morning, Cassie snipped salad greens in her garden, humming a tune to herself as she worked. The joy she experienced while working with the plants lifted her soul, easing the concerns and tensions surrounding her. She carried the basket of greens into the kitchen to prepare them for the afternoon rush. Matt Simmons, one of Giles' friends, stood by the side table, examining the new pair of hinged waffle iron plates.

The muscular young man looked up at her with curiosity in his brown eyes. His short curly black hair framed his angular features. Matt and his brother Zander had arrived a few weeks back when Giles came to the inn. Both former slaves, they owed their freedom to her brother, a fact she was very proud of on his behalf. She wished all slaves were freemen but wishes wouldn't change the minds of those who benefited from the practice. If only. Matt nodded in greeting and then resumed his work.

Flint had ordered the waffle irons so the inn could offer the next level of cuisine like some high-brow hotel he'd heard of in one of his magazines. She liked the idea of improving and expanding the menu but Sheridan resisted too many changes. He preferred for events to unfold in a manageable order rather than all at once.

"Have you sorted out how to use those things?" Cassie set the basket on the scarred work table in the center of the kitchen.

"Just about." Matt glanced at her and pivoted to place the two long-handled cast-iron plates on the smaller wood table. "It's a matter of mixing the batter to the right consistency and to grease these plates well. But I'll manage."

"Those look right heavy." Sheridan Drake, the most popular cook the inn had ever employed, pointed the tip of a butcher knife at the plates, a wry grin spreading on his medium brown face. He, too, used to be a slave until her father had bought and freed him. Tall and strong, the older man's brown eyes laughed at the younger cook. "Are you strong enough to make waffles?"

Matt propped his fists on his blue jean-clad hips as he gave a gap-toothed grin to the other cook. "Don't be silly. I don't need to hold it. I'll use that metal stand to rest the plates on over the flames." He gestured toward a round metal stand with long legs he'd positioned in the fireplace.

"We'll see how well that might work." Sheridan plunged the blade into the large smoked ham on the board in front of him. "I have my doubts as to whether you can find a good recipe let alone bake them properly."

"I know the recipe, thank you for your concern." Matt snared a large bowl from a stack on the new set of shelves Flint had installed the week before. Another improvement to the organization and operation of the inn's kitchen. "Just you watch me."

"And I'll see what? Thin runny pancakes instead of crisp waffles, I bet." Sheridan grinned at Matt, revealing he was really engaged in some good-natured joshing.

"Leave Matt alone, Sheridan." Cassie tore the lettuce into small pieces and added them to the wooden bowl in front of her. "He's a fine cook. Just like you."

"What did you say?" The older man reared back and

flashed a pretend glare her way. "I'm a trained cook unlike that young wannabe."

"I've been taught by a real chef as well. One who knows actual cuisine from other countries, I might add." Matt beat the batter with a wooden spoon, using rapid strokes that blended the ingredients into a smooth, thick consistency. "I'm most likely an even better cook than you as a result."

"I doubt that." Sheridan resumed slicing the ham and arranging the pieces on a platter. "My former massa made sure I know what I'm doing. He was very particular."

"What's your best dish?" Cassie picked up a bunch of watercress, inspecting the tiny green leaves for any signs of wilting, and added it to the mix of greens in the bowl. "Both of you."

"I think the favorite dish I make is crispy hoe cakes made using my wife's recipe." Sheridan set the knife aside as he met Cassie's gaze. "She made them with a secret ingredient that she only ever shared with me."

Sheridan longed for his wife Pansy so very much it made Cassie rather sad. The mere memory of her spiked grief and longing through Sheridan. If only her pa could locate the woman while he was in Savannah where she'd last been working, maybe there was some way to reunite the couple. If they were together, what would they do then? With luck they'd build a home nearby. But what if Sheridan went to live where his wife resided? Her heart sank at the idea of him leaving, taking his friendship and guidance with him. How would she manage without him to confide in as she'd done for so many years? On the other hand, she couldn't deny him the love he so deserved. She had so many questions and so much to hope for on their behalf. Her biggest desire remained for them to be reunited no matter what else happened as a result.

Matt opened the waffle iron on the table beside the bowl of batter. "My mom made wonderful hoe cakes. She'd add a pinch of nutmeg to the batter which really perked up the flavor."

Sheridan tilted his head as he studied Matt. Cassie sensed his curiosity and surprise build the longer he looked at the younger man.

"That's what my wife added, too. What an amazing coincidence." Sheridan shook his head slowly. "I suppose it wasn't such a secret after all."

"Maybe your wife and my mother learned the recipe from someone they both knew." Matt greased the plates with lard then wiped his hands on his apron.

He appeared nonchalant but Cassie detected his puzzlement and surprise, much like Sheridan felt. She grinned to herself at the realization the control of her own abilities had improved. She could effortlessly ascertain how they felt. Such an ability gave her insights into others so she could more easily provide what the customers needed or wanted. She used her gift for the good of the inn and the people who frequented it. But it would also prove their banter and debating who the better cook really was, she hoped they'd found a new basis for their growing friendship.

The darkness of a new moon serves my purposes well. I can hide in the shadows and plan my attack. My prey won't see me coming. There will be no witnesses to my actions. It's worked so far. I watch the old witch move about inside her evil abode, lit by the dancing flames of the fire in the fireplace. She's plotting who knows what mayhem with her potions and spells. It's my mission to rid this area of magic. I wait for the right moment. I know it's coming. Almost here. When the witch begins to chant, I make my move. Easing onto the rickety front porch of her cottage, I silently make my way to the door. Grab the knob and slowly turn it so she won't hear me coming while she's in her chanting trance. I pull it open far enough to slip through. I rush inside and grab her, slit her throat, and then stab her through the heart for good measure. Wiping the knife on her black robe, I leave, closing the door behind me before I slip back into the shadows until next time.

Peering into the freshly polished window to seek out any smudges, Flint folded the drying rag. Over the past two days, he'd identified a few more things he wanted to rectify before the senator's anticipated visit. Like replacing the older front windows with clearer panes. They reflected the active scene behind him, wagons and coaches carrying patrons to and from the inn. The sounds of the activity gladdened his heart. The rattle of harness and the occasional bark of a dog or the lowing of the cattle in their pasture provided a background to the voices of men all blending into a pleasing symphony of business. Suddenly he spotted a lone rider cantering up the lane toward him. Recognizing the horse, he pivoted and strode to the porch steps and down to the carriageway. The hefty man dismounted from the sturdy bay gelding and strode toward him, his dark eyes worried.

"Deputy Parker, it's a pleasure to see you." Flint tucked the rag into his back pocket as the deputy stopped in front of him.

Barney stuck out his hand to shake briefly with Flint. "I'm here on business. To warn you, in fact."

"What's happened?" A sliver of concern pierced his heart at the serious expression on the deputy's face.

"Another murder not too far from here." Barney glanced up the lane with a quick lift of his chin. "A couple miles that way."

"So why the warning? What's that to do with us?"

"It's so close I thought you should know. I don't know whether they'd come after Miss Fairhope or Miss Crawford way out here." Barney pulled his wide-brimmed hat from his head to wipe his palm across his brow. "Someone is attacking these women but I have no idea why. Seems like it's mostly women who live isolated, often alone, for some reason."

"Makes them an easy target." Flint crossed his arms over his chest. He hadn't considered Mandy's safety in her travels to and from the inn. Something he'd need to correct. "What else do you know about this latest victim?"

"She was home alone when she was killed. But..." Scrubbing the back of his hand across his brow, Barney shrugged. "The neighbors didn't know much about her. She lived alone but they said she acted different. Frequent suspicious comings and goings."

"Suspicious in what way?" Women living alone shouldn't pose a concern to anyone. He needed to find out more about their neighbors, get to know them better. Then maybe he could help sort out the motivation for these senseless killings.

"People arriving late at night, for instance. Why would they not arrive earlier like decent folk do?" Barney tapped his hat back onto his head, his concern echoing in his words.

"I suppose they could have been delayed..." The more he thought about it, the less he liked it. "How many people are we talking about?"

"A handful, not a lot. But still, one neighbor saw them pass by approaching midnight on at least one occasion. She thought it very odd that a woman living alone would have visitors so late."

"And what was this neighbor doing watching outside at such a time?" Most folks he knew didn't venture outside after dark let alone so late in the night.

"Her dogs started barking so she got up and looked out, her husband went out with his rifle to make sure all was secure. That's apparently when they saw the group passing by."

"Still, I don't think we're in danger here. There's only a few women here and they are never alone. There's always men around. I should think they'll be safe enough." Flint studied the sweating man for a beat. "You look like you could use a drink. Go on in. It's on me."

"Very much appreciated." Barney looped the gelding's reins around the hitching rail. "I'll only stay a minute."

The deputy hurried up the steps and inside. Flint spun around at the sound of an approaching rider. A shaft of surprise and alarm raced through him at the sight of the young lady arriving. Haley Baker trotted her palomino up to where Flint waited to greet her. Haley was the pretty daughter of the man Reggie Fairhope had asked to keep an eye on the place for him and report via letter as to the job Flint did. John Baker owned the next plantation, Riverwood, and made a point of coming to the inn for a meal several times a week to inspect Flint's efforts. An annoying and somewhat insulting situation but one he had no power to alter.

Haley had become a frequent visitor of late, always arriving alone to seek out Giles for a conversation. At first, he'd assumed they were courting but their quick exchanges no longer seemed romantic so much as furtive. Perhaps he should speak to Giles about his intentions toward the young lady, just to be clear as to what they were about. When she stopped her mare, Flint took hold of the bridle as she dismounted. Her charcoal gray riding habit with long split skirts and black braid trim graced her slight form. A refined black hat perched upon her curls. But by far the most striking feature was the fear simmering in her amber eyes.

"Miss Baker, what is the matter?" He pulled the reins from her hands and led her mare to the rail, wrapping the leather around the wooden rod. Turning back to her, he swiftly rejoined her where she fairly trembled.

"Mr. Hamilton, I've come to talk to Mr. Fairhope. I

must see him right away." She clasped her hands together, knuckles white against the gray skirt. "He's the only one I can tell."

His earlier concern spiraled into deep-seated worry. Giles may need to hear her message, but he wasn't the only one. Flint also needed to know what she had to say in case it impacted the inn and its customers. "I believe he's in the barn. I'll escort you there myself." He motioned toward the barn across the carriageway as he started toward where Giles was supposed to be grooming his horse. The crushed rock crunched under their shoes as they started toward the weathered barn. Hogs rooted in the grass and mud in their pen while the ever-present flock of chickens pecked and squawked nearby.

"Thank you. I can find him if you have other business to attend." Haley didn't smile as she stared at the barn's shadowy doorway.

"Not at the moment." Noting the worry etched between her brows, he hurried his pace. "Come, I'm sure you want to have your say."

"Thank you." She met his stride with quick steps as they crossed the threshold into the barn.

The aromas of sweet hay and manure greeted him as they entered. A swallow darted past and disappeared into the rafters above. He let his eyes adjust for a split second and then took Haley's arm to escort her down the wide dirt aisle. Abram's black horse watched him stride past, alert to every sound until it would grow accustomed to the new place.

Flint stopped outside of the stall where Cassie's brother stood combing his dapple gray gelding's mane with a comb. "Giles, Miss Baker is here to see you."

Giles laid the comb on the stall wall and stepped out into the aisle. "It's nice of you to pay me such an unexpected visit, Miss Baker."

"I must speak with you. In private, if you don't mind." Haley stared into Giles' calm expression.

"Flint, would you mind giving us a moment?" The worry Flint felt echoed in Giles' deep voice.

"I believe whatever Miss Baker has to say I should know about." Their secretive tête-à-têtes had evolved into secrets, ones he needed to be included in from then on. "I'd rather stay."

Giles considered for a long moment, glancing between Haley and Flint. "Miss Baker, I believe Mr. Hamilton does need to hear your concerns. It's time."

Haley clutched her hands together at her waist, the strain inside revealed by her clenched jaw and glittering eyes. "Very well, if you think it best."

Giles nodded and crossed his arms over his massive chest. "Go ahead. What has happened now?"

"My father—" She swallowed hard then squared her shoulders, keeping her fearful gaze on Giles, as if it was easier to speak to him than to Flint. "He went out late the other night and didn't come home until early morning. He's being so reticent about where he goes. I'm worried about what he's doing."

More late night doings. Was it possible John Baker attended the latest murdered woman's gatherings? He couldn't imagine what purpose the man would have for doing so. Surely, he had his wife and daughter to consider. He didn't seem like the kind of man to engage in assignations of such an indecent sort.

"I wouldn't worry, Haley. I'm sure he had business on one of his other farms that he had to manage."

She leaned closer to Giles, lowered her voice to a whisper. "Dressed all in black?"

Even Flint knew John rarely dressed so formally. He preferred brighter colors to the somber tones. On his last visit to the inn he'd been attired in dark blue trousers with a cream dress shirt, embroidered vest, and a tan suit coat with a matching top hat. He couldn't imagine John in all black heading out at night to meet a woman. So where did he go?

"That does seem out of character for him." Giles met Flint's frown. "This isn't the first time Haley has been concerned about her father and his activities."

"Is that why you two have been having frequent conversations in the gazebo out front?" Flint studied Giles and then Haley. "I thought you were courting."

"Sir, don't be impertinent." Haley aimed shocked eyes at Flint. "If that were true, which it is not, it would not be a secret."

Giles regarded Haley with a half-smile quirking one corner of his mouth. "It wouldn't, eh?"

"No. But that's beside the point." She huffed a sigh. "Can we continue, please?"

Giles grinned at her with a shrug. "As you wish."

"So what do you think your father is doing?" Her next words would determine which direction Flint would proceed. He had his own concerns about John and his scrutiny of the inn's business.

"Well, I don't honestly know what he's doing. He will say he's checking on his other farms, like Giles suggested, but is he?" She wrapped a hand around her elbow, her voice low and trembling. "Mother and I know he's talked before about rumors of witches in the region but I didn't think he was worried about…them. I thought he was merely observing their existence. Now I'm not so sure."

"Witches? In this area?" Giles shifted his gaze to Flint. "I didn't know there were others."

"Giles, what are you—"

"It's okay, Mr. Hamilton. I know about Giles and Cassie, and everyone, really." Haley peered up at Flint and then smiled. "Mother and I both are aware. We've been aware for some time now."

"How is that possible when we just learned ourselves?" Giles stared at her, confusion plain on his face.

"We can sense the presence of magic, that's how." Haley drew in a breath and let it out slowly. "But Father doesn't know that Mother and I are witches also. Do not tell him either. He's not fond of witches."

John didn't like witches when his own wife and daughter counted themselves among them. The simmering worry flared into fear for Cassie. If John suspected her of being a witch, what would he do? Haley's concern over his clandestine excursions may indeed be connected to the murders in the area. He'd witnessed the way John Baker observed Cassie closely, how he'd noticed the effect of her singing on her audience. She could be one of his targets.

"I have to go." Flint took a step and then spun back to Haley and Giles. "Thank you for risking yourself to warn us of the possible danger, Miss Baker."

"You're welcome. But please, call me Haley. We're in this together." She strode closer and laid a hand on his arm. "I think we should use our given names, don't you?"

"Very well, Haley." Flint briefly smiled at her and then started walking toward the sunshine outside. "See you later. I have to find Cassie."

Chapter Four

Something was up. Abram straightened in the chair on the front porch of the inn as Flint hurried from the barn toward him. Two of the dogs trotted after him, ears up as if they sensed an adventure at hand. Giles emerged from the open doorway of the barn with a well-dressed young woman beside him, one who had been visiting nearly daily for some time. They paused as they continued what appeared to be an intense conversation. Several white feathered chickens flapped and squawked to one side. Flint reached the steps and took them two at a time. The dogs—he didn't know their names yet—padded up to stand with him, waiting for direction.

"Where's your sister?" Flint barely halted long enough for an answer.

"Working in the garden. What's wrong?" Abram rose, the tension in Flint making him nervous.

"Ask Giles. I've got to talk to Cassie." Flint pivoted and went back down the steps and strode briskly around the side of the inn. The dogs loped after him.

Giles escorted the lady to the hitching rail where she easily mounted her striking palomino. With a wave of her hand, she reined her horse around and trotted away. Giles watched for a moment and then turned toward the steps, his stride faltering when he spied Abram observing him. He slowly climbed the steps.

Giles had certainly changed a lot since the last time they'd been together. Taller, broader, stronger, more reserved. He could only wonder what his life had been like wherever he'd gone. So many questions sifted through Abram's thoughts. Asking them required his brother to be open to a conversation, something he doubted would happen any time soon. Not with the other issues they faced, the new abilities they were trying to come to terms with.

"Flint seems upset by whatever you were discussing." Abram sensed his brother's reluctance to trust him. But if he was forced to assist, he needed to know what the situation entailed. "Who's the girl?"

"A neighbor's daughter." Giles crossed to sit on the other wooden chair flanking the small table with a grunt. "Her name's Haley Baker."

Abram drew in a deep breath, striving for calm and patience. The smell of hot earth and horse manure came with the breath and he blew it out slowly.

"Are you seeing her?" Abram resumed his seat, his back tight.

"I just saw her." Giles lifted a brow at him, the corner of his mouth lifted in a wry grin, but didn't relax into the chair. "What's it to you?"

Abram shrugged off his brother's quip but not his challenge. "Don't keep me in the dark."

Not again. The real reasons for why Giles had left home so many years ago remained obscured from him. He'd watched his brother walk away that morning, never looking back to where Abram stood with Daniel and Silas. Abandoned by their oldest brother without an explanation, only farewell. He thought they were close. He thought they shared everything. He thought he could rely on him. Then his friend, his confidant, his big brother was gone.

"I'm not. It doesn't concern you." Giles swatted at a black fly, shooing it away from in front of his face.

"But it does Flint?"

"Yes."

"He told me to ask you what the problem is, why he's so worried." Maybe throwing in the request from someone he trusted would help his brother open up. "Why won't you tell me?"

Giles glared at him. "You don't know anything about it and don't need to. Drop it."

Anger flared hot and fast inside at the harsh tone and rigid frame of his brother, forcing him to his feet. "You bastard."

Giles jumped to his feet and squared off with Abram, fists clenched at his sides. "You have no right to call me that. Ever."

"When your brother abandons you without saying why, I do."

"I didn't abandon you or anyone."

"From where I'm standing you sure as hell did. You left all of us behind."

"You don't get it, do you?" Giles took a step toward him, then spun around and marched several strides away. "It was... Never mind."

"What?" He needed answers from his big brother, not sparring. Not more secrets.

Giles faced him from across the porch, slowly relaxing his fists. "You didn't care then and you don't care now. You're just being selfish. It's obvious you want to be the center of attention. Like always. Just leave it."

"I am not. You are a no-good brother. You abandoned us without any explanation and you think I'm selfish?" Nauseated from the roiling anger in his gut from the absurd accusation, Abram turned away from Giles. "Just go away. I can't even look at you right now."

"Glad to before I say what I really think about you and those ridiculous clothes you insist on wearing." Giles stomped inside the inn, slamming the door behind him.

Abram startled at the sound then slowly turned to stare at the closed door. A physical barrier echoing the emotional barrier weighing down his gut.

Giles was wrong about him. He glanced down at the beautifully tailored black trousers and blue coat over his pristine white dress shirt. His girdle snugged his waist to its thinnest size, enhancing the appearance of the wide padded shoulders of the coat. He'd even chosen to wear a red satin vest to compliment the color of the coat. He tapped one of his glossy square-toed black shoes in frustrated anger. He didn't wear fine clothes to bring attention to himself. He wore them to present the best appearance possible, to assure those he worked with of his professionalism and worthiness to perform his duties for the senator.

He couldn't help it that his brother's attire showed him as a mediocre sort of man. His trousers made from cotton instead of linen with no crease or sheen. His shirt more similar to the hunting shirts worn by the militia back in the last century. Scuffed brown boots that surely he'd worn for eons. Giles simply didn't care about his appearance in the same way Abram did. That didn't make Abram wrong for dressing the part. It made him better, in fact, because he understood the significance and importance of making a good impression.

Now that he could hide his scar, he'd make an even grander impression. Practice changing himself would indeed make him perfect. Smoothing the points of the vest, he sat back down to observe the flow of people coming and going about their affairs. After the anger dissipated into the morning air, sadness settled on his shoulders. He glanced to the closed door. When it opened and the mousy girl sauntered out toward him, he realized he'd hoped Giles would come back outside. He missed his brother. Wanted him back in his life more than he'd known prior to that moment. Somehow, he would figure out a way to bridge the gap in their relationship. He must.

"Hello, miss." He rose to greet her properly. "How do you fare?"

"I'm well, thank you." She motioned toward the closed door. "Sheridan asked me to see if you required any refreshments."

"No, but I do have a question for you." He regarded her curiously intriguing eyes.

"Yes?"

"What's your name?"

"Mandy Crawford." Her musical voice lingered on the warm late morning air, softening and brightening the day.

"Abram Fairhope." He stuck out his hand. "Nice to meet you properly."

"Oh, so you're Cassie's brother." She let him take her hand in his.

He lifted her hand to press a light kiss on the back of it, surprising himself almost as much as her. Her light brown eyes twinkled at him, entrancing him for a moment with their sparkle of pleasure. Was she laughing at him? Or merely happy? He searched her eyes until he confirmed she enjoyed the sudden kiss to her hand. He released her hand and straightened his shoulders.

"Yes, that's correct." Abram sniffed, which he regretted when her delicious perfume filled his nostrils. He really needed to manage his reactions better. "Thank you for inquiring as to my needs. If you'll excuse me?"

She gripped the edges of her apron with both hands.

"Of course. I'll probably see you later when you come in for your dinner."

So, she was a serving wench. Probably a lonely one given her lack of appeal. Though when she smiled at him, her eyes briefly captivated him. He'd need to see that smile again in order to know if she only sparkled when surprised or every time.

"I look forward to it." He touched his hand to his brow in farewell and then strode away, a slow smile easing onto his lips at the unexpected yet pleasant interlude with the girl he'd originally dismissed. Possibilities for how to answer his intriguing question flitted through his brain as he went inside.

The flock of chickens scattered with agitated squawks and flapping of feathers. He didn't care. Flint spotted Cassie in her garden, bent over a row of plants. Oblivious to her surroundings. Alone. He trotted the last few steps and rested his hands on top of the gate. She didn't even look up from where she hummed to herself, snipping dead blooms from a row of marigolds.

Even after her mother's murder and hearing about the recent deaths in the area she didn't even take the simple step of being aware of who else might be nearby. With customers coming and going around the inn, anyone could have approached her, accosted her, or even harmed her. How would they ever know who was at fault? What if John Baker threatened or hurt her? She would be easy prey for him since she trusted him. How long would it take before someone noticed her missing and sought her out? The idea of her being killed in her own bountiful garden left a cold metal ball of fear in his gut.

"Cassie, what are you doing?" He tried to keep his deep concern from his tone but failed.

"Oh, hello. I didn't see you there." She straightened and slipped the snippers into her smudged work apron pocket. "What's wrong?"

"Deputy Parker has informed us of another woman murdered. And not far from here." Flint clutched the warm metal rail, striving to remain calm even as concern for her safety rocked his shoulders.

"That's horrible." She tilted her head to one side, her smile of greeting fading as a brow slowly rose in silent query. "What does that have to do with me?"

"Hopefully nothing, but we must take precautions." He dropped one hand to rest on the butt of his flintlock pistol hanging at his side. "This may not be enough."

"You're scaring me." The quaver in her voice alerted him to her reaction even more than her words.

"Good, because I need you to do as I request."

"That depends on what you ask." Her frown deepened as she regarded him, lips pressed firmly together.

"It's simple. I don't want you to be outside without someone with you."

"With so many people around all the time, I doubt being outside is as dangerous as you seem to think." She crossed her arms over her bosom, erecting an emotional barricade to his concern.

Her assumption that having many people around protected her battled with his own views and lost. He must convince her to take precautions. For her own good and his peace of mind.

"The deputy disagrees or he wouldn't have ridden out to expressly warn us to be careful."

She looked sharply at him, squinting in surprise. "Really?"

"That's why I came here as soon as I learned of the threat to you." He kept to himself the possibility of John Baker also being a threat. He didn't need to alarm her unduly. He and her brothers would protect her from that direction.

"I don't like making somebody have to babysit me when I'm working in my garden. It's my private time when I can think." She dropped her hands to slip into her apron pockets. "Must I? Truly?"

A slight whine emerged on the last word of her plea. She had a right to privacy but not during a time when she was in danger. He'd ensure his girl stayed safe no matter what it might cost in terms of her pride. He'd see to it one way or another.

"Until the killer is found, yes." He opened the gate and beckoned for her to come out of the fenced garden. "I must insist."

She sighed as she joined him. "Fine. I will ask Teddy to come out whenever I need to work in the garden or want to read in the gazebo."

The boy had a keen eye and knew the regular customers since he'd worked at the inn for the last several weeks. Flint would have a talk with him about his duties with regard to safeguarding Cassie, to be sure the boy kept alert. And to make sure he reported any suspicious activity directly and immediately to Flint.

"That's a good idea. I'm sure Sheridan can spare him for an hour or two a day." Relief at her ready acquiescence swept through him. He took both of her hands in his and pulled her closer. "Thank you."

"For what?" She tilted her face up so she could meet his gaze.

"For trusting me and accepting that I only want, no—need to keep you safe." He pressed his lips to hers for a long moment, savoring her sweet sun-warmed lips. "Because I love you with my entire being and I don't want anything to happen to you."

"I know." She pursed her lips for a second and then smiled widely. "I love you too, but this restriction is only for a short time. Or I'll be forced to break my promise to you."

41

He blinked slowly at her as she pulled her hands away and propped them on her hips. "I have no control over how long it will take for the sheriff to arrest the killer, Cassie. You can't renege on your vow to have Teddy with you until then."

"Perhaps, then, you should encourage the good sheriff to act faster to find the villain." She started walking toward the back door of the inn. "I need to get to work. See you later."

He slowly trailed after her, his thoughts a jumble. She'd told him she loved him. She promised to do as he requested. But only for as long as she felt like it. He had no control over how long it would take to find who was responsible for the killings. He raked a hand through his hair as he realized he also had no control over Cassie. Now what did he do?

Exhausted, Cassie made her way out to the gazebo a couple days later to rest and reflect on the events of the past week. The Saturday morning rush had been unusually intense. The lovely refreshing morning air brought folks from their homes. Teddy ambled beside her, his long legs easily keeping pace with her. She'd keep her promise to Flint. For now. Even though she felt rather silly having a boy as her watchdog. She couldn't ask Giles to stand around even though he was her appointed Guardian. But she had to escape the hustle and bustle of the inn in order to process everything.

"Sit over there, Teddy." She pointed to the metal bench on the far end of the gazebo as she took a seat on the middle one. "I'm sorry to make you stay out here with me when you have other, better things you could be doing."

"It's a nice break, so I don't mind for a time." The young boy dropped onto the hard surface with a grimace. "After a bit, though, I imagine my bum will be worn out."

She nodded as she arranged her skirts around her legs.

"That may be our signal for when we go back inside and get back to work."

Cassie perused the front of the inn with its lively comings and goings of guests and customers. Many lived close by and came for the fine food and entertainment. Others stopped over on longer journeys through the northern wilderness of the state, refreshing themselves in the mineral springs or simply relaxing on the back porch viewing the foothills beyond. The number of horses and vehicles of every description belied the inn's location out in the wilderness. Yet it proved the inn provided a needed stopover for those traveling. On their way to wherever their business took them. Memphis. Nashville. Montgomery. Or other points in between. Thankfully, they went about their days not knowing about the Fairhope's abilities and how they might impact them.

Not only her own siren and empathic talents, ones she worked on frequently to learn to control and to use effectively. But also the surprising concept of Abram's ability to change into another person or animal. She couldn't fathom how such an ability would prove useful but he seemed to very much like the idea. He needed to practice on controlling it but he'd eventually sort out the ins and outs of shapeshifting. He was smart and persistent when he set his mind to something. All the while Giles stood guard over them all, prepared to defend them should the need arise. Lately he seemed to have developed some kind of sixth sense, appearing out of nowhere whenever she wanted him. Her ma seemed certain of the need for his protection and the deputy had also forewarned about dangers. Threats from all sides, or so it seemed. Threats against her person and thus her future.

Flint's declaration of love warmed her heart as much as the sun warmed the air around her. All encompassing, blanketing all of her with the comfort and hope his love afforded. With the worries and fears associated with the looming danger, did they have a future? Could they overcome the perils ahead?

She heard the front door of the inn close with a distant thud. The afternoon's cooler than normal air meant Flint hadn't bothered opening up yet. But the last week of August would still be warm, perhaps even hot. The doors would be left open yet again as the temps climbed. If not today, then on the morrow. Flint trotted down the front steps and started toward her, an envelope fluttering in his hand.

Looked like he had a letter for her. Otherwise why would he be carrying it out her way? Most likely from her father but it could be from her aunt. She longed for Pa to return home but knew from his previous communications his intent to not return until closer to Allhallows Eve. But with her aunts planning to visit, she could really use the emotional support having her father around would provide. So many threads of family and danger and hope and fear woven together into a tapestry of uncertainty. At least she had the man she hoped to marry one day at her side during all the turmoil.

He briskly strode across the lawn and jogged up the few steps of the gazebo. He smiled at the boy as he halted in the center of the gazebo in front of Cassie. "Thank you, Teddy. You may go, but I appreciate your diligence."

"Thank you, sir." Teddy whistled as he sauntered back toward the inn and his duties.

"He's so anxious to get back to work, isn't he?" Cassie chuckled as she watched the boy dawdle his way inside.

"I don't blame him, really. It's such a nice day." Flint sat beside her and gazed across the grassy expanse separating the gazebo from the carriageway and inn. The roaming flock of chickens pecked their way around the side of the inn, hunting in the grass for whatever tasty tidbits they could find. "Not even the usual humidity to contend with."

"I'm glad you came out. I was thinking about you." She tilted her head as she turned to peer into his captivating eyes. "About us, really."

He clasped one of her hands in his. "Anything I need to know about?"

She glanced away as she shrugged lightly, then met his gaze. "Wondering if we'll even have a future what with all the dangers descending on us."

He shifted, laying the letter on the bench beside him as he held both her hands. "Do not fret so, my love. All of us, me and your brothers, will protect you."

Love and confidence shone in his eyes as she studied his expression. She didn't even need to use her empathic ability to know how he felt. Despite her initial plan to marry him as a means to escape her mother's dictatorial ways, she'd fallen for him. She couldn't deny she had feelings for the man sitting beside her. Only she'd recently found out about family she'd never known she had. Who were they and how did she fit into the much larger group? Would he be accepted? She knew without one scrap of doubt he'd protect her to the best of his ability. But could he? So many questions yet to be answered.

"I know you'll try and I appreciate it. But Ma seems to think it's not going to be enough." She squeezed his hands and then pulled them free. "I think I'm going to need to defend you all as much as you'll defend me. We'll be stronger together."

"We'll have to wait and see." Flint rested his palms on his knees with a sigh, then picked up the envelope with strong fingers. "In the meantime, you've received a letter from your father."

"Good. I've been wondering how he's faring." Unfolding the proffered note with a slight tremble in her hands, she took a deep breath before reading it aloud.

August 17, 1821
Savannah, Georgia

My dear Cassie,

I only have a moment to dash off this note before the post will be picked up but I know you're anxious on a particular topic and wanted to let you know what I've uncovered. I believe I have a lead on where Pansy Drake may be working. I'm going to pay the woman a visit and determine for myself whether she is indeed Sheridan's wife. Please keep this to yourself until I can confirm as I do not want to raise the poor man's hopes should it prove to be a wild goose chase.

More later.

Love,

Your father

She folded the letter and leaned back in her seat. Her heart swelled with hope, buoyant as a chocolate soufflé. "Wonderful news."

"If he's found her." Flint's tone held a caution as he regarded her.

She bristled at the subtle rebuke, irritated at the implication. "I'm not going to say anything."

Telling Sheridan about the hunt for his wife would not be the right thing to do. He'd become even more anxious than she was at the idea that Pansy may have been found and a chance existed of reuniting the couple after all these years. Who knew what the man might do once he learned of her whereabouts. He might…no, he'd probably go find her himself. Cassie's confidant, friend, advisor might leave. Then who would she turn to for guidance? No, better to keep the uncertain news under wraps for the moment. Until Pa was sure.

"Just a reminder. It'd be better to know for certain before saying anything. That's all." Flint grasped one of her hands with a gentle tug, pulling her closer for a quick kiss. "I know you'll do the right thing."

"I'm happy Pa may have found her, too." She contemplated Flint's strong jaw and kind eyes, reminded of his inner strength and gentle nature. She leaned against him, drawing on both to center herself. Sensed his contentment surrounding her which actually helped her to relax even more. "But I don't want to hurt Sheridan if he's ultimately disappointed."

She imagined revealing to Sheridan the happy news of her pa locating Pansy. Of Sheridan and Pansy being able to live out the rest of their lives together as they should have all along: as husband and wife. Sharing their lives and their love for one another. Being able to confide in each other all the good and bad happenings in their lives. At least they'd have each other. She longed to give him the very happy news. When it happened. If it happened. In the meantime, she'd remain mum.

Chapter Five

S ome discussions leave a person with much to ponder. It had been two days since Reggie's letter revealed the happy news that Sheridan's wife may have been located. Which made Flint think more about marriage and who he wanted to spend the rest of his life with. But he had to finish several projects and identify others and wait until the lady in question agreed. He strolled back inside the inn, debating his priorities. Protecting Cassie had taken precedence over improving the inn in preparation for the senator's visit. But both must be accomplished. As he closed the door behind him, he heard raised voices coming from the kitchen. Now what? Frowning at the disrupting sound, he hurried across the entrance hall to push the door open.

"What's the problem?" He braced his fists on his hips as he glanced between Sheridan and Matt, squared off across the work table. "I could hear you two arguing from the front door."

Piles of vegetables and hunks of meat graced the surface in bowls and platters. The delicious smell of baking bread made his stomach growl. Meg and Myrtle hunched over the sideboard, peeling more carrots and potatoes. The ubiquitous simmering kettles of stew and soup hung over the immense cook fire, adding aromas of garlic and onion and meat into the air. His stomach rumbled again. Still a few hours until dinner would be ready, so he'd have to wait.

Sheridan speared the butcher knife at Matt. "He's being impertinent."

"No, I'm being honest." Matt's wry grin suggested the depth of humor he found in the banter. "I am better."

"No, you're not." Sheridan dropped the knife onto the table with a bang of the blade against a porcelain bowl. "You don't know near as much as me."

"Why don't you prove it?" Matt pressed his fists onto the work table on either side of a mound of dough and arched a mocking brow at the older cook.

"Why should I? I have nothing to prove." Sheridan crossed his arms, his deep bass voice rumbling with confidence.

"Maybe then you think I do. So let's have a cookery competition." Matt pushed away from the table to mirror Sheridan's stance.

The tall man glared at the younger man with quiet disdain. Flint glanced back and forth between the obstinate glare and the challenging quirked brow. With any luck they wouldn't come to blows over who made the better gravy. But the more he contemplated the idea of a chef's challenge, the more he liked it.

"Yes, why don't you." Flint stepped between the two men, hoping to keep them from slugging it out. "Just make a meal, so we can compare, and we'll see which is better."

"A competition?" Sheridan straightened his shoulders, wary questioning in his eyes.

"I think that's a good idea." Matt lowered his arms as he peered at Sheridan. "Are you up for such a challenge?"

"If I can choose the menu." A thread of steel underlay his voice as Sheridan provoked the younger man.

"Not on your life." Matt shook his head and then motioned to Flint with his chin. "Flint will choose the item, then let the best cook win."

A lump of congealed pasta settled in Flint's stomach. What did he know about the caliber and quality of food let alone choosing the menu? Sure, he had ideas about food items but not entire meals. He left that up to the expert. Sheridan always had final say. Except now the younger cook had arrived and challenged Sheridan's abilities and authority. Mayhap Flint would find himself in the uncomfortable position of refereeing skirmishes. He couldn't be in the middle and yet he would encourage the friendly rivalry for the inn's benefit.

"Flint should judge our efforts to decide who the best cook at the inn is." Sheridan's brown eyes rested on Flint for several tense seconds. "What do you say?"

Doing so would leave him stuck like the cream in a donut. Both of the men regarding him with anxious gazes were worthy of preparing fine meals. Of that he remained certain. But how could he choose between their offerings? He blinked as an idea occurred to him, a slow smile spreading across his lips.

"I tell you what let's do. You each devise a menu." He grinned at their matching arched brows over wide eyes. "Then we'll have a tasting event in one week. We'll invite our customers to come out for the special event and they will be the ultimate judges. The cook with the most votes wins."

Matt met Sheridan's sharp gaze. "Sounds good to me. Are you willing?"

"Of course." A shaft of pride blended with confidence in his tone. "I'll win hands down."

Matt chuckled, one corner of his mouth twisting up. "We'll see."

"Grand. I'll start spreading the word about the tasting

next Monday afternoon." Flint pivoted to head out of the kitchen to his office, then hesitated at the doorway to turn back to the two men. "Make your menus and a list of what you need to prepare them. You have a lot of work to do to plan and prepare your special menus in addition to the typical fare, so I hope you're both up for the challenge ahead."

He grinned at their serious expressions and pushed through the swinging door. Either way, the inn's fare would benefit from the friendly battle, perhaps some new menu items, and customer feedback. While he hadn't thought up the idea of a cooking contest, he would take all the benefits from the event possible. If it worked out, it might be something to repeat quarterly, expand to include a competition between hostelries. Anything was possible. His boss would have to approve when he learned of the concept. After all, what could be more fun than gathering the customers and guests together to sample a variety of foods over a friendly rivalry? It would be an event for the record books.

"Next week? And you just decided to do it today?" Abram accepted the mug of ale from Flint with a nod of thanks. It had been a busy morning and he was parched. The dining room was fortunately empty between the major meals of the day except for him and the innkeeper. Soon though others would begin arriving. "Is that enough time?"

"It will have to be. What kind of a challenge would it be otherwise?" Flint mopped up a small puddle of froth on the bar with a clean rag. "That should be enough time to decide on what they'll fix and gather the ingredients."

Abram swallowed a gulp of his beverage, then spluttered when Mandy strolled into the dining room wearing a pretty gingham dress with an easy smile aimed at him. The smile transformed her eyes and enthralled him. He couldn't keep an answering smile from his lips even as ale dribbled onto his chin. He broke eye contact and wiped his mouth dry. Better to focus on the conversation with Flint.

"What do you think will happen once the winner is announced?" The two cooks might have been joking around with each other about who was best, but once one was named the winner it would be a sore point the other would never forget. "I'd think the loser wouldn't be as eager to cook."

Flint draped the towel on the rail behind the bar. "Let's hope that doesn't happen. Having two cooks has been a blessing."

"You managed with one before."

"Yes, but I do not wish to go back to only one."

Abram shrugged, his attention caught by the mousy young woman moving about the room. "Say, what can you tell me about the serving wench over there?"

"She's not a wench. She's a woman." Flint pressed his hands onto the shiny surface of the bar. "Show some respect for my employee."

Abram blinked at the umbrage in Flint's tone. "I only assumed since she is a female. Finer establishments typically hire men as servers. At least where I come from."

"Now you know." Flint pivoted to select a bottle from the collection on the sideboard behind the bar. He snagged a small glass and turned back to face Abram. Pouring some of the amber liquor into the glass, he recapped the bottle and set it aside. "We do things differently here. My servers are respectable young ladies, including your sister."

"With your precious senator scheduled to visit, you might reconsider your approach."

"Why is that?" Flint returned the bottle to the sideboard and then lifted the glass to take a sip.

"His expectations will likely be the same as mine are… were." Only the lowest dining establishments resorted to hiring women as servers. He'd need to adjust to the idea of his sister waiting on customers and not demean her reputation. "Perhaps you could forewarn him?"

"I do not have the authority to contact him." Flint sipped again as his gaze followed Mandy's progress in covering the tables with fresh cloths. "So, what did you want to know about her?"

Mandy moved to the next table and unfolded the table cloth, snapping it open and letting it float down to cover the wooden table. Her hips swayed with each flick of her hands and each step she took, going from one table to the next. Abram met Flint's questioning gaze. "How did she end up working here?"

"She heard I was looking for more servers and applied for the job."

"She's very young, isn't she?"

"Eighteen, I believe."

"What about her parents? Why would they let her work in such a…"

Flint cleared his throat.

"Nice place?" Abram caught the censure in the innkeeper's demeanor. He corrected himself in order to not offend but really the inn wasn't of the same caliber as the elegant Tennison's Hotel on Pennsylvania Avenue in the Territory of Columbia. The inn would never measure up to the standards of the highly respected establishment.

"Better. She doesn't have any parents. She was raised in an orphanage in Nashville. Then moved south when she turned eighteen and met Haley Baker at church. They became friends and that's how Mandy learned of the opening here."

Abram frowned as he took a drink, remnants of foam swirling in the mug. "Where is she currently living?"

Flint shrugged. "With friends, but I'm not sure where or who. I need to talk to her about that, come to think of it."

"So she comes to work each day by herself?" With the ongoing threats, the idea worried him. Not that he cared about her personally, but every woman was apparently a target.

"Yes, she does. Poor girl doesn't own a horse so she walks." Flint sighed as his gaze returned to the girl in question. "I imagine as soon as she saves up the money, she'll buy herself a suitable mount."

"I don't like that she's putting herself at risk." Abram tapped his forefinger on the bar several times. "And you shouldn't let her do it. You're her boss and need to ensure she's not at risk so she can continue to work for you."

"I agree. But what do you think I should do?" Flint huffed. "Make her stay here?"

"Why not? You have the room."

"Are you interested in her?" Flint leaned closer to him, studying him intently. "Is that why you're asking so many questions?"

"No, not at all." The very idea. Like he'd want to be associated with such a plain little thing. He glanced again at her, seeing the same mousy woman he'd run into. Even if she did have an extraordinary smile. "But look at her. She must be lonely. Probably doesn't even have anyone interested in her let alone a suitor."

"If you're thinking about trying to become better acquainted if she is around more, then think again." Flint pointed a finger at Abram, an uncompromising expression settling on his features. "She is not the woman for you. You're not good enough for the likes of her."

"You shock and affront me with such a claim." The nerve of the simple innkeeper to denigrate his personality and person. He straightened his shoulders and raised his chin. "I believe it's the other way around."

Flint chortled as he gestured at Abram's entire being.

"You're an actor, aren't you? All dressed up and playing a part. All your fine clothes and sideburns, all about how you look and act. Acting the part of a dandy in the countryside. Grow up, man."

"How dare you—"

"Because I know the people you call family. This…"— he gave another wave of his hand at Abram—"is you pretending to be something you're not. The sooner you realize that, the better for everybody."

Flint tossed back the rest of his drink and strode out of the room. Abram gazed after him, reeling from the man's ridiculous, presumptuous, *outrageous* opinion. Abram was not play acting at anything. He'd built a good, decent life for himself. One every man would be proud of. He had a fine woman waiting for his return, one who outshone the serving girl in every way. Fashion, etiquette, connections, and a fine family. Mandy finished covering the last table and hurried out the door without a backward glance. A sense of disappointment filled him as a result. She'd left him alone with his fuming thoughts and the niggling feeling he was missing something.

Chapter Six

*L*ater that afternoon, Abram forced his steps to be light as he followed Cassie and Giles up the stairs. While his insides quivered with nerves and reluctance, he whistled a ditty and maintained a curious expression on his face. Giles kept glancing back at him, a quirk in his brow, watching his reaction to the idea of entering his parents' bedroom. He wouldn't give him the pleasure of revealing how the looming event unsettled him.

"It's still difficult for me," Cassie said in a low voice as she hesitated with her hand on the door knob. "But let's go."

Pushing the door open, she strolled inside, each step slow and measured. Abram silently drew in a bracing breath and eased through the doorway behind Giles. A tall wardrobe stood at the foot of a spiral staircase off to the right. Centered in the room, the bed with a tree of life quilt on its thick mattress waited for his parents to return. Knick-knacks rested on the vanity table along with...the looking glass he'd sent to his mother years ago. Drawn to it, he moseyed across the floor to the table.

"She loved that mirror." Cassie joined him, smoothing away a fine layer of dust from the wooden framed edge of the reflective surface. "She always thought of you whenever she gazed into it."

"That was the point." Abram stifled the urge to chuckle as he nodded solemnly. "Not that she'd think of me, mind. But I wanted her to be able to see herself clearly."

"When did you give her the glass?" Giles moved to the window and slid it partway open, letting a rush of cool rain-scented air into the stuffy room. Then he turned to gaze at his brother, crossing his arms over his chest. "When did you see her last?"

The defensive nature of his brother's stance and demeanor bespoke the level of his care. His role as Guardian suited him well. His steady regard from serious yet calm eyes. His feet apart and braced yet apparently set to spring into action at a hint of trouble. Never mind his immense strength, both muscular and emotional. Truth be told, his mere presence proved a comfort.

"I shipped it to her, actually. Several years ago, after I landed on my feet in the national capital, the Territory of Columbia." Times had been tough until he'd learned of the opening as a junior aide to a senator. His previous jobs as waiter, salesman, and even newspaper boy had provided him the skills necessary to be of use to the good man. Definitely better pay than any of his previous employment. "I thought she'd appreciate being able to ensure her appearance was sufficient."

The window panes rattled in a sudden gust of wind. He could see the trees whipping about outside. Perhaps a summer squall was blowing up.

"Very kind of you." The query in Giles' expression revealed his suspicions of an ulterior motive. "I'm sure she appreciated it."

"She did." Cassie tapped the table lightly with her fingertips before she sauntered toward the bed. "Abram, we want you to see the family heirlooms while we're up here."

"Heirlooms?" Abram peered into the mirror, imagining his mother primping and patting and preparing for the day. The visage staring back at him looked perfect. The dreaded scar nowhere in sight. The slight effort it took to maintain the glam was definitely worthwhile. He met Cassie's eyes in the reflection. "What heirlooms?"

"They're in trunks in the attic. Ma told us about them the last time we came here." She glanced toward the staircase and then back to him. "You won't believe what's up there."

"Handed down from previous generations of witches." Giles unfolded his arms and started toward the stairs. "Powerful artifacts of one kind and another. Come on."

A low rumble rolled across the heavens as the wind whistled through the open window, the tinging of rattling glass panes filling the room. Abram held his breath, aware of his heart racing at the thought of magical heirlooms hidden away in the mysterious attic. The idea of entering his mother's private lair and exploring the items she'd secreted away for an untold number of years distracted him from everything else. Studying his reflection, he winced when the scar appeared as vividly as ever. He took several slow breaths and focused on the image he wanted to present until the scar faded away. Perfect. Again and finally. His image in the mirror showed a flawless face. He steadied himself before following his brother across the bedroom, his footsteps echoing in the brooding space. He placed a foot on the bottom step as lightning flashed, blazing into the bedroom and illuminating the concern on his sister's face where she stood on the upper landing.

"That was close." She rubbed her arms with jerky movements. "Did you bring the lantern?"

Giles glanced down and then hefted an oil lamp. "Right here. Open the door and let's get this over with."

"Anyone else hungry?" Abram blurted out the first excuse he could conjure. Anything to delay what seemed inevitable.

Giles huffed. "No chance. Let's go."

"Just a thought." Abram refrained from muttering by silently chanting his mantra. *Make it look good. Make it look good. Make it look good.*

Cassie pulled a key ring from her apron pocket. A flash of lightning preceded a boom of window-rattling thunder. She jumped, clutching the railing with one hand. Abram grasped the railing at his side, striving to not display the jolt of panic the storm outside had initiated inside. Climbing higher in the building, toward the source of light and sound and lashing rain, felt illogical. Selecting an ornate key from the many on the ring, she shoved it into the lock and turned her wrist, the bolt withdrawing with a loud click.

She smiled reassuringly over her shoulder at him. "Ready?"

Giles, too, glanced over his shoulder and down the spiral stairs at Abram. "Be brave."

Of all the things his big brother could suggest, bravery was the farthest thing from his mind. He didn't consider himself brave. Determined. Persistent. Dogged, even. Not daring. His Adam's apple slid violently in his throat. Lightning flashed yet again, several blinding strokes illuminating the bedroom, followed by a thunderous crash of sound from above the quaking building. Almost as if Mother Nature warned him against taking another step toward the secrets buried in the trunks above. His brother and sister waited, knowing looks lurking in their eyes.

Abram forced his hand free from the railing. "Lead on."

She didn't blame him. Abram's mild expression contradicted the sheer terror racing through him. The raging storm outside in fact reflected his true feelings far better than the careful mask he wore. The fury of the wind and rain battering the sides of the inn added a sense of urgency to their mission. Without another word, she turned the door knob and pushed inside the dim interior, slipping the key ring back into her pocket as she stepped forward. Giles sidled past her with the lit oil lamp, shedding light into the attic and chasing away the remnants of shades and ghosts. At least until Ma appeared.

Everything looked as it should, thank goodness. Several trunks of varying sizes and designs were positioned around the room. Shelves of leather and cloth bound books hung on one wall. A fancy wooden chair with a cream-colored crocheted blanket draped over the back waited beside a matching table by the window, a small oil lamp centered on it. The floor was covered with a fine carpet bearing a floral pattern woven into the wool with a black Franklin stove nearby. The largest trunk sat by the door, made of walnut wood, with a flat top and the front wall decorated with carved flowers and arches. Three other similar trunks were spaced around the small room but only one of them contained the artifacts she wanted Abram to see.

She reached out with her senses, verifying they remained alone in her ma's private quarters. Or at least, they had been her private space. Until they'd discovered the hidden and secret family heirlooms which they claimed as their own. No longer solely belonging to her mother. Last time, Giles had pocketed the fancy watch. She'd declined to take anything, not feeling an affinity with any of them as of yet. She may never be drawn to one, which was a somewhat sad realization. But would Abram be attracted to a specific heirloom?

She sensed Abram's deep disquiet with each stride behind her. She needn't turn to see the guise he'd painted on his features. His emotional turmoil revealed far more than his expression would. The dichotomy between his appearance and his reality created a chasm in his personality, one he seemed unaware existed. Or perhaps denied even to himself.

"Wait until you see the variety of items Ma squirreled away all this time." She kept her tone light and fun to counter the weight of concern in his wide-eyed gaze.

The three trunks glowed in the incandescence of the lightning flashes from outside the small windows. The blond wood trunk hunkered across the room near the window. The domed lid took on a luminescence unlike anything else in the room. The flying owl design on the front beckoned to her, the open beak of the bird of prey calling her name as it appeared to fly toward her, talons outstretched and wings wide. She edged closer and slowly eased the lid up.

"I doubt there's anything in there for me." Abram slid his hands into his front trouser pockets, shoulders hunched as if warding off a cold breeze.

"You may be surprised." Giles strode across the floor to the side of the open trunk. "Come take a look and see what you like."

Abram shrugged and slowly shook his head, but didn't move any closer to the assortment of items gleaming in the lamp light.

"Come on, Abram, don't be afraid." His emotions ricocheted from brave to shrinking away, careening inside of her until she raised her own barrier against them.

"I'm not." He pulled his hands free from his pockets and squared his shoulders, a calm mask falling into place on his features. An echo of the small scar appeared and then vanished as he placed one foot in front of the other until he stood at her side. "See?"

Indeed. His inner turmoil had distracted him enough to affect his ability to glam. A weakness in the use of his gift, one he'd need to work on. She studied him for two seconds before restoring a grin to her lips. "You know I can tell how you're feeling, right? I can see when you're upset and distracted, too. Just rummage around in the jewelry and see what might appeal. Giles kept the pocket watch because he needed one. What might you need?"

"What kind of watch?" Abram pinned his gaze on Giles, tilting his head as he waited for his brother's response.

"Some fancy thing. It's not my style, but it will do for now." Giles motioned toward the open trunk with one hand. "Anything of interest?"

Abram perused the contents of the trunk for a brief moment before lifting a silver jewelry box from its depths. "This is rather pretty."

"There are some lovely pieces in there." Cassie glanced to the window when a boom of thunder shook the house and lightning flashed again. "That's quite a storm."

"Sudden, too." Giles followed the direction of her gaze. "I hope it's short-lived."

Abram inhaled sharply, shock flooding his core, which drew Cassie's attention back to him. He'd slipped a filigreed silver ring onto the fourth finger of his right hand.

"What's the matter?" She took a step toward him only to stop when he put up a hand. "What is it?"

"I don't understand what I'm feeling." He raised worried eyes to meet her gaze. "It's weird."

"You must be very careful, son." Mercy shimmered into view, hovering inches above the carpeted floor.

Dragging in a calming breath, he addressed his mother's ghost. "You really should knock or something, Ma."

"I agree. Your sudden appearances are disconcerting." Cassie pressed her palms to her waist. "Now why must he be careful?"

"Because that ring comes with immense power when wielded correctly." Mercy pointed to the tarnished ring and it slowly burnished until it gleamed. "If used incorrectly, it can cause great damage."

"Wow, Ma, I didn't know you had that kind of power." He pulled the ring from his hand and dropped it back into the box. "Perhaps I shouldn't wear it. I don't want to cause trouble."

"Too late for that." Giles started to chuckle at the jibe to his brother but fell silent as he stared at the wall. "We've got trouble coming."

"What do you mean?" Cassie followed the direction of his gaze but didn't see anything. "What's wrong?"

"I'm seeing the owl warning again but it's different this time…" He closed his eyes, holding still and silent for several moments. When he opened his eyes again, they glittered with intent. "We're going to have company soon and it's not going to go well. I can feel the danger approaching."

"What kind of danger?" Abram clasped the silver box with tense fingers.

Giles looked around the room, slowly nodding to himself, before pinning his gaze on Cassie. "Our aunts pose a threat to you."

She blinked in surprise and even denial. "I don't believe it."

"I do." Giles glanced at the ghost, his features tight. "Do you think Aunt Hope has forgiven me?"

"That one doesn't forget and rarely forgives." Mercy's voice filled with regret. "You must prepare yourself."

Giles merely nodded.

Cassie sensed the sorrow well up inside of her mother's spirit. "Do you miss seeing your sisters, Ma?"

"No. I wish they would stay away."

The sorrow vanished to be replaced with worry and deep anger. Cassie strengthened her barrier to better protect herself. "But I don't understand. Why would they be a threat to me?"

"Trust me, dear." Mercy shook her head once. "Those women are my sisters. I know just how very powerful and dangerous they are."

Abram's brow furrowed deeper as he stared at Mercy. "You're afraid of your sisters?"

"You should be as well." Mercy floated a foot closer to Abram. "You will need to raise a defense to protect your sister from their manipulation and machinations. The ring can help you."

"That's nonsense. I can protect myself." The very idea that her brothers, newly arrived, must protect her sent unease washing through Cassie. "What could he do that I can't?"

"We don't know yet what my sisters may attempt when they arrive." Mercy moved to the open trunk and studied the contents for several moments in silence. Then she looked at each of her children in turn. "Keep these trunks and the door to this room locked. The heirlooms come from the most powerful witches, male and female, in the region. Just because those witches happen to be related doesn't reduce their threat."

"Can you teach me how to use the ring?" Abram asked Mercy.

She nodded in response. "I can but you must promise to only use its power to help others."

"You have my word." Abram opened the box and retrieved the ring. "I'll do what's necessary. If there is indeed a threat."

"There is." Giles crossed his arms over his massive chest.

"I'll have to take your word for it, Giles." Abram studied his brother's set features and then met Cassie's quizzical look. "And you need to stay close."

She nodded once as fear sparked in her core. What or who was coming for her?

Chapter Seven

$\mathcal{T}$he storm moved off as quickly as it arrived, but not before it had dampened the afternoon dinner rush. Flint suppressed a sigh as he polished the already clean bar. Cassie had yet to make an appearance after begging off to show Abram the secreted items in the attic. But Mandy had the group of four men seated at one table in the dining room taken care of for the moment. He'd already chastised one young man for flirting too suggestively with her. He didn't need anything happening to chase her off. The young woman moved easily through the tables, pouring coffee or giving a quick smile before threading her way to the next patron. She'd adapted to the role of waitress quite easily, in fact, and the customers seemed to enjoy her quiet manner. He intended to keep it that way.

A gust of cool air drew his attention to the opening front door of the inn. Sterling and Abigail Nelson, each dressed impeccably, strolled toward the dining room, arm in arm. Sterling enjoyed an esteemed reputation and thus was an invaluable client for the inn. Sterling greeted the group of men, pausing at their table for a minute before continuing toward Flint. He squared his shoulders as he dropped the white towel on the bar and headed toward the couple.

"Mr. and Mrs. Nelson! What a delight to see you both again." Flint motioned toward the nearly empty dining room, keeping a welcoming smile in place. "Come, have a seat and let me get you a beverage."

"Thank you, Mr. Hamilton. I'm pleased we survived that ferocious cloudburst." Sterling removed his top hat, dripping water on the wood floor, and followed Flint toward a nearby table. "I would have stayed home were it not for an urgent meeting with those fine gentlemen."

"Indeed." Flint looked at the group a bit more closely. All prominent men of the county based on their attire and bearing. But why would they be meeting at the inn instead of in town? Curiosity piqued, he resisted the urge to pry but he'd keep his eyes and ears open. "What would you like to drink?"

Mandy hurried past carrying a tray laden with two bowls of pheasant stew, the delicious aroma wafting past his nose and teasing his appetite. The growl from his stomach reminded him he'd skipped his midday repast. Days like this one made him long for the assistance Reggie Fairhope would provide upon his return. In a little more than two months. A long time yet for him to juggle all the responsibilities of running and also improving the inn and its offerings. Preparing for the much anticipated visit by the senator. All while trying to assist in protecting his woman from an unspecified threat, possibly from her own relatives but also from the very man Reggie entrusted as overseer of Flint's endeavors. Such a mess to manage.

"A couple ciders would hit the spot, don't you think, dear?" Sterling glanced to Abigail and grinned at her nod of agreement. "I'll have mine over there. Abigail, darling, please make yourself comfortable. I shall join you in a little while."

"All right, but please don't take too long." Abigail sat down on the chair Sterling held for her, helping her push it closer to the table.

"I'll do my best." Sterling patted her shoulder and then walked over to sit with the other four men.

As Flint lifted the cold pitcher full of cider, Abram appeared at the entrance hall door in his fancy clothes and slicked hair. He'd been all worked up about a tiny scar Flint hadn't even noticed until the fop pointed it out. Not that a single hair would dare to defy Abram's specific and precise arrangement. The man needed to pay more attention to what was really important in life, which wasn't whether his appearance seemed perfect. Nobody could be flawless. Not even Abram Fairhope.

Abram scanned the room and then followed Mandy with his eyes as she checked with each guest. The man's finely tailored coat and vest along with the fancy trousers with boot straps to keep the crease sharp and crisp irritated Flint. In fact, Flint didn't like the way the young man half smiled and moistened his lips with a flick of his tongue as he regarded the waitress. Like a rattler preparing to strike. Not if he had anything to say about it.

He also didn't like the tone of the discussion emanating from the table by the door. The men spoke with a tenor of both anger and fear in their voices. Flint poured the beverages and carried one to Abigail and then approached Sterling to set his before him.

"The problem must be resolved and soon," Sterling said with a nod of thanks to Flint. "We must rid this area of the threat these women pose. If we work together, we can force their hand and banish them."

Flint froze in the act of turning away to go back to the bar. What women? He quickly snatched an out of place chair at a nearby table and righted it, giving him time to listen to the conversation.

"I agree, but how?" one cultured yet unfamiliar voice asked.

"Ah, there he is." Sterling stood up and intercepted John Baker who had just entered the dining room. "Come, sir, join us."

Flint peeked over his shoulder to see who he referred to, then spun around to greet John properly. "I wasn't expecting you today."

"I hadn't planned to come but received a last minute request to attend this meeting." John shook hands with Flint. "Might I trouble you for a whiskey?"

"Of course." Flint would take any excuse or reason to return to hear more of this conversation. "I'll be right back."

Abram strode over to intercept Mandy as she started for the door. He had a quiet exchange with the server, but sent sly glances toward Flint. The man was taunting him by flirting with the girl despite his warnings. Flint bristled as the two talked for a spell before Abram stepped to one side to let her pass. He slid behind the bar and reached for a rock glass. Mandy hurried out of the room with a quick look over her shoulder as she disappeared from view. With a smirk firmly in place, Abram sauntered toward the bar.

"What was that about?" Flint pressed his palms on the glistening surface.

"I don't know what you are referring to." Abram rested an elbow on the polished bar.

Flint tapped the mahogany with his hand. "You were flirting with Mandy a moment ago. I don't like it."

Abram waved off his objection. "I wasn't flirting with her. I was asking her to get me something to eat."

"Don't hurt her by teasing her and then leaving like you keep saying you'll do at the first opportunity."

"You have my word as a gentleman," Abram said. "I'd like something to drink."

Flint bit back the retort forming on his tongue. He poured amber liquor into the glass and set the bottle back on the bar. "Just a minute."

He hurried John's drink to him and set it carefully on the table. The conversation halted on his approach as six men waited for him to depart. Damn. He didn't know these men and no introductions were offered. Time to go. "Gentlemen."

Once more behind the bar, he kept one eye on the intent group of men, wishing he could hear their discussion without being obvious. Instead, he met Abram's expectant expression. "What can I get you?"

"An ale would be appreciated."

"How did it go upstairs?" Flint stifled the impulse to bring him down from his high horse as he poured an ale, careful to scrape the foam from the top, and slid it and a cloth napkin toward Abram. "Everything work out all right?"

Giles appeared in the doorway, pausing for a moment to survey the room. His gaze landed on the six men for a long moment before he ambled toward the bar.

"I've acquired a new ring, one which should prove useful." Abram sipped the brew and then wiped his mouth with the napkin, his gaze sliding away to land upon Mandy as she carried a tray of steaming plates into the room behind Giles' burly frame. He took another gulp and met Flint's assessing gaze. "What is bothering you now?"

"Your attitude toward Mandy." Flint snatched up the towel and rubbed the bar counter dry rather than go eavesdrop on the startling and worrisome group. "Leave her alone."

"Why? That's up to her, isn't it?"

Giles slid onto a stool at the bar, angling his body so he could peruse the activity within the room. "An ale when you have a moment."

"Sure." He acknowledged the request then turned back to Abram. The temptation to plant a rumor of some defect or illness blazed inside as Flint contemplated the self-obsessed fop. "Don't even think about getting involved with her. She's my employee, not your next conquest."

"If you and Cassie are together, why do you care?" Another sip of ale preceded a slithering glance at Mandy as she came toward the bar with a bowl of stew in her hands. "Hmm?"

"Who are we talking about?" Giles asked, a slight frown in place.

The conversation broke off as the girl in question set the bowl before Abram, pulling a napkin and spoon from her apron pocket and placing them on the bar. She dipped a quick curtsey.

"Thanks, miss." Abram touched two fingers to his forehead in salute of her efforts. He lifted the spoon and scooped up the fragrant mixture as Mandy hurried away to dispense the remaining meals. Holding his spoon aloft, he peered at Flint. "Did that meet with your approval?"

"It's better." If only the man wouldn't act like he was so superior to the rest of the people around him. Then maybe he wouldn't be so irritated by him. Somebody needed to make him understand the effect he was having on others. "What happened to your itty-bitty scar?" Flint gestured at the man's chin, barely refraining from landing a punch there.

"I understand now." Giles nodded and sipped the ale Flint set before him. "Mandy."

"Yes, Mandy. Flint is being an ass." Blinking slowly, Abram lightly touched his chin before gripping the mug with both hands and staring at Flint. "Why do you ask?"

He noticed Abigail motion for a refill of her cider, so he grabbed a clean mug and poured the cold liquid into it. Then he leaned closer to Abram, peering into the man's guarded expression. "I'd be careful using your powers on yourself for too long."

"Why would you care?" Abram pushed away from the bar, tugging his coat down to lay smoothly against his hips.

"You don't know how staying in 'costume' might impact you." He placed the full mug on a small round tray and then shrugged at the dandy. "May even weaken you and prevent you from doing what's necessary to keep your sister safe. Who knows?"

"I doubt it. I have to go. I need to take care of a few things." Abram stepped back and turned to head out of the dining room. "See you later."

Flint shook his head as the man disappeared out the front door. The entire conversation upset him but he had more important things to think about.

Giles drummed his fingers on the surface to draw Flint's attention then tilted his head toward the group of men. "What's going on over there?"

"Nothing good. I only heard something about banishing women." Flint peered at Giles seeing concern reflected in his hazel eyes. "Could they be referring to witches do you think? Is that why women are being killed? Because they're witches?"

"But they look like they are well-respected men." Giles turned to assess the neatly attired gentlemen in their suits and ties. He stiffened, eyes widening. "Damn, the owl."

"Owl?"

"Never mind." Giles turned back to look at him, but worry lingered in his eyes. "But surely they're not killers. Their gathering may not even be connected to the murders."

"I wish I knew. I thought it might be John working alone, but now…" Flint raked his fingers through his hair and then dropped both hands on the bar. "I hadn't anticipated an organized effort like that gathering might indicate."

"I'll see what I can find out." Giles drained his mug and pushed away from the bar, then turned back to lean closer. "Keep this between us for now."

"I will. Let me know what you learn." He watched Giles stroll out of the room and then carried the fresh drink over to Abigail. She looked bored sitting all by herself. Then he had an idea. "Say, we're having a cookery competition between my two chefs next week. Would you and your husband be interested in coming to taste their meals and then vote on your favorites?"

"A cookery competition?" Abigail accepted her glass of cider with a nod. "Sounds intriguing. Why are they having a competition?"

"Just a friendly contest, actually. They're both excellent." Flint pulled the towel from his shoulder and held it in one hand. "But if it will help identify some new menu items for our customers, then I'm all for it."

"I'd love to try whatever they prepare," Abigail said with a grin. "It would be fun."

"Wonderful, Mrs. Nelson." Flint glanced to where Sterling was in an intense exchange with a quirked brow. The men were winding down their meeting, shaking hands all around as if they'd reached an important decision. If only he knew what it was. "Would your husband like to as well?"

"I'm not sure he can get away. When is it?"

"Monday afternoon right here in the dining room." Flint gestured with both hands as he gazed at the banker's wife.

Abigail swallowed some cider. "I'll be sure to ask him, but I think he'd enjoy it. Actually, I'll talk him into it." She smiled at him to seal the bargain.

"Then I'll put you both down." Soon, he'd have to figure out who those other men were and what they were up to. He draped the towel over his left arm and patted it smooth. "You never know what might come from such a fun event."

"Now, ground and center."

"How do you expect me to do both?" Abram sat cross-legged on the carpeted floor that evening, hands resting on his knees as he tried to follow his sister's instructions. He gazed at her, wondering if she believed the mystical nonsense she'd spouted over the last several minutes. "And what do you mean by center?"

"Relax and breathe. Picture a glowing golden taproot connecting your spine to the earth beneath you." Cassie perched on the edge of a chair in front of the fireplace in the parlor, her expression serene and gentle. "Close your eyes and concentrate." She paused for several seconds as he let his lids drop. "Can you see it?"

He inhaled slowly, struggling with the conflicting desires to dismiss her guidance as utter rubbish or to follow her instructions and see what might happen. Despite his reservations, the image of a thick, strong taproot like that of an ancient pine tree formed in his mind's eye. "Now what?"

"Feel the earth's energy flowing gently and warmly to the base of your spine."

A slight tingling warmed his hips as he sat with his eyes closed, seeing the energy like a glowing golden stream flowing up along the taproot and into his body. Squeezing his eyes tight to ensure he didn't open them and lose the image, he waited for her next directions.

"Now feel the energy flow through your legs down all the way to your feet. Then let it flow up your spine and through your arms and hands."

"It's so warm. I didn't expect to feel that." He flexed his fingers then relaxed them on his knees. The gentle warmth surged through his entire body, filling him with a sense of peace and security but mostly a surprisingly deep connection to the earth.

"That's perfect. Now, push the excess energy back down the taproot but keep your own energy alive inside." Her soft voice drifted to his ears and assisted him in easing the unnecessary energy back into the earth through the golden taproot. "When you're done, open your eyes."

He pictured the last of the excess energy evaporating into the ground even as a sense of completion and readiness filled him. He opened his eyes and grinned at her. "That was amazing."

"Now, you're ready to try shapeshifting." Her voice sounded both keen and wary, like a young girl about to be kissed for the first time.

"I don't know how to start." He grasped his knees as his thoughts careened inside. "I'm not sure it's a good idea."

"Abram Fairhope, you need to practice shifting if you have any hope of doing so when you need to." She rose to her feet and strode closer to him. "If you don't figure out how to use and ultimately control your gift, then you won't be able to employ it effectively when you need it. So, let's try."

She was right but that didn't mean he had to like it. Did shapeshifting hurt? How did it work? How long would he be in the other shape? How did one learn to become something or someone else?

Mercy shimmered into view a few feet from him. "Abram, before you try to shift let me tell you about how you can use the ring to help you succeed."

He sucked in a shaky breath at her sudden appearance. "Very well."

"Close your right hand." She demonstrated with her ghostly hand until he did as instructed. "Then say,

'I summon the protections of this ring

To guard me and aid me in my intent.

By Earth, By Sky, By Sea

By the ancient Law of Three,

As I Will, so mote it be.'"

"What will that do?" He needed some reassurance of the intent and outcome behind the spell before he'd follow her instructions. Even though he had become adept at adjusting to quick changes, the more he knew beforehand the smoother his adaption to the new direction.

"This spell protects your true nature so you can return to it when you're finished." She drifted a little to one side, pressing her lips together. "It doesn't increase your ability but it does provide a layer of protection."

He frowned at the idea of casting a spell. Of acknowledging his witchy inheritance. "I don't know…"

"You do want to be able to shift back into your true self, right?" Her arched brows and slight shake of her head made him feel like a fool.

He steeled his courage. "Of course."

"Then memorize the spell so you can invoke it when you feel threatened and uncertain." She smiled at him and then shimmered. "I'll see you later."

She vanished as he was about to ask her to repeat the lines. He cast a glance at Cassie. "Did you catch the words of that spell?"

"Yes, they're easy." She repeated them for him.

The ease with which she rattled off the unfamiliar words made him feel even less capable. "Thanks. Maybe I should try this some other time." He shifted to start to rise but Cassie hurried to him.

"Abram, come on." She grasped his shoulders and gave him a little shake. "Think about becoming something else."

"Such as?"

"Whatever you'd like to try." Cassie strode across the room to perch on a chair in front of the fireplace. "Choose and visualize every detail. Then will yourself to become what you see."

Before he did anything else, he closed his hand and repeated the spell. If there were any time he was feeling uncertain, it was at that moment. Then, feeling slightly calmer, he thought for a moment until he settled on one of his favorite creatures. A powerful and beautiful animal, one both admired and feared. He pictured a sleek black panther with large paws and fangs prowling through the forest. Imagined its yellow eyes and pointed ears, whiskers bristling on either side of its open mouth. He concentrated as hard as he could on the mental picture of the big cat until he heard Cassie chuckle. He glanced at her and saw a lopsided grin and twinkling eyes.

"Almost." She gestured with a hand at his body.

He looked down to find whiskers poking out from his face and large clawed paws for hands. Otherwise, he was still in his own body. "Don't laugh."

"It is quite a sight though. You must admit as much." She folded her arms over her chest as she wrestled the grin from her face.

"I tried my best. What went wrong?"

"I don't know. You'll figure out how to do it with time and practice. I couldn't control my empathic abilities at first but I practiced subtly on the guests from time to time until I learned how to work with it."

"Maybe it was the cat. I'm not a cat nor even acted like one. I want to try again."

"All right. Maybe try shifting into me, since I'm right here. It might be easier with a model to concentrate on."

"Shifting into another human form may be easier, too." He nodded to himself as he scanned his sister's form. Noted her long curly blond hair and pale blue eyes, a dimple in one cheek. "Here goes."

He kept her image in mind as he closed his eyes and willed himself to become her. Focused on having long blond hair instead of dark brown and growing shorter to match her height as the tingling increased. Pictured himself in a flowered dress with heeled leather shoes. He felt himself change, become smaller with long tresses hanging down his back. He smiled as he opened his eyes.

"Nice try, but not quite." She laughed out loud the longer she met his distraught gaze.

Glancing down at himself, he saw the hair he'd felt and even the dress but his legs hadn't changed. "Blast it all. What else didn't shift?"

"I've never had side burns for one thing." She waved at his face with humor sparkling in her eyes. "Nor bright blue eyes and bushy eyebrows."

Embarrassed and affronted by her laughing at him, he stopped trying to be her and willed himself back to normal. Relief flowed through him as the prickly energy left his body. "Never mind. Perhaps I can't do this after all."

Her mirth evaporated. "Oh, don't give up. You have to keep trying."

He smoothed his waistcoat with a tug fueled by annoyance. "Not if I don't want to. I'm finished."

He left the room with quick strides, desperate to escape her taunting and his own failure.

Chapter Eight

The next morning, Cassie worked on mending a tear in one of her work dresses, grateful for a few minutes alone in the parlor. Abram's embarrassment shouldn't have made her laugh at him. She'd apologize to him when she saw him next. Pulling the needle through the gingham fabric with sure strokes calmed her anxiety regarding his failure to use his gift to completely shift.

A small pop sounded at her elbow. An envelope rested against the vase of fresh flowers on the table. She frowned as she lifted it. It hadn't been there before, she was sure of it. She sniffed, detected a hint of rosemary in the air. The combination of its sudden appearance and the change in the air could mean only one thing. Magic was involved. A thrill of foreboding swept through her.

Flint strolled into the room carrying a small tray bearing a silver pot and two cups. Just the person she needed as she studied the envelope, reluctant to open it. Having Flint's calming presence helped settle her disquiet at the sudden appearance of the mysterious letter.

"Good morning, Cassie. I thought you might enjoy some tea." He set the tray on the low table and then turned to face her. "Who is that from?"

She angled the white envelope, glancing at the return address. "From my aunt."

"I hope she's decided to forego coming here."

"Ma would like that." Opening it with care and caution, she unfolded the single sheet of paper and quickly skimmed the note. "Ma will be disappointed, I'm afraid."

"They're still coming then?" Flint sank onto the chair opposite Cassie's.

"In a few days, in fact." She perused the letter, her eyebrows arching of their own accord. "They want to speak to Pa and demand a clean room near mine so 'we can best ascertain your well-being'."

Abram strolled through the open door as she finished reading from the letter. "Morning. What's that?"

She jiggled the page in her fingers, pondering the particular demands it contained. "Our aunts are on their way." She filled him in on the other details in the missive. "What now?"

"Let them come if they want to." Abram shrugged lightly before dropping onto the settee by the front window. "You can't stop them."

"I wish you could." Mercy appeared out of nowhere to float in the center of the room.

Cassie couldn't stop the gasp or the hand clutching her throat. "Please stop doing that, Ma."

"What?" Mercy grinned conspiratorially as she settled to the floor near Cassie. "I can't help it if you scare easily. And you should be scared...of my sisters."

Flint's scowl aimed at the ghost made Cassie grin in response as her heart stopped racing in her chest "Anyway... Abram is right. I can't stop my aunts from coming. What do you suggest?"

Mercy shimmered but stayed in the room. She aimed her troubled eyes at Abram. "At least prepare some form of defense. Get Giles to help you."

"What do you expect us to defend against?" Abram relaxed on the lounger, legs crossed and arms folded. "They're family even if they are witches. Why would they harm us?"

The nonchalance streaming from her brother gave her pause. He discounted the possibility of the threat her mother feared from her sisters. Surely Ma had a better grasp of what they were capable of than her brother. She reached out to sense the emotions in the room and confirmed worry from Ma but a wariness beneath the calm façade Abram presented. Flint also stood on alert to the question of her safety as her aunts verged on arriving.

"They are powerful witches." Mercy glared at her son, shimmering with distress. "They will stop at nothing to have their way. Mark my words, they want Cassie to fill the role they'd tried to have me take on for their benefit. They will try to steal her away."

"Do you want to work with them?" Abram asked, gazing steadily at Cassie.

"No." She couldn't imagine even being tempted to work magic that might harm others.

"Then there's nothing to worry about, Mother." He shrugged and picked at a fingernail.

Mercy drifted over to stare down at her son. "Don't underestimate them."

"Cassie is a big girl. She'll do what she wants to, not what they demand."

Her brother's insistence on denying the impending threat sent a wave of impatience through her. "At least listen to Ma's concern. Please talk to Giles."

Abram examined his thumbnail for several seconds before sighing and sitting up. "About what exactly?"

His attitude defied reason. But then, what did they really know about the witches? "Ma, I think Abram has a point. What do you think your sisters will try to do?"

Mercy drifted closer to Cassie, her image wavering in streams of concern that flowed from her spectral form into Cassie's core. "They will attempt to persuade you to work with them. To go back south with them and leave the inn. You mustn't fall into their hands. They'll change you and not for the better."

"How will they try to persuade me? What arguments will they use?"

"My guess is they will convince you that their goals are for the betterment of the family in one way or another. That your skills and talents will complement theirs and make the resulting trinity of witches all-powerful."

"So as long as she doesn't agree, then all should be well." Abram stood and smoothed his suit coat into place. "Problem solved."

A brief knock on the door preceded Mandy striding into the parlor. "Hey, Cassie, there you are."

Cassie glanced at her ma's ghost, hovering near the fireplace, and raised a brow. Her mother nodded once before shimmering and vanishing. Cassie turned to Mandy, relief flowing through her knowing that even if Mercy hadn't left the girl couldn't see the haint.

"Did you need something?" Cassie frowned at the other woman who came to an abrupt halt, trying to recall if she'd forgotten she'd promised to do something for her.

"Just wondering about the uniforms you're going to make. It would be lovely to have something nicer to wear than these worn out frocks." Mandy hovered near the door, shifting her weight from one foot to the other.

The girl had suddenly realized she'd interrupted a heated discussion. Cassie sensed her dismay and embarrassment over walking into a family squabble. But she still stood there, waiting for an answer, uncertain how to remove herself from the scene. Abram simply stared at the girl without saying anything but Cassie could tell he was intrigued by her. Flint cleared his throat loudly, drawing Abram's wry look. What was going on between Flint and Abram? Mandy fidgeted more and Cassie shook off her own musings.

"I need to purchase the materials but hopefully soon." She smiled at her, lifting her brows. "If that is all?"

"Yes, that's all." Mandy dipped a curtsey. "If you'll excuse me…"

With that the girl fled the parlor. Abram chuckled softly as Flint glared at him.

"Now, Abram, let's talk about what you're going to do next." Cassie blinked slowly at her brother, upset at his dismissal of their mother's concern ricocheting inside. His entire demeanor suggested he simply didn't care whether her safety or very life might be at risk. He acted as if he cared more about his manicure and his attire than her. She sensed his resistance to the idea that their aunts posed a threat to them. Disappointment settled in her stomach like a rotten tomato, oozing and souring her happiness at seeing her brother after so long. He came at her request, but had no plan to help her.

"Don't be an ass." Flint rose from his chair and stalked across the parlor to confront Abram. "Let's go find your brother and devise a plan to defend your sister. You can do that much."

"Please, Abram." She studied her brother's careful front as he glanced between her and Flint. His mask of disinterest remained firmly in place although the hint of his scar revealed the level of distraction he fought. Perhaps he cared more than he allowed himself to believe let alone demonstrate. Was that why she didn't sense his concern? Interesting.

"Very well, but it seems a waste of time until we know if there is actually a threat that these two women might pose to you." Abram sighed and shook his head. "Let's find Giles and rope him into pretending to erect a useful defense."

"I think he's upstairs, so let's check there first." Flint glanced up at the ceiling above the parlor. "Come on."

As Flint led Abram over to the staircase, Cassie could only wonder which approach was right.

"There he is." Flint didn't bother knocking on the open door, but led Abram inside the bedroom. "Giles, we need to talk."

He strode into the fair sized room where Giles shared bunk beds with Matt and Zander. When the three men had first arrived at the inn, they had taken two of the guest bedrooms on the other side of the building. But as they settled in, Flint realized it would be better for the three of them to be on the family side with Cassie. If indeed a threat presented itself, having her protectors, including himself, nearby would prove the best deterrent. Besides the two sets of bunk beds flanking the lone window, a small table with a ewer and basin and four cushioned chairs occupied one corner. An oak wardrobe stood beside the door, its doors and drawers graced with carved ribbons and flowers.

Giles sat on the edge of the lower bed, his stockinged feet on a green braided rug. "About?"

"Your mother is very worried about her sisters coming here." Flint planted his feet and crossed his arms. "We need some kind of plan or approach to face whatever threat they might bring with them."

"Why the hurry?" Giles reached down to retrieve one scuffed boot and pulled it on his foot.

"Cassie received a letter stating they will arrive in a couple of days," Abram said, his tenor voice dripping with doubt. "Though Ma has no real idea of what kind of threat they might be. We should wait until they arrive and then develop a response to whatever happens."

"That leaves us flat footed and unprepared." Giles

stomped his foot to slide the boot firmly in place. "It would be too late to devise a strategy once they are here."

"How on earth do you think we can prepare when we don't know what's coming?" Abram paced the room, his agitation and defensiveness evident in his stiff shoulders and scowling features.

Flint watched him prowl back and forth for several seconds. "What do you think we should do then?"

"Wait and see what happens." Abram hunched his shoulders and then squared them as he continued striding to and fro.

Giles pulled his other boot on and stamped his foot before standing. "As Guardian of this family, I say we figure out all the ways we can imagine two witches could put Cassie at risk. And then determine what weapons we have in our arsenal to raise a defense."

Flint nodded as relief flowed through him. Having a starting point, a basic plan if nothing else, gave him a sense of purpose and hope. "Where do we start?"

"We know Ma thinks they will try to convince Cassie to leave with them," Abram offered reluctantly. "But we also know she doesn't want to go."

"Mercy claims they are powerful witches so we don't know to what extent they'd use magic to gain their objective." Flint raked a hand through his hair and then rubbed his chin. "I have my pistol but what good would that be against whatever they can conjure?"

"Cassie has some abilities she might be able to wield but what if they enchant her?" Giles glanced at Flint and then Abram, a frown firmly in place. "What if they do convince her to go with them?"

Flint's heart dropped to his feet at the mere thought the women could possibly steal his girl away from him. He'd go after her. Without a doubt, he no longer wanted to live without her. If she'd have him, of course. Doubt slipped into the cracks in his plan. She kept putting him off, asking him to wait. Perhaps she entertained her own doubts about the future. Their future and hers.

"We have Mercy, too, don't forget." Flint grasped at whatever hope he could find as he struggled to maintain his own emotional balance. "She knows them and can help us find ways to thwart any attempts they make on her daughter."

Abram shook his head as he stopped pacing to address the two other men. "Like I said, without knowing what exactly we may face we're just speculating and conjecturing."

"But now we have a better idea of what we have to fight back with." Giles crossed the room to grab his hat from the coat rack on the wall. "If you'll excuse me, it's time for my rounds."

"Somehow I don't think the threat is outside, but it does make me feel better knowing you're keeping an eye out." Flint dragged in a deep breath and let it out. "I've got to get to work, too."

Chapter Nine

$\mathcal{R}$ esentment simmered in his chest. The discussion or, rather, argument with Giles left him out of sorts. Abram strolled into the dining room later that afternoon, keeping a pleasant smile on his mouth despite how he felt. No matter what else, he knew from personal experience how much appearances mattered. The whole concept of protecting his sister from their aunts made his skin crawl with irritation. Why on earth would family hurt family? Well, other than his mother and father chasing their sons out of the house as soon as they were of age to survive on their own. That was different. That was for their own good. Wasn't it?

His stomach grumbled loudly as he hesitated at the open doorway to scope out an empty table during the midday rush. Mandy bustled about the room, pausing to check on first one customer then another. She managed the tray with dexterous skill as she handed out drinks and collected dirty plates and bowls to carry back to the kitchen. Someone needed to teach her how to dress to enhance her features instead of hiding them. She really was a plain girl, all brown and tan with hardly any sparkle about her. Except when she wore that entrancing smile.

Cassie hurried into the room with two bowls of stew in her hands, her expression serious as she balanced them until she reached a table where three men bantered. They could use several more servings, what with their clothes hanging on their scrawny frames. Abram watched the two girls, as different as he was with his tailored clothes, refined hair style, and classic education from a simple working man. Cassie's golden hair and vibrant blue eyes contrasted with Mandy's brown hair and eyes. How unfortunate for the plain girl to be so...well, plain. Shrugging off his musings, he spotted a table on the far side and quickly secured a seat.

Moments later, Mandy approached his table and a smile lit her face. He blinked rapidly as the impact of her radiant smile smashed through him. That smile illuminated every feature, from her eyes to her skin glowing with life. But honestly, when the woman smiled, she transformed into a real beauty.

"What can I get you? Some ale? Or cider?" She propped the tray on her hip as she waited for his order.

Not a freckle marred her pale glowing skin. Her brown hair was pulled up into a neat bun at the back of her head, a style that emphasized the nearly black lashes framing her lively, light brown eyes. Her lips formed a perfect curve, perfect for kissing he'd bet. What would her kiss taste like?

"Mr. Fairhope?" Laughter sparkled in those lovely eyes as she quirked a brow at him.

"An...an ale, please." *Get a grip on yourself, man.* He wasn't some young buck fawning over some chit. "Do you like it? Working here?" Her scent enveloped him, something light and floral with an underlying essence of vanilla.

"Yes, though the others can be somewhat mysterious at times." She shrugged and glanced around the room, obviously checking on the other customers.

"Mysterious?" His turn to quirk a brow. "How do you mean?"

"I don't mean anything, honest. I've just learned to read people, being an orphan. I need to be able to figure out those who are telling me the truth and those who aren't."

"Is someone lying to you?" Now both brows rose to inquire as to her meaning.

"No, no. Sorry! I don't mean to mislead." She grabbed the tray with both hands, holding it like a shield in front of her. "Anything else you want along with the ale?"

A quick change of the subject suggested her discomfort with the direction the conversation had taken. "Whatever stew you have."

She gave him a nod and spun on one heel to scurry from the room. The sway of her hips set her long skirts swooshing side to side until she disappeared from view. He swallowed and glanced around him. Had anyone noticed him staring after her? Nobody else paid him any mind except for Flint, who stood at the bar with a scowl on his face. His hunger vanished at the foreboding expression.

Cassie strode up to the bar and caught Flint's attention, effectively breaking the staring contest between the two men. Abram breathed easier without the hostile glare weighing on him.

"So Mandy and I were thinking about those uniforms. We have an idea." Cassie hopped onto a tall stool and propped her elbows on the bar. "We need your approval, of course."

"What do you have in mind?" Flint's wary tone revealed his uncertainty.

"Something refined yet useful. A blue dress with a white shirt and a pale yellow apron. Oh, and pockets in the apron." She tapped a finger on the polished surface of the bar. "It's bad enough we're women waiting tables. Some folks object to that. I don't want anyone to think we have loose morals because we pitch in to help."

Abram's ears pricked up at his sister's comment. The colors she mentioned would make all the difference for the other server's appearance. Clothes spoke volumes about the wearer if one knew how to listen to the message. He scanned the others in the room, noting their sturdy yet clean and neat attire. Compared to his fancy tailored ones, they were nothing to brag about. Still, he really stood out in the crowd and not necessarily in a good way. He suddenly felt very overdressed and uncomfortable as a result. He'd speak to Flint about where he could find more appropriate clothing to wear while he remained in the area.

"As long as the skirts cover your ankles...I won't have you appearing in anything inappropriate." Flint brushed her hand off the bar and rubbed a towel over the surface to make it gleam once again. "I may need to look into hiring some men to serve when the senator arrives, come to think of it. He may be offended otherwise."

"I do not wish to be inappropriate but neat and pretty." Cassie pressed her palms onto the counter, a daring arch of a brow challenging him to argue with her.

"Cassie, what are you thinking?"

"That it's not your decision as to the proper length." She tapped the bar with her forefinger. "We know what's right for us."

Mandy returned carrying a steaming bowl of stew. She stopped at the bar on her way past. "Could you get an ale for Abram, please?"

Flint met Abram's gaze, lingering mistrust in his eyes. "Of course."

Cassie gestured to Mandy to wait before she had chance to deliver the food to Abram. "I've told Flint our idea for a uniform and he's approved it. Now we just need the cloth and trim and we'll be set."

"Sounds wonderful." Mandy indicated the bowl in her hands. "I need to give this to Abram before it gets cold."

"Let Cassie give it to her brother." Flint snapped the towel and then slung it over his shoulder. "You can see to those new arrivals just coming in."

Mandy frowned lightly but handed the bowl to Cassie. "If that's what you want me to do."

"It is." Flint nodded, his eyes conveying to Abram a warning to stay away from the girl.

Why did he care? It wasn't like Abram had designs on wooing her. She was simply a girl, a more enticing female than he'd first thought, but still just a girl. The more he saw of her, however, the more he found to like. The more her personality shone forth and revealed the light within. She had depths he hadn't appreciated when he'd first seen her. Perhaps first impressions weren't all he'd been led to believe.

The kitchen door swung shut behind her, blocking out the remainder of the jovial argument between the two cooks. Those two had high hopes of beating each other out in what was supposed to be a friendly competition. Cassie heaved a sigh and hurried to find Flint. He obviously expected the caliber of the inn's menu to improve as a direct result. Which given the list of ingredients needed, it had better also increase the number of customers in order to offset the cost.

"There you are." Cassie paused in the open doorway to the office. "Why are you hiding in here?"

Flint looked up, blinking, an open ledger on the desk and a nub of a pencil in his hand. "Catching up on the finances."

He looked so cute sitting at the desk, all owl-eyed and hunched over his work. She walked into the room and rested her fingertips on the corner of the wood desk. A stack of magazines occupied the far corner, the top one featuring a grand red brick building. Probably one of his architecture magazines he liked to study for ideas to improve the inn. The sound of horse hooves and harness jangling as well as that of the lowing cattle in the field behind the barn drifted through the open window.

"Am I interrupting?" She gestured to the stack of magazines. "I can come back later if you're too busy. Looks like you were studying up on something."

He saw where she pointed and shook his head. "No, I'm almost finished." He sighed as he dragged his attention away from the magazines. "I'm not going anywhere anytime soon. Those can wait."

A wisp of sadness spooled through him, surprising her, and she looked more closely at his expression. "What do you mean? Had you planned on going somewhere?"

He raised his eyes to meet her surprised gaze. "I had hoped to but not until your father returns, if then. Now everything has changed and I can't."

"But want to, though."

"I did but now I won't. I can't. You're too important to me to follow that path."

Relief washed through her at his declaration. She'd come to depend upon him. "I am glad to hear that. But I hope it's not too great a sacrifice, one you'll end up regretting."

He pressed his lips together and shook his head. "I won't regret my decision. I can promise you."

"Okay, but if something changes so you can follow your dream, let's talk about it."

"So what brings you in search of me this morning? I could use a little break."

The change of subject was not lost on her. Lightening her tone, she pressed her hand onto the wood desk. "I hope there's money on account to purchase what those two battling cooks want from the market." She held up a paper in her other hand. "It's quite a list."

He squinted at the paper, his mouth forming an O when he detected the length of the list. "I'm amazed you can carry such a weighty collection of items."

"It's been a struggle." She winked at him for good measure. He seemed tense and yet quiet. She sensed he was somber yet hopeful. Something weighed as heavily on his mind as the list of items in her hand.

"What on earth are they preparing and for how many people?" Flint's voice sounded weary and a touch concerned.

"They told me what they need but have sworn me to secrecy. And you, too, of course." She angled the paper so the soft glow of the oil lamp sitting on the desk illuminated the contents. "Sheridan's dinner features duck with huckleberries and watercress salad, and Matt's is something called East Indian Curry and a fancy salad." She smiled at Flint's open mouth and raised brows. "There's more…"

Flint waved off hearing more. "Let them surprise me."

"Want to hear what they need?" She glanced at the paper in her hand and then back to him. "Or part of it? I don't want to take too much of your time."

"May as well. That way I can mentally prepare for the expense."

"All right. Other than the obvious duck I mentioned there are lots of seasonings like thyme, ginger, turmeric, cardamom seeds, etc. Fruits and vegetables such as onion, shallots, corn—which we have in the garden—huckleberries and blackberries, bananas, grapes, oranges… Shall I continue?"

"No." He fingered the pencil, wiggling it back and forth. "That's enough to tell me what I've signed up for with this contest."

"You did ask for it." She chuckled at his strained expression. "Tomorrow is Wednesday, market day. Would you take me into town so I can pick up what they need?"

"I suppose there's no other option. I did agree to this

battle after all." He tapped the pencil on the ledger before dropping it on the page. "Do you want to select the bolts of cloth and the trim you need to make the uniforms at the same time?"

She laid the paper on the desk and moved to stand beside his chair, resting a hand on his shoulder in silent compassion. "That's a fine idea."

"I do have them occasionally." He grimaced before pushing away from the desk and standing to face her, his expression gentle and serious. "The drive will give us time to talk."

She found herself holding her breath at his words. Reaching out to him with her senses, she detected a quivering anxiety. Yet she couldn't get a clear read as to what he might be anxious about. Or more worrisome, what he wanted to discuss. What she clearly sensed was his desire for her, which sparked her own.

"And to do this." She lifted her lips to press against his, savoring the warmth and taste of mint.

She belonged with him yet she held back, needing her father's approval since her mother wouldn't give hers. Cassie's juvenile idea of finding a man—this man—to marry solely to escape her mother's domination had changed to a sincere desire. But with her father so far away and her mother's objections fresh in her mind, she simply couldn't succumb to the temptation of marrying. Especially after learning of her witchy family and new abilities. So many changes had happened amidst so many revelations her head still whirled. After several moments, she pulled back, searching his expression for hints of his emotions at the same time she reached out with her senses.

"Yes, and that." He glanced away to the open ledger then met her eyes again. "I need to finish updating the ledger in order to prepare for some major expenses apparently, so if there's nothing else for now?"

"Just this." She kissed him again, holding onto his upper arms to steady herself, then ended the kiss and stepped away to point at the paperwork. "Now, get to work."

"Yes, ma'am." He mock saluted her as she turned to leave. "I'll see you later."

She strolled out of the office, pondering why she couldn't sense his emotions more clearly. She'd improved her control over her abilities and yet somehow he seemed closed off to her. What exactly did he need to talk to her about?

Chapter Ten

The morning sun hung high in the sky, relentlessly beating down on the passengers in the open wagon. Flint gripped the leather traces in his gloved hands and urged the pair of horses into a steady trot. Steering around the worst of the holes and ruts required concentration. The more the wagon bumped and jounced the more likely something would come apart. He scanned the road, searching for the smoothest path on the badly maintained lane. Grimacing at a splintered wagon wheel off to one side of the road, he hoped they'd not experience any such problems.

"It's hot this morning." Cassie slowly waved a hand fan so the breeze would cool them both. Or try.

Flint grunted, annoyed with himself for chickening out of saying what he needed to convey. He didn't know how to start the conversation. Halfway into town and he still hadn't raised his concern. His burning question. Afraid of her views on the matter. He'd tossed and turned in bed instead of sleeping, leaving him disgruntled.

"Are you feeling all right?" Concern laced her question as she laid the fan in her lap and peered at him. "You're awfully quiet."

"I'm fine." When she continued staring at him, he added a shrug. "I didn't sleep well."

"Ah, I see."

Not clearly. She couldn't know how he felt, not even with her empathic ability. He'd hidden it, effectively buried it in his soul. The dread increased in his gut with each passing minute until he couldn't bear the pressure. He swallowed to force the words back inside but they burst from him.

"You know I love you." Those three tiny yet weighty words hung in the hot, humid air like a challenge.

She picked up the fan and languidly waved it in front of her face. She stayed quiet for what seemed an eternity, not responding other than to glance at him and then away.

"I do. I want you to be my sweetheart, my girl." He clutched the traces to keep himself together. The horses trotted faster, as if sensing the urgency inside his chest. "What do you say?"

She turned to look at him with serious eyes, the fan slowly moving up and down. "We've talked about this. I love you and am with you, just not officially. Not yet."

A ball of frustration weighed his core as he glanced at her and then back to the road. "That's just it. I want it to be official."

"Why? Because my brothers are here?" The fan never paused as she looked away again. "Or because you feel like you must make it official in order to protect me? Claim me? Or what?"

"None of that. I love you. All of you."

"Including my magic?" Now she stared at him, the motion of the fan speeding up the longer she considered him.

"Yes, of course." Which raised the other concern he'd wrestled with in the dark. "Do you love me, Cassie? Even though I am not a witch, just a guy?"

Given his lack of any special abilities or even a stellar career path, he could imagine she didn't. Couldn't. Not really. Despite her affection toward him. Compared to her brothers, he must be a poor substitute for a man who could better provide for and protect her. All his grand visions and plans crumbled to dust because he'd fallen for her and would do everything in his power to keep her safe. Knowing she wouldn't leave the inn meant he wouldn't leave it either. Doing so would tear the tenuous connection they shared in two. Something he never wanted to do.

"I'm very fond of you, Flint. Truly." She swallowed and looked away toward the forest they passed.

"But love?" He hated to push her but he must know what his future with her might hold. After their conversation the previous day, he struggled with her question about regrets. He'd never regret loving her. Never. But if they had no future together, then perhaps he needed to rethink his plans. "Do you love me enough to marry me, Cassie?"

"I—"

A loud crack and snap interrupted her reply. The horses neighed in terror and bolted at the sudden loud noise behind them, ripping the traces from his grasp as they galloped away, dragging the broken yoke behind them. The wagon dipped as the front left wheel splintered and the bed crashed to the rutted dirt road, tossing him to the hard-packed pitted ground in a painful heap. Cassie screamed as she flew past him when the wagon tumbled across the road and into the ditch, landing pitched up against several pine trees.

He struggled to sit up, finally managing to brace his arms behind him. Then he attempted to stand only to fall back when his leg gave out. A long splinter from the broken wheel stuck out from his thigh. It obviously couldn't stay there. Gritting his teeth, he gripped it and then yanked before he could second-guess himself. Blood flowed down his pant leg and into the dirt to form a red puddle. He pressed a hand to the wound while he pulled a handkerchief from his pocket. Wadding it into a messy pad, he applied the makeshift bandage to his leg to staunch the flow. Then he surveyed the road, searching for where his girl had landed after the rolling wagon halted.

She lay on her back, unmoving, at the edge of the road. Was she dead? *Dear God.* He tried to stand but his leg wouldn't support him and he flopped back down, his heart thundering in his panicked chest. "Cassie!"

Trapped and put on the spot. How had he let himself get roped into assessing the elegance factor of the inn? Abram surveyed the largest bedchamber with disgust. No respectable government official would deign to sleep in such a dowdy and austere accommodation. The furniture most definitely needed refinishing at the minimum. Replacement would be far better. The bedclothes were faded and worn, with merely a quilt thrown over the thin mattress. The bare wood floor offered no comfort other than a paltry braided rug on either side of the bed.

"Looks nice, don't you think?"

Abram turned to pin a disbelieving look on Giles. "Nice? I don't think so."

"What's wrong with it?" A frown settled between Giles' eyes as he scanned the room. "If you mean the furniture, you don't need to worry about that. Pa is having new beds and such made. He'll bring them when he returns in October."

"That's some relief." Still, imagine lying beneath the thin quilt trying to sleep while one's teeth chattered. "Flint has his work cut out for him upgrading everything before that senator arrives in two months."

"Cassie said he's been making incremental improvements." Giles shifted his weight to one hip as he regarded Abram. "That's why Flint asked your opinion about what more he should consider."

Put on the spot more like it. How could he know what the mysterious senator would find appealing? Abram only could judge based on the senators he worked with. His own taste clamored for more refined furnishings. Duvets instead of homey quilts, for instance. Heavy, decorative drapes at the windows to both block out unwanted light and keep in the warmth. A fine porcelain ewer and basin to wash away the road dust upon arrival. Perhaps even a plush carpet to cushion and fend off the chill from tired feet.

"Is he only concerned with the sleeping accommodations?" From what he'd seen of the dining room, he hoped the answer was no. He had some opinions on that topic as well.

"He's looking at the entire presentation of the inn, so I'm sure he'd want you to survey the whole property." Squaring his shoulders, Giles strolled to the window and peered outside. "Probably the outbuildings and stable, too."

"I'll need paper and pencil."

"For what?"

"The list." He crossed his arms over his chest and shrugged. "You can't expect me to keep such a lengthy list all in my head, now can you?"

Giles twisted his mouth into a wry grin as his eyes twinkled with mirth. "There's not much else to keep in there so…"

"Very humorous, brother."

"I hope you won't take too long to compile said list since you'll want to also practice with your newly discovered abilities." Giles sobered as he crossed the room toward Abram. "We must do all we can to defend our sister."

"Here we go again." Against what exactly? No one had clearly defined what type of threat two women might present. Let them come and he'd judge for himself.

"You need to take this seriously." Giles' deep bass voice reverberated with tension. "Ma's concerns can't be dismissed given she knows her sisters and we do not."

"I suppose there is a measure of truth to your words." People were people, after all, and if someone felt threatened they might lash out. Or if they were desperate, they might do things they wouldn't in other circumstances. "I have attempted to shapeshift but with little success to date."

"Thus the need to practice so you'll be ready when—" Giles stopped and spun around to skim his gaze through the room. His entire body went on alert as he searched for something in the air. "What's that?"

Mystified, Abram scowled at his brother. "What?"

Closing his eyes for a moment, Giles stood still and then his eyes flew open. "Cassie's in danger. She needs me, I can feel it."

"Now? She's with Flint. She's fine."

"No. Look." Giles pointed to the wall behind Abram.

Pivoting, Abram followed the direction of Giles' frown. "There's nothing to look at."

"I forgot. You can't see it. But it's the owl again." Giles shook his head slowly. "As Guardian, I'm the only one who can see the symbol of imminent danger."

"Figures only you can. What now?"

"I just know she's in peril." With a grimace, Giles clenched his fists. "I need to go to her."

"You're going after them?"

Giles stared at him for a moment. "Yes."

"But—" Abram started to argue but suddenly he was alone. Giles had vanished. "Giles?"

He spun around, skimming his gaze quickly around the empty bedroom. Where did he go?

Something was wrong. The world was dark and she hurt all over. The sound of fear when Flint called her name made her frown. Slowly, she opened her eyes and then squinted at the blinding sunlight before closing them again. Why was she lying outside? She blinked open her eyes and saw the remains of the wagon on its side against a battered pine. Large pieces of wood covered the grassy ditch. The accident. Where was Flint? She struggled to sit up, placing a hand on her forehead to try to calm the swirling sensation inside.

"Cassie! Are you all right?"

She peered across the space separating them, shocked to see the red pool surrounding his leg. He'd been hurt. Her heart stopped to see him injured and vulnerable. What if he'd died? Her heart restarted, racing frantically at the mere thought of him not surviving. She drew in a breath, willing her fear to subside. He sat there waiting for her response, his loving concern evident. When her heart started beating in a normal rhythm again, she realized how much she cared for him. "I think so, but what about you?"

"I can't stand on it." He shook his head with a grimace. "Can you get up?"

She scrambled to her feet with cautious movements, and then walked slowly to where he sat on the road. "What happened?"

"A wheel broke apart and scared the horses." He motioned toward the empty road they'd been traversing. "They're long gone."

She stared down the dirt road as dismay filled her. Surely someone would happen along and help them. They were halfway between town and the inn with no transportation and Flint unable to stand, let alone walk. Then Giles appeared in front of her. She blinked at the sudden vision of her big brother.

"Giles?"

"Are you okay?" Giles looked her up and down and then met her surprised gaze. "I knew you needed me and here I am apparently without even having to think about it."

"But how?" She frowned and then shook her head. "We can sort that out later. Flint is hurt."

Giles pivoted to address the wounded man gaping up at him, taking a few steps closer. "Is it bad?"

"I don't know." Dropping her gaze to examine Flint's leg, she stifled a gasp. The blood looked even worse close up. Just how bad was he injured?

Squatting down beside him, she eased the soaked bandage up to inspect his wound. The bleeding wasn't too bad after he'd pressed on it for several minutes. She pulled the long white collar around her neck from where it was tucked inside the bodice of her day dress.

"Lift your leg so I can slip this under." She removed the soaked pad and wrapped the fabric around his leg then knotted it in place. "I hope it helps."

"I'll be fine. Don't worry about me." He aimed a reassuring grin at her, but she was unconvinced.

"We need to get you either home so I can treat your leg or into town to the doctor." She pushed to her feet and rested her fists on her hips. "I could walk to the nearest farm. We passed a pretty spread not too long ago."

"Where are the horses?" Giles asked, looking about to see if they were nearby.

"They ran off up the road," Flint replied. "I hope they didn't hurt themselves in their fear."

"We need some way to transport you, Flint, since you can't walk." Cassie glanced back up the road they'd come down. "Do you know who lives back at the last house?"

"No, but what choice do we have?" Flint interjected.

"It's not safe to approach an unknown property." Giles shook his head. "Someone will come along. There's always people on this road."

"I'd have thought we'd have seen someone by now." She shaded her eyes with one hand and peered up and down the road for a moment. "Wait, there's a man with several horses heading this way."

"Good." Giles moved to stand beside her.

She stared at the approaching man, driving a one-seat carriage pulled by one horse and leading two others. She was relieved to have Giles' formidable presence in case the man wasn't friendly. He looked familiar but was still far enough away to make it difficult to determine if she knew him. But the horses, those she recognized. "He's got our horses in tow."

"Even better," Giles said, relief in his deep voice.

After a couple of minutes the black man pulled to a halt with a worried frown etched on his features. He met Giles' challenging look with a tilt of his head and then glanced at Flint before looking at her. "Miss Fairhope, are you all right?"

The man's deep voice confirmed his identity. She'd recognize the rich melodic sound anywhere. Relief flooded through her. Help had arrived.

"Yes, but Mr. Hamilton can't walk and needs a proper bandage." She smiled up at Tobe, Mr. Baker's very helpful well digger. He and another man had worked together to dig a fresh well for the inn several weeks back when Teddy's father had spoiled it. "Thanks for catching our horses."

"Glad I knew them when they galloped past. What spooked 'em?"

Flint pointed to the bits and pieces of the wagon. "The wheel shattered right behind them and they took off."

Tobe set the brake on the carriage before stepping to the ground. "Let's get you home, Mr. Hamilton."

"I'll give you a hand, too." Giles eased closer to where Flint rested on the ground.

The two big men helped Flint to his feet, supporting him

with their massive strength into the small vehicle. After Flint was situated in the carriage, Giles stepped away several strides. Tobe turned to assist Cassie into the vehicle but she shook her head. "I'll ride one of our horses and—" She looked meaningfully at her brother until he started toward her. "Giles will ride the other."

"But...but astride, miss?" Tobe's wide eyes revealed his disapproval.

Cassie pulled her skirts up between her legs and tucked the ends into the waistband. "Help me up."

She would not argue with the man about propriety when there was an easy solution to the problem. She didn't dare look at Flint or Giles until Tobe lifted her up onto the back of the horse wearing a saddle for situations such as the one they found themselves in. When she met Flint's gaze, she detected his pride in her.

Giles offered her a small smile of approval. "Let's get you both back to the inn."

"Agreed." Cassie tightened her fingers on the reins in preparation for setting off for home as Giles swung up onto the other horse's bare back and gathered the reins of its bridle.

"Let's go." Flint addressed Tobe with a wave of his hand. "I'll be sure to let your boss know how helpful you've been, too."

"Thank you, sir." Tobe clucked to the mare and the carriage started toward the inn.

At least Tobe had no reason to question Giles' presence but accepted it. But she had questions. Specifically about his sudden appearances. The most likely answer being that she'd established a psychic connection with her Guardian, allowing her to summon him when she needed him. A useful ability when faced with looming challenges.

Cassie urged the gelding beneath her into a walk. All the way back to the Fury Falls Inn she pondered the revelation she'd experienced when she saw Flint injured and vulnerable. Felt his love and fear combined into a living, breathing thing. He wasn't afraid for himself but for her. An all-consuming emotion that arced through the air and charged her own heart. His love energized her heart with a returning love and fear for his well-being she'd never before experienced.

When they reined to a halt in front of the inn, Abram rushed from inside the stable to meet the beleaguered party. His urgent steps stuttered to a halt when he spotted Giles. "Oh, there…" He cleared his throat at Cassie's quick shake of her head. "Glad you made it back."

"Without any further incidents, too." She let Giles lift her off the horse and set her gently on the ground, fully aware the entire time of his deep concern for her.

"Are you really all right?" He scanned her head to toe and back to meet her gaze. "Were you injured?"

"I'm fine. Really." She laid a hand on his arm to convey her sincerity. "I was just dazed from being thrown from the wagon. No cuts or anything. Thank you for your concern, though."

"Glad I could help." He placed one hand on top of hers. "I knew when you were in danger and you needed me. Something I've been feeling more and more often, I might add."

"It's possible my empathic ability works to reach out for your help when I need it." She mulled over the concept for a moment. "That would explain how you seem to appear when I'm thinking about you and wanting your assistance."

Giles merely nodded without further comment, but she could tell he was contemplating the ramifications of the newly discovered ability.

"I knew Flint was with you so didn't worry too much until Giles…left." Abram pressed his lips together when he spotted the bandage on Flint's leg. "Guess I should have worried a bit more."

105

"Tobe came to the rescue." Cassie grinned at the man as he helped Flint out of the carriage. "He recognized the horses and came looking for us."

Giles nodded at Tobe as the man assisted Flint up the front steps to the porch. "You were definitely in the right place at the right time. Thank you."

Settling Flint on a chair, the big man took a deep breath before he acknowledged Giles' grateful words. "Glad to, but I need to be on my way. I've got chores yet."

"We won't keep you then. Thank you for taking care of my sister." Abram shook Tobe's hand, bringing a wary smile to his face. "I have my own tasks to do, so I'll be off."

Shaking hands with slaves didn't happen, but Cassie kept her observation to herself. Tobe had earned their respect and gratitude and deserved both.

"I'll ride with you and explain to Mr. Baker." After Tobe's nod of agreement, Giles hurried to the stable, Abram following with the pair of horses.

Cassie climbed the steps of the porch to sit with Flint for a moment, until the other men departed. Then she'd take him inside and properly clean and dress the gash on his thigh. Take good care of her man. She gazed at him for a long moment and then tapped the table between them.

He raised his eyes to meet hers. "Yes?"

"That's what I was going to say." She eased a smile onto her lips when confusion replaced the inquisitive look. "I'll be your sweetheart. Officially."

"What changed?"

"I realized that I love you more than I could ever put into words. I've always known I want to be with you." She tapped the table again and leaned closer so she could lower her voice. "I'll even marry you if you still want me to."

A happy smile met her last statement. "I do indeed. Whenever you say."

"After Pa comes home and I know more about who my family really are." She couldn't tie the knot with anyone until she and he knew more about the kind of family he was marrying into. It wouldn't be right. "Then as soon as we can make the arrangements. Agreed?"

He took hold of her hand and squeezed. "Yes, ma'am."

Chapter Eleven

S triding out of the stable later that day into the afternoon sunlight, Abram squinted at the flow of
customers arriving in carriages and on horseback for dinner.
He paused at one side of the carriageway to jot down a few
thoughts about improvements to the barn and paddocks on
the small pad of paper Giles had scrounged up for him
earlier after he'd returned from the Bakers. A couple of dogs
slept on their sides in the grass nearby, oblivious to the
activity around them. He finished writing and slipped the
pad and pencil into his back trouser pocket. Stepping
toward the inn in search of his own meal and to evaluate the
dining room, he scanned the area. Then frowned when he
spotted Giles and Haley Baker in what appeared to be an
intense conversation on the steps of the gazebo nestled
among a few shade trees at the front of the inn. Vines of
climbing pink and red roses draped over its roof and
columns, lending it an air of privacy.

Why had she come calling so soon after Giles had been
to see her father about Tobe? Was aught amiss? His brother
looked very serious and tense as he strode down the steps
and then turned back to continue the heated exchange.
Something had happened to upset both of them. Striding

toward the gazebo, he tried to fathom the cause of their debate. One so intense they didn't notice him until he stopped at the steps.

"What's going on?" He propped his fists on his hips.

"Nothing for you to worry about." Giles pivoted to address Abram, then shooed him away with a wave of one hand. "Go on with you. Go practice or make your list. Just go."

Haley moved several feet farther into the shade of the gazebo, folding her arms over her chest. Why did she appear to feel guilty or at least worried? What conversation had he interrupted?

"Stop telling me to mind my own business when whatever you two are discussing is so serious. What's going on with you two?"

The veins in the sides of Giles' neck strained into view. "Back off, brother."

Something in Giles demeanor alerted and alarmed Abram. His brother was worried about some mysterious thing involving Haley. Every time she appeared, the concern Giles displayed seemed to deepen. Why was it a secret? He'd had enough of those after coming to the inn. No more.

"Stop hiding the truth from me then." Abram poked a finger in the center of his brother's chest. "Tell me what's going on."

"You're being a pest, Abram, that's what is going on." Giles shoved Abram with a hand, pushing him back several steps. "Leave us alone."

Abram had momentarily forgotten about his brother's amazing strength but the building anger inside overpowered reason. He rubbed the sore spots on his chest as he closed the distance between them. "Make me."

"Don't push it, Abram." Giles fisted his hands and shook his head once. "You won't win."

Gritting his teeth, Abram launched himself at Giles, the surprise move knocking the bigger man to the ground. Haley gasped and called for help but Abram ignored her. He had his hands full defending himself against the blows from his older and stronger brother as they rolled on the ground. Giles somehow ended up on top. He grabbed hold of Abram's silk shirt and pulled, the fine fabric tearing with a heart-wrenching sound. Abram prized the white shirt but at the moment he needed to guard his face from more punches. But he landed a few punches of his own when he managed to maneuver on top before Giles rolled them over again and pinned him to the ground. Damn the man, he wasn't even breathing hard as Abram tried to catch his breath.

"What are you two doing?" Flint halted beside where Abram lay on the ground. "I heard Haley calling for help and I find you two brawling. Making a scene before our customers, too."

Abram chanced a quick look toward the front of the inn and found a small crowd, gawking from a safe distance. He didn't care. He must stand his ground and let his brother know he was in the wrong to exclude him from the family.

"It's his fault." Abram pointed at Giles but didn't dare attempt to move until his brother stopped acting all tough guy.

"I told you." Giles glared at him for several seconds before pushing away to tower over him. "Believe me now?"

Heat infused Abram's face as he struggled to his own feet. Inspecting the shredded shirt, anger swept through him like a wildfire. He'd never replace it as long as he was trapped at the inn. The meager offerings in the new town couldn't possibly compare to what he could purchase in the big cities. He'd probably end up wearing cotton or worse, linsey-woolsey. He lifted his eyes to glare at Giles. "Look what you've done to my shirt. It's ruined."

"It's just a shirt." Giles brushed his hands on his jeans, obviously unconcerned. "Cassie can make you another."

While he loved his sister, he doubted she could sew as finely as the tailor who made the ruined shirt. "This one was very expensive. I can't replace it here."

Giles shrugged. "Perhaps you should have thought of that before you attacked me."

"You didn't have to tear it. I was merely trying to prove a point."

"Which was?" Giles arched a brow at him, his tone dripping with sarcasm.

He scrambled to come up with a plausible point he might have been trying to make by jumping his brother. He'd really not considered the consequences of his actions, something he rarely allowed himself to do. But his brother's haughty dismissal had infuriated him to the point of losing his patience and common sense. He wanted Giles to take him seriously, not consider him a pest. He wanted to be included.

"You insist I need to be part of this family and yet you won't keep me informed." That sounded plausible... "Why are you keeping secrets with that girl?"

"I'm not." Giles glanced to Haley and then met Abram's disbelieving expression. "Not really."

"I'm sure Giles isn't trying to keep you in the dark, Abram." Flint made a placating noise in his throat before gesturing to Haley. "They're just getting to know each other better. Right?"

Haley eased to the edge of the gazebo floor, looking down on the trio of men. "I didn't mean to cause a rift between you two."

Abram crossed his arms over the torn shirt, to hide the gaps as much as to present a defensive posture. "What did you mean to do by coming here?"

"That's between her and Giles." Flint stepped between Abram and his brother.

Irritation simmered in Abram's belly as he landed his gaze on the innkeeper. "Stay out of it, Flint. You've done enough damage of your own today."

"What is your meaning?" Flint frowned at him.

"You put my sister in danger this morning. You need to inspect the vehicles more carefully before you use them. If you even bothered to do so before taking Cassie to town."

Flint blustered as he tried to respond. Good. He'd made his point with regard to the constant interruptions from the man who wanted to be part of the family but was not. Not yet anyway. And one more thing...

Abram fished in his back pocket and pulled out the notebook, flinging it at Flint's feet. "And there's your damn list of recommendations you wanted."

Flint bent to scoop up the small book and tap it on his palm. "Thanks but that doesn't excuse your behavior in front of my guests."

"I don't much care but you need to take better care of my sister if you want my approval of your intentions." Abram fairly shook with anger and a growing sense of isolation from his own family.

"It's not Flint's fault the wheel broke, for goodness sake." The contempt in Giles' voice seared through Abram. "Be fair."

He considered his older brother's uncompromising features for several moments. "You want me to trust everyone but you won't trust me enough to share what's really going on. Why were you arguing with Haley?"

"Fine. I'll tell you, but it's between us. Understood?" Giles waited until Abram nodded and then glanced around to make sure they were alone. He lowered his voice to a near whisper. "Haley keeps me informed of her father's nighttime activities, or at least the timing of them."

"Why?"

Giles huffed an annoyed sigh. "Because we don't know what he's doing."

"So you're thinking he's doing something he shouldn't be?" A wave of concern washed through Abram at the fear glinting in his brother's eyes. "He's up to no good?"

Haley chewed her lower lip and shrugged. "I hope not."

"If so…" Giles glanced at each person in the loose group before continuing. "Is it related to the many women killed recently? Or something else?"

"John Baker, our father's trusted colleague, a killer?" A flood of fear replaced the wave of concern inside as Abram considered the dire implications.

Flint carefully steered the team around the crowded public square several days later. A politician stood on a stump giving a speech on the corner. A crowd had gathered farther down the street for an auction of some sort. Dogs chased a man on horseback up another street. He avoided an approaching cotton wagon pulled by oxen to halt at a hitching rail across the street from the general store. Market day always brought out a lot of people in search of goods they couldn't raise or make themselves at home or that they wanted to sell. A sense of belonging filled his chest at being back home again in the thriving town. He climbed down from the front seat of the carriage and secured the horses, favoring his injured leg. Cassie joined him behind the vehicle, a pair of large woven bags hanging on one arm. Abram jumped down from the back of the wagon, brushing off his maroon trousers.

"Well, you managed to get us here safely this time," Abram said, rounding the vehicle to stand beside him.

"I normally do." Flint bristled at the man's tone. "You didn't have to come with us."

"I intend to visit the tailor, if you'll point me in the right direction." Abram trailed his gaze around the square, disapproval tightening his lips.

"It's that small store front on the other side of the square, second from the left." Flint pointed back the way they'd come. "The tailor's upstairs."

"Fine. I'll catch up with you later." Abram tipped a finger to the brim of his top hat and strode away.

"Well, at least I don't have to put up with his cheek for a little while." Flint shook his head and turned to face Cassie. "Where do you want to start?"

"Let's go into the general store and see what they have." Cassie gazed at the front door of the shop at the end of a row of brick storefronts near the hotel. "I know they sell striped linsey and leghorn bonnets, so they may have what I need for uniforms."

He checked the flow of wagons and carriages before snaring her hand and leading her across the dirt road. "Definitely a busy Saturday for a market day."

"It's exciting. The energy flowing through the town." She waited while he pulled open the door, then slipped past him into the brightly lit store.

Her perfume teased his nose as he inspected the interior of the bustling shop. "Let me know what you find."

"I will." She strolled away, heading toward the back of the store where there was a corner dedicated to bolts of fabric and notions.

Flint lingered by the front door, observing the friendly merchant behind the cash register. After the financial difficulties a few years previous, the Brick Row addresses had become known as Cheapside. Bank notes from Tennessee and Alabama were accepted but a high premium was offered if one paid with gold or silver. Thankfully, business at the inn thrived so he had a quantity of gold to pay for the uniform material Cassie required. Then they'd go to the other corner of the square to the market building and hope to find the ingredients necessary for the cookery competition.

"Flint Hamilton, saints above, is that you?"

Startled out of his musings, Flint turned to greet the familiar sultry voice. Dressed in her favorite color of burgundy with pale gray lace and trim, Adelle Wharton's come-hither smile made him want to flee. "Miss Wharton."

"I didn't know you'd returned to town." She tapped her folded fan on his shoulder as she batted her lashes over her blue eyes. "When did you get back?"

"I'm only visiting for a short while." She didn't need to know any more about him than that. "How have you been?"

"Lonely without you." She smiled up at him as she spread open her fan to hold in front of her chin. "Did you miss me while you've been away?"

He'd not even thought about her. Once he'd contemplated a future with her. A long time ago. "I'm afraid I've been very busy. I'm pleased to see you looking so fetching. Is that a new dress?"

"How kind of you to notice!" She patted her blonde chignon as she simpered at him. "I'm glad you like it. It suits me well, I think."

He never said he liked it. She had a way of putting words in his mouth or twisting them into something entirely different from what he'd meant. "I'm sure you must have errands to complete, so I won't keep you."

"Silly. I can spend a few minutes talking with you." Adelle put on her most flirtatious grin and assumed a hurt tone. "I haven't seen you in months."

"I'll be away for several more as well." He perused the young lady smirking at him and found her wanting. Yet again. But after falling in love with Cassie, he would never look at another woman. He tipped his hat to her with a half grin. "I'm here with my betrothed while she selects some fabric and other incidentals. If you'll excuse me."

Without another word, he turned away from the astounded woman and went to inspect a display of new top hat fashions. Anything to end the uncomfortable conversation. He heard Adelle mutter "bless you" without any shred of religious blessing included before she stomped away. He grinned, he couldn't help it. With good fortune that would be the last time she bothered him. He whistled a tune as he examined the merchandise and waited for his love.

After a few minutes, Cassie hurried toward him, a bolt of blue cloth and several lengths of lace and other small notions hanging out of one bag. "Who was that?"

"Nobody."

"She didn't seem to think so."

He shrugged. "She would like for there to be something but there is not. Did you find what you needed?"

She regarded him for a moment and then nodded once in acceptance of his dismissal of the other woman. "This should serve the purpose though I'm not sure it will be enough."

"Enough to start." He led her toward the register, guiding her by her elbow as they made their way through the many displays and tables of wares.

She sat the bag on the counter and smiled at the clerk. "I'd like to buy these, please."

Before long the purchase was completed and they strode outside into the morning light. And heat. Sweat accumulated under his hat brim as they placed the filled bag in the carriage. He lifted his hat and ran his palm over his brow and then settled the covering back in place.

He offered his arm and was pleased and proud when she wrapped her hand around it. "Ready to market?"

Chapter Twelve

$\mathcal{T}$he stroll down the street toward the tailor's shop amused him. Abram fairly chuckled at the antics of the children with their dogs and large hoops. A cluster of men debated the politician's points with gestures reminiscent of an auctioneer accepting bids. He paid particular attention to what the other men in town were wearing. After all, he wanted to fit in. The men were dressed in tidy yet unprepossessing attire. Casual frock coats in dark blue, brown, and dark green over a waistcoat in a solid color beneath. Trousers instead of pantaloons with a white shirt and tall collar and, of course, a cravat. He nodded to himself. He could work with those elements and still have his own style.

He tipped his top hat to a group of ladies approaching him with shy smiles and a plethora of skirts and parasols. They giggled and hurried past him, leaving him wondering what they found amusing about him. Glancing at his bright blue coat and fancy waistcoat he grimaced. He stuck out in his bright colors and intricate embroidery. He quickened his pace toward the narrow two-story building where the tailor worked.

He climbed the steep narrow stairs to the second floor, a fine sheen of perspiration beading his forehead by the time he reach the upper landing. Why the hell did the tailor have to choose such a difficult place to conduct his business? Pulling his handkerchief from a pocket, he mopped his face before entering the shop.

"Good day, sir." The young man rising from a chair beside a sewing dummy had a voice that could cut glass. "How may I help you?"

Abram skimmed his gaze from head to toe of the tailor's work clothes and shoes. His hair was cut short and allowed to curl in whichever direction it chose, appearing as if he'd just risen from bed. A white shirt was smothered by a heavy work apron, lengths of lace and trim dangling from its pockets. Brown trousers flowed down to cover half of the brown leather shoes on his feet. The man's entire appearance was of one interrupted and unprepared. Still, Flint had assured him he was the best tailor in town.

"I need to replace a few items in the fashion of the town." He motioned to his outfit with one hand. "Something quieter and more befitting the sensibilities of the people of this town, perhaps?"

The tailor blinked slowly, a crease forming between his eyes. "Excuse me?"

Stifling a sigh, Abram pasted a patient expression on his face, the one he reserved for difficult senators. "A couple frock coats in brown and dark blue to begin. And I'll need two white shirts with cravats, and of course several pair of trousers. Can you help me with such a request?"

"Oh, yes, of course." The delighted tailor bobbed his head several times. "When do you need them?"

"As soon as possible. I do not know how long I'll be in town and I would like to make use of them."

"Let me take some measurements and I will begin on them immediately." He glanced away to the work table and the dummy. "Those projects are not urgent."

After the man had jotted down Abram's measurements,

they agreed on a price and a day for Abram to return to be fitted. He said his farewells and strode back out into the heat of the morning, relieved to be outside the confines of the shop. He paused on the edge of the street to soak in the view, his earlier mirth returning until he spotted a familiar sway of hips approaching him. But Mandy wasn't alone.

She smirked at him with a challenge in her expression as she and a tall, handsome man neared. "Why, Mr. Fairhope, how delightful to see you here in town."

He took a moment to size up the other man. Clear blue eyes returned the inspection. The man looked like an Adonis. Almost beautiful he was so perfect in form and appearance. No need to have the magical ability to hide a childhood scar from sight, either. The man stood tall in his perfection, from his assessing yet inquisitive eyes, high cheekbones, and clear skin to the cut and color of his clothes and the way he carried himself. Damnation. The man was indeed a perfect specimen of the male species.

Something hot and sharp and unfamiliar sliced through his gut as he bowed to Mandy. "My pleasure as well. Pray introduce me to your companion."

He straightened to continue his assessment of the competition. The man wore a gold stick pin in the rolled back collar of his dark brown frock coat. A chain and fob from a pocket watch stretched across the front of his fine gold waistcoat. Even his brown trousers sported a sharp crease. He'd attended to every detail. And caught the attention of the plain little woman at his side.

"Mr. Fairhope, may I present Caleb Pyke. Caleb, this is Abram Fairhope." She continued to smirk at him with a knowing look. "Caleb, Abram is visiting the inn where I work."

"Ahh! Nice to meet you." Caleb stuck out his hand to shake with Abram. "Mandy has told me all about you."

Abram tried not to wince at the strength in the other man's hand. What had she told him? "Pleasure is all mine."

"What brings you into town?" Mandy asked.

He gestured to the brick building behind him. "I visited the esteemed tailor to replace a few items."

Caleb nodded. "Good choice."

The man's endorsement should have bolstered Abram's confidence and yet it rankled. He didn't want to like the man nor agree with him when he was obviously interested in Mandy. There could be no other reason they'd be in town on market day together. Shopping and dining and spending time together. But then again, he wasn't interested in her so it didn't matter if the other man laid claim to her.

"What brings you into town, Miss Crawford?" He kept his expression friendly with an effort as the knife continued to move about his gizzard. The man took Mandy's elbow to move her a little to one side to let a couple pass. Abram couldn't stop the sharp look he aimed at Caleb. He shook himself and took a calming breath. "Looking for anything in particular?"

"Oh, Caleb is taking me down to Lloyd's Bookstore where he's started working." She clasped her hands together. "It's on the other side of the square, next to the auction house where that crowd is."

"Are you fond of books?" Why didn't he know this about her? "I haven't seen you reading."

"Yes, I enjoy books. They provide an escape when things are…" She glanced away for a moment and then up at Caleb before meeting Abram's gaze. "Well, let's leave it at that, shall we?"

She didn't want to share her reasons but he surmised she had implied them nonetheless. She must spend much time alone and books helped pass the time. "Very well."

"If you'll excuse us, sir, we must be on our way or we'll be late." Caleb half bowed to Abram in farewell. "I'll ensure Miss Crawford is safely delivered to the inn shortly thereafter."

"Wait. Please." A sort of panic consumed Abram at the thought of her walking away with this perfect man. Even knowing it was only for a small span of time. She'd chosen Caleb and he her. He'd thought she was attracted to him, even though he didn't return the favor. A twist of his gut accompanied the point of the blade. What was the matter with him?

"You look quite pale." Mandy reached out as if she would take hold of his arm and then let her hand fall away. The smirk disappeared to be replaced with concern. "Are you all right?"

He inhaled deeply, struggling with the nausea in his gut. Quelling the emotions with more effort as Caleb studied him with a frown marring his features. He must squash the unnecessary and unnerving feeling. After another moment, he regained control of his composure and nodded once.

"Please forgive me, Miss Crawford." He took another steadying breath and let it out slowly. "I have forgotten what I wanted to say, so I apologize for detaining you both. I hope I have not caused you any inconvenience."

"It's of no consequence, I'm sure." She examined his features and then inclined her head. Her earlier air of teasing and conquest left behind a sad smile. "I will see you later at the inn. Until then, farewell."

"Again, it was a pleasure to make your acquaintance, Mr. Pyke." Abram tipped the brim of his top hat to the other man. Then he nodded once in farewell to Mandy. "Until later at the inn."

She waved a hand and then turned to stroll away from where Abram stood rooted to the dirt street like some sapling tree. The farther she and Caleb withdrew the more certain Abram knew why he'd panicked. He couldn't believe it. Didn't want to believe it. But there could be no other explanation. He'd experienced jealousy for the very first time ever. But why?

Flint escorted Cassie up the square away from the courthouse and toward where the jail once stood. His leg throbbed from the accident, but he subdued any hint of a groan as they strolled down the street. The corner had been transformed into a green space where children could play and people could pause to have a picnic lunch on a nice day. Turning the corner, an amazing mass of people milled about the two-story building where the market was held twice weekly. Produce and other wares mounded on the back of wagons hitched to mules, or carried in saddlebags, or even brought in a backpack. He knew from experience the variety to be found at the market. Depending on the season, people offered fresh vegetables, fish, tame and wild fowl, tallow, eggs, butter, honey, meal, nuts, grapes, wild fruits and berries for preserving, freshly-butchered meat, wild game, and whatever else they could bring in to trade or sell.

"I've never seen so many people in one place." Cassie dragged on his arm, slowing their progress. "It's a bit overwhelming."

"And useful." He patted her hand as he escorted her closer to the throng. With each step, though, his leg hurt more. He bit back the urge to stop.

"How?"

"There's safety in numbers." Less chance of anyone attempting to harm his girl with him at her side and so many witnesses. "Do you want me to help you find anything?"

He slowly steered her around a cluster of women haggling over a haunch of venison. Locating a stone bench tucked up against the market building, he drew her to a halt in front of it. A place to rest and recover without making his discomfort obvious. Out of the flow of marketgoers. The outing was proving more taxing than he'd anticipated.

"No need. I can manage." She squinted up at him from

beneath the brim of her bonnet. "How are you feeling?"

"All right." Relief and love swept through him at her words. She cared enough to ask after his health. "Have the merchants bill the inn and have the bulkier items delivered."

"I will. I don't expect there to be all that much to carry home, mainly bunches of herbs and bottles of spices. I should get going because I know how anxious Sheridan and Matt are to begin."

"I'll wait here for you." He gestured to the bench with a hand. "Then help you carry your purchases back to the wagon."

"You have a little rest." She squared her shoulders, the second bag on her arm. "I'll be back."

Off she went, her trim figure and frilled black bonnet dodging through the crowd. Nobody seemed to pay her any attention. Good. She worked her way from table to booth to display, adding this and that to the soft-sided bag on her arm as she went. He eased down onto the bench with a sigh. Some minutes passed before the throbbing stopped and he felt more like himself. He rose to his feet when he spotted the deputy making his way toward him.

"Doing a little marketing?" Deputy Barney stopped and shook hands with Flint.

"Guard duty." Flint rested his hand on the butt of the ever-present flintlock pistol at his side. "Cassie's over there."

Barney followed the direction of his nod and then met his gaze. "I'm glad you're taking the situation seriously."

"What's going on?" He tensed at the concern in the deputy's expression, gripping the pistol in preparation for drawing it from the holster.

"Nothing new, so relax." Barney gestured to let go of the gun. "Those three guys you brought in for killing Mercy Fairhope are scheduled for trial in a week but don't trouble yourself with them. They'll do time or be hanged for their crimes."

Those three rogues had started the whole mess at the inn by murdering Mercy in cold blood for an imaginary treasure. They should hang not rot in a jail, mooching off the public for room and board. Especially the one who pulled the trigger. Poor Teddy. At least his father hadn't killed the woman, but the boy still lost his father. Good thing he'd found a second home with the Fairhopes.

"What about the recent killings? Any news?" Flint dropped his hand to pat his thigh, then glanced to where he'd last seen Cassie's bonnet. A jolt of unease zapped through him. She'd disappeared. After a moment he spotted the frilled bonnet again coming slowly toward him.

"Nothing. It's like the criminals are ghosts. Nobody's seen anything and there are no clues left behind at the scene of the crime." Barney regarded him for several moments. "I'm worried there's a vigilante on the loose. There's something tying these killings together but it's unclear what it might be."

Should he reveal their suspicions to the deputy? Or wait until they had some link to the murders? Accusing the wrong man could lead to much trouble all the way around. Especially if he accused the friend of his boss and he was wrong. That would cost him his job and his reputation. They really only had conjecture to go on. Better to bide his time.

"That's frustrating. Anything I can do?" Flint returned Cassie's hesitant smile as she joined them, her bag sagging with bunches of fresh herbs and small clinking bottles.

"If you hear anything, let me know, will ya?" The deputy wiped the concern from his face as he greeted Cassie.

"Hello, Deputy." She held the bag handle with both hands. "Is anything wrong?"

"No, miss. I was just giving Flint an update but nothing for you to worry about." Barney tipped a finger to the brim of his hat. "You take care of her, Flint, and I'll take care of the rest."

"I intend to do so. My leg may be hurt but I can still hit what I'm aiming at." Flint tapped his gun again, reassured by its presence.

"What happened to your leg?" Barney asked, a pair of vertical lines appearing between his brows.

"A wagon accident the other day, but I'm fine." Flint returned the deputy's nod of understanding. "Let me know if you need anything."

"Will do. If you'll excuse me." Barney nodded to Cassie and then eased into the crowd.

So the threat remained even if law enforcement was on the job. He'd keep his girl close. With so much uncertainty and mystery surrounding recent events, he'd prefer to hole up at the inn where he felt more in control. Time to head home.

"All finished?" Flint peered at the bulging bag and then met Cassie's frown. "What? Did you forget something?"

"Something's happened. What?" She searched his eyes.

"No, nothing." He schooled his features to prevent his concern from reflecting in his expression. Turned his attention away from his worry and focused instead on his love and concern for her. Hoped she'd sense his love instead of anything else. "If you have everything, let's get going. We need to find Abram and go home."

She glanced at the contents of the bag. "Don't tell me, then. But I'll find out."

He took the heavy bag from her and then grasped her hand. "There's nothing to find out. Let's go."

Chapter Thirteen

$\mathcal{T}$he ingredients for both fancy meals and the new dresses weighed on her arms as Cassie entered the inn early that afternoon, Abram trailing behind her. The trip to town had taken longer than she'd anticipated and now she had chores to deal with before the afternoon rush. A light breeze brushed her cheeks. Sheridan and Matt both wanted to get to work on their new menus. Setting the bag with the fabric and notions on the table by the door, she turned toward the kitchen. Abram tensed, she felt his concern wash over her in waves.

"What did you find?" Mandy strolled down the hall to peer into the other bag. "That's a pretty color."

"I think so, too. It will make lovely dresses, don't you think?" A ripple of disappointment mixed with an echo of delight flowed from the other woman. "What's wrong?"

"I didn't say anything was wrong." Mandy met Cassie's questioning gaze with a frown. "Why did you ask that?"

"Something in your expression I guess." Inwardly, Cassie rolled her eyes at her lapse. She mustn't reveal her abilities to everyone. They would not react well if they knew how much she could sense their feelings. "So?"

"If you ladies will excuse me... I'll leave you to discuss

feminine concerns." Abram touched his hat and strode out of the entrance hall toward the covered passage, apparently heading to his room on the residence side of the building.

Cassie stared after him for a moment, aware of his unease but unsure of the cause.

"I know we talked about the skirt length, but..." Mandy pressed her lips together, hesitating for several moments. "I was thinking maybe we could shorten them a bit. Make them flirtier? You know, show a bit of ankle."

"You want the hem to be above the ankle?" Ah, now Cassie understood what she'd been sensing from the other girl. "Who do you want to flirt with?"

Pink infused Mandy's neck and then inched into her cheeks. "No-nobody specifically. I thought the men would be more likely to come back more frequently if we did."

"Nobody special in mind, hm?" She pursed her lips, reaching out to probe Mandy's real reason. Then she understood her brother's quick departure. "Not even Abram?"

Mandy looked away and then cleared her throat. "Maybe..."

"You like my brother, don't you?"

"Yes." A dare glittered in Mandy's eyes as she faced Cassie. "Is that a problem?"

She had no say in what her brother did with regard to relationships. Maybe she didn't much like the idea of Abram being with Mandy, but they might make each other happy. Was Mandy seeking her approval of the match? Or merely daring her to disagree and put a rift between them. One thing remained certain. She had to work with her either way.

"No, it's not." In fact, she liked the idea of being a bit flirty with the skirt length. "Let's be flirty, shall we?"

"There you go again, being a slattern." Mercy shimmered into sight beside Mandy.

Cassie huffed a sigh. "I've asked you not to do that."

"I've asked you to be more modest and now you're talking about shortening the hem?" Mercy shook a finger at her as she hovered several inches off the floor.

Mandy frowned at Cassie, her gaze darting around the space. "Who are you talking to?"

She'd forgotten. Mandy couldn't see her ma since they hadn't known each other before her mother was killed. Perhaps it was just as well.

"Nobody." She glared at her ma's ghost and then regarded Mandy's wary expression. "We can talk later. I've got to get the marketing into the kitchen. I know the cooks are anxious for what I found for them."

Nodding slowly, Mandy offered a weak smile. "All right. I'll see you for the dinner rush."

After Mandy strode away, glancing back at her once as she went into the dining room, Cassie addressed her mother. "Did you need something? Other than to badger me, that is."

"I came to warn you. But if you don't want to hear it…" Mercy shimmered, preparing to vanish.

"Warn me about what?"

"My sisters will arrive soon. You don't have much time to prepare."

She had her doubts as to how much of a threat her aunts posed. Abram definitely didn't believe they could cause too much of a problem. They couldn't make her go with them, even if they pressured her. Her life and love remained here at the inn.

Hefting the bag, she shrugged. "There's nothing I can do to stop them, so we'll just have to deal with it when they get here. If you'll excuse me, I need to deliver these condiments and spices."

Mercy frowned as she shimmered more and then vanished without another word. Well, what did her ma expect her to do? Run around tearing her hair and acting upset and afraid? She didn't know her very well, if so. She had her own abilities and capabilities. And she had Flint and her brothers as well as the three black men to help her if she needed. Between all of them, what did she have to fear? She strode into the kitchen, pasting a smile on her face as the door swung shut behind her. The scene before her made her smile. Meg and Myrtle peeled potatoes and carrots at the side table. Matt kneaded more bread dough, punching it down and folding it over. Sheridan used his large knife cutting up rabbits into chunks for yet another stew. The normal and familiar sight eased the tensions she'd experienced in the entrance hall.

"Here you go. Everything you asked for." She plunked the bag onto the work table.

Sheridan hurried over to pull things out of the bag and place them on the table. "Goat cheese, gherkin pickles, shallots…"

"Some of that's my stuff." Matt wiped his hands on his apron as he marched over to peer into the mass of herbs and spices. "Like this ginger root and the cardamom seeds and oh, good you found the chutney I asked for, too." His voice trailed off as he selected various herbs and spices from the items arrayed on the table.

"I couldn't carry everything on that massive list. The rest will be delivered in a little while." They acted like little boys receiving gifts, matching open mouths as they picked through the offerings.

"I can start with this, but the old man may need help." Matt grinned at her and then glanced at Sheridan with a wry lift of his brow. "Right?"

Sheridan's eyes lit with good humor as he shook his head. "Once I have the rest of what I asked for, I'll be fine. You're not going to win. Trust me on that."

"You two." She shook her head and grinned at them.

"You do know this is supposed to be a friendly competition, right?"

"Who said?" Sheridan carried his selections around the table to his side. "May the best cook win."

Matt started transferring the quantity of spices and herbs to his work space on the opposite side of the table from where the older cook had already started to sort through his bounty. After several trips, he arranged them in groups but didn't offer any explanation as to the system he used. At some point, perhaps, they'd compare notes about new menus rather than competing. Not yet, obviously.

"If you don't want anything else from me, I'll be on my way." She needed to take the material up to her room and start making the pattern for the dresses.

"Go on with you." Sheridan waved her away with one hand. "I've plenty of help in here."

She glanced at Meg and Myrtle working at a side table for confirmation and they shook their heads at her, keeping a steady rhythm with their paring knives. "Matt?"

"I'll help the old man out if he needs it." He aimed a wry grin at Sheridan. "Which I'm sure he will."

"Hey!" Sheridan pointed the knife at the younger man, a twinkle in his eyes as he acted affronted. "I got along fine without you. Maybe you should go take a hike or something, kid."

"Maybe I will." Matt crossed his arms and chuckled. "After all, I have plenty of time unlike some cooks around here."

"On that note, I'm going to excuse myself." She chuckled as she pushed through the swinging door.

"Thanks for coming with me." Abram sauntered up the path leading toward the falls. "Sheridan seemed glad you were getting outside for a while."

"I decided to take him up on the idea of getting outside

for a spell." Matt chuckled as he walked along. "We're having a bit of a friendly rivalry. He's glad I'm not there to see what he's planning to make."

"You don't know?"

"Not based on the ingredients he's gathered. Other than the fact he's most likely including some kind of greens and he muttered something about needing to hunt some ducks."

"What are you making?"

He rather envied the good-natured relationship the two men had. They joked and made fun of each other's abilities but only because of their mutual respect. They recognized their talents were of equal merit so they could push each other to try new things. New ways. Having such a relationship was outside of his own experience at work. In fact, the senator didn't joke with him about much of anything. Always serious, that one.

Matt glanced around as though afraid of being over-heard. "My main course is a curry dish, with a salad and soup to balance it out, but don't tell anybody."

"I won't." Abram stepped over a rock in the path. "I don't even know what it is."

"You'll find out in a few days when we have the tasting. Everybody gets to try it and then judge whose is best."

Judgement. One word he detested. One of the reasons why he worried and fretted about his appearance. People always judged based on appearance. Whether a person acted professional enough or of high enough society to engage with. How one dressed, behaved, and spoke all contributed to the overall impression. He'd once felt lacking on all counts. He'd worked hard to improve and become a fine man and senator's aide. But to judge the efforts of others? He tried to avoid such undesirable trials.

"We'll see." Perhaps he could go for a ride or take the waters instead. Abram drew to a halt at a small clearing to one side of the trail. "Here's a good spot."

Far enough from the path to not be easily visible and yet convenient. The ring of trees would provide a curtain to keep prying eyes from noticing, too. Space to move about in case things didn't go as planned. Of course, it would help if he actually had a plan. Other than visualization and focus. How did a person become something else merely by thinking about it?

"For what?" Matt halted beside him, scanning the grassy expanse in the middle of a copse of trees.

"You keep watch while I practice. Okay?" Abram cleared his throat as he walked into the grass. "I need to figure out how to control my gift."

Matt frowned slightly as he strode over to stand nearby. "You want me to keep watch…for what?"

"Let me know if anybody comes this way." Cassie had cautioned him more than once about being discreet in using his powers. If the guests saw him shifting, they would likely never return to the inn. Which would hurt business and upset not only Flint but also their father. And he really didn't want his father mad at him. He'd had enough of being on the receiving end of his father's anger or, much worse, disappointment. He pointed to the side of the trail. "Stand over there so you can see down the path."

With Matt facing the path, Abram invoked the ring's protection and then concentrated on forming the image of a gray cat with white paws and long whiskers. Yellow eyes and pink nose. Short, medium-gray fur and a long tale with a white tip. He visualized the tom cat and soon felt himself changing. It didn't hurt exactly but the tingling and pricking spread through him. His hands shifted into paws with claws and gray fur covered his body. A soft rustle in the underbrush made him whip around to ensure he remained alone. Not seeing or hearing anything after several moments of inspection, he dropped his gaze to assess his progress.

Pleased with the beginning of the transformation, he

focused more on the image in his mind and felt whiskers grow on his face. He shrank in size to that of a tom cat but no tail or sharp teeth appeared. He closed his eyes and tried harder but the tingling and pricking stopped. Opening his eyes, disappointment filled him. Nearly there. What must he do different to complete the shift?

"Hey, there's people... Um, are you all right?" Matt leveled shocked eyes at Abram as a tom cat.

Damn. Failed again. And with guests nearby. Something he'd been warned about not letting happen. The ramifications could be devastating all around. He shook off the cat image and felt himself shift back to his normal form.

Embarrassed and disappointed, he drew in a bracing breath as he ambled over to stand by Matt. "I'm sorry you had to see that."

Matt blinked at him from wide eyes that held a hint of fear. "You're a shapeshifter."

"Not a very good one." He bit back the self-reproach. "Not yet, anyway."

"Thus the practice session?" Matt crossed his arms but managed to stay still despite his apparent unease. "Why didn't you tell me earlier?"

"Would you have come with me?"

"I dunno but it would have been nice to be forewarned."

"Granted."

"So why the secrecy?"

Abram scanned the perimeter as he struggled to put his reluctance into words. "Have you ever disappointed anyone?"

Matt unfolded his arms and shoved his hands into his front pockets. "Probably."

"I've learned to lower expectations by not revealing my intentions ahead of time." Abram brought his gaze back to meet Matt's. "That's why I didn't tell you. So you wouldn't be disappointed when I failed, like I did."

"Hard to make friends that way." Matt glanced to the path as the sound of voices reached their ears. "Who'd you disappoint?"

"My pa, back when I was a kid. I'd tried jumping my pony over a log and fell off." The pony trotted away and started grazing while he'd cried on the ground, rubbing his shoulder after rolling on the hard earth. "I never want to see that kind of sadness and disappointment on anyone's face again."

"Everybody falls off when learning to ride." Matt shrugged, pulling his hands free from his pockets. "At least I think they do at one time or another."

"Did you?"

"More times than I could count." Matt chuckled. "But the massa wasn't disappointed, he was upset I might hurt myself."

"Very considerate of him, to be concerned on your behalf."

"Nah, he didn't want me hurt 'cause then I couldn't work." The humor in Matt's eyes disappeared.

"I see." What more could he say? "You ride fine now, though?"

"I get by." Matt shrugged again, dismissing the compliment. "I don't fall off any more."

The small group of customers, nattily dressed men and women with their arms full of covered baskets and blankets, nodded in greeting. They passed by the two men, heading farther up the trail to the springs for a long soak and continued lively conversation.

"You'd make your father proud." Abram acknowledged the group's greeting and then grinned at the other man, trying to lighten the mood.

"I hope so, but I don't have a father either."

So much for bringing a bit of levity to the conversation. "You can have mine…"

Finally, a twinkle lit in Matt's eyes. "He's not here either."

"Cassie said he'll come back in a couple months, so if you can wait until then…?" He grinned sheepishly at Matt. "In the meantime, I should practice now that the guests have gone by."

"Go on, get to work. I'll let you know if anyone else approaches."

With a nod of agreement, Abram strolled back to the center of the clearing. Time to be serious. He really didn't want to disappoint anyone. Most of all, himself.

Finally, I had proof. The Fairhopes were indeed practicing in magic and spells. The shapeshifter had used both when he transformed into of all things a cat. But what would he do next? That was the worry, the fear. What else would they conjure and evoke into being? Like all witches, though, they simply couldn't be allowed to remain, contaminating my beautiful state with their devilish ways. I'd see to it.

Chapter Fourteen

B rushing his hands on his jeans, Flint left the stable and crossed the crushed stone carriageway. His ears pricked up at the sound of male voices and the strumming of guitars. Giles and Zander occupied the chairs on the front porch of the inn, playing a country folk tune he hadn't heard in a long time. The merry melody evoked fond memories from his childhood when his mother and sisters would sing at the piano of an afternoon. The songs changed with the seasons and with their increasing abilities but his enjoyment remained constant. He smiled at the pleasing sound and quickened his pace.

The song ended with a flourish as Flint mounted the few steps. "That was nice."

"We've been working on the harmony." Giles rested his arm on the guitar. "It's a little shaky yet."

"Speak for yourself." Zander gripped the body of his guitar. "I kept mine in tune."

"It sounded good to me, but I'm no expert." Flint leaned against the warm post, folding his arms across his chest. "How did you learn to play so well?"

"Zander taught me." Giles strummed the strings slowly, a gentle sound floating on the warm air.

136

"How did you learn, Zander?" He shifted to a more comfortable position. "Did you teach yourself?"

"No, my father taught me the basics so I would be able to sing our people's songs." Zander strummed a few chords, complementing those of the other guitar. "He taught me enough that I could sing along before…"

A movement in the open door to the inn drew Flint's attention. Sheridan strolled out onto the porch and joined the trio. He seemed a touch wary of being accepted into the group so Flint motioned for him to take a seat. Sheridan briefly shook his head and crossed his arms. If that's the way he wanted it. Flint returned his attention to Zander, who hadn't finished his sentence.

"Before what?" Flint glanced at Giles to gauge his reaction to Zander's hesitation.

Zander stroked the strings several times before slowly raising his eyes to meet Flint's. "Before me and Matt were taken away."

Sheridan moved closer and laid a hand on Zander's shoulder. "I'm sure it was hard for your pa to see you taken, too."

Zander nodded as he strummed but didn't look at Sheridan as the older man lifted his hand and slid both into his front pockets.

"Did you need something, Sheridan?" Flint straightened away from the post, ready to manage whatever issue brought the cook out to the porch.

"Yes sir. Do you know about when the rest of the groceries will be delivered?"

"I understand by midafternoon, so it won't be much longer."

"Good. I need to get started." Sheridan grinned at Flint, his conspiratorial expression revealing his competitive nature.

"Hey, Zan, why don't you play a song your pa taught you?" Giles stopped picking at the strings to rest his gaze on his friend. "The one that's so haunting? I really like that one."

"This one?" Zander started picking on the strings and then added his voice to a slow, mournful song.

Chills inched up Flint's spine at the sound. Haunting, indeed. The lyrics painted a sad and lonely picture of a man mourning his long-lost lover. The want and desire of a man bereft of his woman. Flint glanced around, suddenly wanting to connect with Cassie. Hold her close. Keep her at his side. Never let her go. Where was she?

As if on cue, Cassie emerged from inside the inn and strode over to stand by Flint. The singing must have drawn her outside, to him. He wrapped an arm around her waist, relieved to have her near. The tension inside from the haunting melody eased.

She squeezed his arm and snuggled closer. "Have you seen Abram? I can't find him anywhere."

"Not for a while. Now hush and listen." Flint squeezed her waist. "Isn't Zander's song wonderful and moving?"

She nodded mutely, turning her attention not to the singer but to Sheridan. She studied him with a quizzical expression for several seconds. What was she sensing from the older man?

Flint glanced over at his cook. Sheridan stood rooted in place while Zander strummed. When the song ended and Zander rested his hands on the instrument, Flint realized the strong black man was trembling. Flint frowned at the older man's reaction to the song. Sure, it was moving, but for him to be quaking in his shoes didn't make sense.

"You okay, Sheridan?" Flint peered closer to better assess his condition.

"What...what was your pa's name?" Sheridan stared at Zander.

"Dan." Zander shrugged and resumed strumming lightly. "So probably Daniel, I'd guess. I don't really know more than that."

"Oh…" Sheridan blinked once and then dropped to the plank floor, fainted dead away.

Cassie knelt beside the sprawled man, checking to make sure he was breathing. The music stopped as the others gathered around. The scent of rain wafted past her, combining with the aroma of bread baking and the warm earth surrounding the building. The click of dog paws on the wooden floor made her glance down the length of the porch. Beau, the chocolate Labrador retriever, and Pickles, a black Lab, trotted up onto the porch at the far end and stopped to watch the show, tongues hanging out of their panting mouths. She turned her attention back to her friend.

She laid a hand on his forehead for a moment. "Sheridan. Can you hear me?"

"What happened?" Giles squatted beside her. "He dropped like a rock."

"He was upset and shocked." She'd sensed his change like a downdraft from a thundercloud, a cold blast chilling him to the core. "He's coming around."

Sheridan blinked and moaned, rubbing his head with a hand. "Where am I?"

"On the porch. Can you sit up?" Cassie eased away to give him room to maneuver.

"Let me help you." Zander held out a hand until Sheridan slowly clasped it.

Sheridan stared at their hands for a minute and then struggled to his feet with Zander's assistance. He kept hold of the hand and stared at him. "I think you're my son."

Zander shook his head slowly. "My pa died."

A flicker of hope lit and died in the young man. Certainty burned inside of Sheridan, though. Followed quickly by joy. Could it be true?

"Are you sure?" Cassie asked Zander.

"He died in some kind of accident is all I know."

"How do you know that's true?" Flint grasped Cassie's elbow as he spoke to Zander. "Didn't you say you were taken away from your parents as a boy?"

Zander pulled his hand free from Sheridan's. "Yes."

"Then how do you know what happened to them?" Flint regarded Zander with a light frown on his face.

"The plantation owner told us." Zander picked up his guitar and held it casually in front of him.

"But the man was no good." Giles tilted his head to one side. "I met the man and trust me. He might have said your pa died so you wouldn't try to run away."

Sheridan strode over to stand in front of Zander. "The song you sang. I made up that song. It's the story of my parents."

Zander searched Sheridan's eyes as hope flared inside. "You're Dan?"

Sheridan nodded and swallowed. "That's what the massa called me. Said it was easier to yell."

"But you said your sons were named George and James." Flint squinted at Sheridan. "Right?"

"Yep, but I know I'm right. Earlier Matt mentioned how their ma made hoe cakes, same as my Pansy." Sheridan glanced at Giles. "Isn't it possible your massa changed your names?"

Giles raised his chin and looked sharply at Zander. "It is indeed. Do you remember being called anything else?"

"I was so young then and terrified. I can't recall…" Zander gripped the guitar harder as he struggled to remember. "I tried to put the past behind me since I couldn't go back."

Sheridan leaned toward Zander with an intense look. "Jim-Jim, is that you?"

Zander's eyes widened. "Pa!"

Joy and elation flooded Cassie's core as the two men embraced, tears on their cheeks. Her eyes smarted with happiness for her confidant. He so deserved to be reunited with his family. All of them. Hopefully, her pa would locate Pansy soon, too.

Sheridan ended the bear hug but stayed close to Zander. "Where's Matt? He needs to know."

"I think I saw him go with Abram up the path a while ago." Flint's grip on Cassie's elbow tightened. "They should have been back by now. I'll go track them down."

"I can't wait to tell him." Sheridan grinned with joy. "I've got my sons back."

Cassie grinned through her tears right back at him despite the question burning in her soul. Should she tell her dear friend about her pa's efforts when he'd requested she not say anything?

Flint jogged up the winding path, eager to retrieve Sheridan's son. Wow. An amazing turn of events happened minutes earlier. Wait until Matt learned the truth. A silly grin spread on his lips when he spotted Matt standing beside the dirt path.

"Hey, Matt. What are you doing standing there?" He slowed to a halt beside the man. "Where's Abram?"

"He's over there. Practicing." Matt pointed behind him to a small clearing where a gray cat sat licking its paw.

Was the cat smiling at him? Or what would pass as a smile if a cat could actually do so. It sure look pleased with itself. Flint frowned, confused, and then he understood. "In plain sight?"

"It's okay." Matt stood with his hands in his pockets, a calm expression on his face. "I'm standing guard."

"It's risky." He grimaced and shook his head. "He should have picked a more private place."

Matt shrugged. "Safe enough."

All his plans to improve the inn's appearance and appurtenances would be for naught if word got round about the goings on. The witchery and haunting would put an end to the entire business. No matter how comfortable the beds. No matter how delicious the meals. No matter how entertaining the musical performances. The guests would not come back and he'd be out of a job. Labeled a failure and unlikely to be hired elsewhere as a result. All because Abram chose to practice shapeshifting in plain sight.

"He's done." Flint marched into the clearing. "Abram. Quit that."

He watched in amazement as the smiling cat morphed into the grinning fop. The whiskers and fur replaced with sideburns and fancy clothing. Paws and pointed teeth becoming human hands and teeth. He mentally shook off the fascination associated with trying to understand the process the man had to go through in order to become another creature.

"What's the matter?" Abram fairly beamed at him. "Cat got your tongue?"

"It's not funny." Flint braced his hands on hips. "You could ruin everything."

"Relax. We took precautions." Abram pointed at Matt who had followed Flint into the clearing. "He made sure I didn't shift while others could see."

"After all, there's nothing wrong with a cat in the field. Is there?" Matt chuckled.

"Don't do it again, you hear me? What if someone witnessed you shifting?" Flint speared Abram with his glare until the fop nodded. Then he turned to Matt. "Sheridan wants to speak to you."

"Can't be anything important." Matt shrugged. "Probably wants to try to find out what I'm planning to make for the competition."

How he'd love to be the one to share the news, but it was Sheridan's revelation to share. "He didn't say."

"Are you finished for the day?" Matt peered at Abram. "Or do you want to keep perfecting your new skills?"

Flint huffed. "Sheridan is waiting."

"He can keep on waiting." Matt arched a brow at Flint. "He's not my boss."

"I was thinking about trying to shift into a bear." The devilish grin on Abram's face challenged Flint.

"You wouldn't dare." Flint pursed his lips and shook his head. "That would be far too dangerous in so many ways."

A rustle in the underbrush had them turning to peer at the low bushes and surrounding trees. After a moment, Flint glanced at the other two men, shrugging off the interruption to continue their conversation.

"Probably a squirrel or something," Flint suggested. "Now…"

"How about a cougar?" Abram winked at Flint. "It's just a bigger cat."

"How about let's go back to the inn." How could he get them to agree without revealing the real reason for the summons? "It's getting late. The dinner rush is about to begin and I need to be there and so does Matt."

"Then go." Abram shooed him with both hands. "We'll be along in a bit."

"Look, I don't have time for this. Matt, please. Come back with me." He peered at Matt, praying he'd agree and stop arguing with him. "I believe it's important."

"I can't imagine Sheridan has anything earth-shattering to say to me." Matt's grin faded as he regarded Flint. "Or does he?"

Did he see something in Flint's expression that tipped his hand? Dang. He forced a light shrug. "I don't know…"

Abram glanced between Flint and Matt. "Something's up. What is it?"

"I don't—"

"Know. I bet." Matt studied him for several moments. "I think you do, don't you?"

Caught between keeping the surprise and telling the truth. He sighed and nodded.

"And?" Abram stepped closer. "Are you going to tell him? Or keep yet another secret?"

"No. I can't tell you." Flint drew in a breath and let it out slowly. "You need to talk to him, though."

Matt crossed his arms and stared at him. "I just met him a few days ago and now you're saying he's got a secret to tell me?"

Flint opened his mouth to reply and then shut it again. It did seem far-fetched. "Yes."

Grumbling, Matt shook his head. "This is ridiculous."

"Trust me." Flint splayed his hands. "Please?"

Chapter Fifteen

What was taking him so long? Cassie perched on a chair with the other men, waiting for Flint to return with Matt and Abram. "Surely he's found him by now."

"Be patient." Sheridan relaxed in the other chair, smiling softly. "I've waited a long time for this day. What's another few minutes?"

"He'll be so surprised." Zander leaned against the post, eyes sparkling. "I know I was."

Giles, sitting on the top step, strummed his guitar, the lively tune reflecting the mood of the group. "Here they come."

"Matt doesn't look happy." Cassie stood and sauntered to stand beside Giles.

The three men strode quickly across the carriageway and up the steps. Abram continued on inside without saying a word. Flint paused at the top of the steps to observe the group before joining Cassie. Matt went straight to Sheridan, a frown heavy on his brows.

"I understand you want to talk to me." He crossed his arms and looked down on the older man who grinned at him. "So talk."

"Have a seat." Sheridan motioned to the empty chair on the other side of the small table.

Matt looked as if he wanted to argue but merely dropped into the chair. "So?"

Cassie turned to witness Matt's reaction to the happy news. Matt's defensive attitude belied the curiosity swirling inside. Good, he wasn't entirely opposed to hearing what Sheridan had to say.

Sheridan cleared his throat and glanced at Zander before fixing his gaze on Matt. "Remember how we were surprised earlier when your mother and my wife both made hoe cakes with the same ingredients?"

"Sure do." Matt drummed his fingers on his leg, impatience simmering inside along with the curiosity. "Why?"

Zander started humming the haunting tune he'd played earlier. Matt looked at him, puzzled. Zander merely smiled.

"That tune your brother is humming…" Sheridan shot Zander a quick grin before meeting Matt's gaze again. "That's my song."

"You wrote a song. That's the big reveal?" Matt gripped his knees with both hands.

Cassie sensed a surge of impatience and disgust in Matt. Sheridan tensed, a bit of humor blending with concern at his son's reaction. By contrast, Zander was laughing inside at his brother.

She stepped forward and smiled at Matt, eager for him to learn why he'd been summoned. "No, just listen."

Matt nodded once to her, eyes wary. "Go on then, Sheridan."

"Zander said his father taught him that song, right?" Sheridan sat up straighter, keeping his gaze on Matt. "He's right. I did."

"But that would mean…" Matt shot his brother a look. "He's your father?"

"Yes. He reminded me of my real name, James." Zander

regarded Matt with calm certainty. "Don't you remember I used to be Jim-Jim when we were little?"

Matt's eyes widened as he stared at Zander. "Yes…"

Recognition and shock catapulted through Matt, sweeping away his defensive attitude like a new broom. Cassie's own joy at the family reunion increased as Matt sorted through the facts and came to a startling conclusion.

"But if he's your father, then—"

"Yes, Matt. Turns out you're my other son George." Sheridan leaned forward in his chair, stretching a hand out toward him. "You found me."

"But we thought you were dead." Matt glanced at the waiting hand and then at Zander. "How is this possible?"

Giles rose and leaned his guitar against the post. "I think the plantation owner lied to you when you were mere lads about your parents to keep you from running away."

Cassie's heart broke at the concept. How could the man be so mean and uncaring to the boys? How tragic for them to believe they were orphans for so many years when they were not. And one more pressing question rattled around in her mind.

"Why the name change?" Tapping her fingers on her crossed arms, she scanned the group of men arrayed around the porch.

"That's a good question." Matt shifted his gaze to Giles. "Any ideas?"

"To keep you from finding your parents or any other family you might have?" Giles shook his head slowly as he glanced at his friends. "Or them finding you. Dastardly move."

"Zan—" A sudden thought stopped Cassie's comment in its tracks. "Which names do you two want to go by?"

Zander opened his mouth and then shut it again as he pondered his response. Finally, he shrugged. "I've lived most of my life as Zander, so let's stick with that one. Matt?"

"I agree. I don't think of myself as George." Matt looked at Sheridan with concern in his eyes. "Is that all right?"

"It's fine with me. No matter what you want to call yourselves, I'm simply glad to have you both back in my life." Sheridan extended his hand to Matt again who accepted it with a firm shake. "We'll have to let the rest of the family know if and when the time comes."

The mention of other family raised the question of Pansy and her whereabouts. Hope soared inside Cassie as she enjoyed the moment between the father and sons. If they could find each other, then her pa must be able to find their wife and mother. She'd been asked to not say anything but with the surprising turn of events unfolding before her refraining from doing so became all the more difficult.

Zander picked up his guitar. Caressing the strings, he played the haunting melody, his gaze bouncing between Sheridan and Matt. "Hey, Pa—man, that sounds fine—whatever happened to Ma?"

Sheridan sank back in the chair, the happy light in his eyes dimming. "I don't know."

But she might. With good fortune, her pa may have already confirmed her existence and location. Even if he hadn't, the urge to share what little she knew swelled inside until she couldn't contain it.

"Pa may know." All eyes turned to her, mouths open. "Maybe."

"What do you know?" Sheridan stared at her, hope sparkling in his dark eyes.

"I asked Pa to see if he could find Pansy." She swallowed, nervous about giving them false hopes but wanting to reassure them as well. "He said he might have found her but wanted to verify it was her."

"Why didn't you say something sooner?" Sheridan pressed his lips together, disapproving and disappointed. "You know how much I want to find her."

"Pa asked me not to say anything until he was certain." The mix of emotions swirling around her threatened to overwhelm her so she raised her inner defenses to protect her equilibrium. "I wanted to but didn't want to raise hopes too high."

"I thought we were friends." Sheridan sniffed and rose from the chair. "I've got work to do before the dinner rush."

"Do you need help?" Cassie ran her hands down her skirts, drying suddenly damp palms on the gingham.

"I'll help him." Matt also stood and, with a quick glance at her, followed Sheridan inside.

"I understand why you didn't say anything, Cassie." Zander moved toward the inn's open front door. "Give him time, he'll understand, too."

"I hope so." She clasped her trembling fingers together as Flint wrapped a comforting arm around her shoulders. Her friend and confidant had never been angry with her before, nor disappointed. What if he didn't forgive her?

After returning from practicing shifting into a cat, exhaustion weighed down Abram's shoulders, his footsteps heavy on the stairs. He went up to his room in the inn to take a nap, but once there he decided to first write a note to his girl waiting for him. The chance encounter with Mandy in town had upset him. Reaching out to connect with the girl back home might settle his anxiety. Touch base with reality and things familiar. After he finished writing the letter, then sanded and dried the ink, he'd flopped onto his bed and fell asleep in moments.

Sometime later the sound of soft sobbing disturbed his slumber. The crying seemed to be coming from the guest room next door to his. A woman but who? A ripple of disquiet moved through him. The sound disturbed his equanimity but he stayed prone on the bed, hoping whoever it was would finish and go on about her day. Sad as it may be. He needn't insert himself into her problems and sorrows. Only, the sobbing didn't stop but grew louder. The disquiet inside continued to grow the longer she cried. The poor woman sat alone and obviously miserable. He should see if he could be of any assistance. Then he would try to go back to sleep. He rolled off the mattress and padded over to open the door.

He eased into the passage and peeked inside the next room to check on the woman. He caught his breath. Damn.

As much as he'd thought he could avoid becoming involved, the truth smacked him upside his heart. He couldn't ignore the bowed head of brown hair, hands shielding her face as her shoulders trembled with each sob. "Mandy? What is amiss?"

She jerked her head up, her fingers covering her mouth as her wet eyes stared at him in horror. "Go away."

Normally, he would take a crying woman at her word. If she didn't want or need his help, then he'd comply with her wishes. However, the tearful woman staring at him had the look of someone who in fact wanted his assistance. How or in what form he needed to discover.

He shook his head and strolled closer, taking his time to give her a chance to understand his intent. Her eyes widened as he drew slowly toward her. "Why are you crying? Did someone upset you?"

She swiped at her eyes, then dried her hands on her skirts. "You have no need to know my private affairs."

"Mandy, please, perhaps I can help in some way?" He squatted down in front of where she sat on a chair by the open window. A light breeze lifted the hair around her face and into her eyes. He reached out a hand, tempted to brush it away, but hesitated when she drew back.

"You can't help." She sniffled and swallowed, tears drying on her cheeks.

"Talk to me? I'd really like to." He'd do anything to stop the tears. Their presence set him on edge, true. But his reaction to them stemmed from feeling inept and unable to solve the problem they represented. "Did somebody hurt you?"

She chewed on her lip and shook her head, keeping her eyes pinned on him. "No, I think I hurt someone though."

He tilted his head as he searched her light brown eyes. "I doubt you're capable of such a crime."

She sniffed as tears began again. "Not on purpose."

"Who do you think you hurt?"

She studied him for a moment before shrugging. "You."

Not the answer he expected. "Me? You haven't hurt me, Mandy."

If anything she woke him up to a new sensation and self-reflection to try to understand his reaction to bumping into her with Caleb in town. She'd made him want to connect with the woman he left waiting for him, too. But she hadn't caused him pain. Had she? He replayed the conversation and her expression during the exchange. Suddenly he recalled how she'd started out with an air of teasing that metamorphosed into chagrin.

"You remember." She pulled a handkerchief from her sleeve and dabbed her eyes. "I hadn't meant to embarrass you, Abram."

He smiled at her as he shifted to grip the armrests of the chair. "Why do you think I was embarrassed?"

"I thought…" She peered at him and then sighed. "I tried to gain your attention by flirting and talking with you. But you didn't seem to notice, or care if you did."

"I noticed." He patted her hand and then enclosed it in his. "Actually, if you want to know the truth…"

She met his amused gaze and he saw a glint in her eyes as her expression lightened. "Go on."

He handed her a dry handkerchief as he smiled. "I actually felt a bit jealous of the man."

Her mouth dropped open as she stopped dabbing her eyes, holding the larger handkerchief in midair as she blinked at him. "Jealous of Caleb?"

He nodded, sobering as he realized something he hadn't considered even a possibility. But now, sitting this close to the girl with tears drying on her lovely cheeks, inhaling her scent, and seeing the beginnings of her captivating smile emerging on her lush lips, he knew. "I realized that I have feelings for you, Mandy Crawford. I didn't like seeing you walk away with another man."

A brilliant smile erupted onto her face, dazzling him into returning it. "He's just a friend from church. There's no need to be jealous."

Squeezing her hand, he pursed his lips for a second. "And yet, I was. What are we to do about such a state of affairs?"

"We'll have to see how things work out between us over time." She pressed her fingers around his before handing him back his handkerchief. "Thank you for your concern."

"Are you quite all right now?" He tucked the damp handkerchief into his pocket and then succumbed to the temptation and brushed the stray hair behind her ear.

"Yes, I do believe so. Thank you."

He rose to his feet and pulled her up with him, the warmth of her fingers in his spreading through him. "My pleasure. I must leave you now as I have an important task. But I will see you later, yes?"

"Yes, I look forward to it." She pulled her hands free and led the way out of the room.

She turned left to go downstairs, he turned right to rush back to his room and tear up a certain ill-conceived letter.

Chapter Sixteen

The dining room bustled with guests, eating and drinking while chatting and laughing. The noise in the room ebbed and flowed around him as Flint scurried to refill tankards and mugs. Mandy and Cassie sashayed between the tables, carrying steaming trays of food to the hungry throng. The proposed uniforms had yet to make an appearance, but in the meantime they wore conservative dresses and clean aprons, their hair carefully arranged and attractive.

He scraped a mound of foam from a tankard and reached for an empty one to fill. The bar glistened from the spilled ale and he itched to mop it up but had little time between customers. He spotted the Bakers hesitating in the dining room doorway, scanning the room for a group of available seats. Topping off the second tankard, he dried his hands on his apron before carrying the drinks to a nearby table. Dodging around a group of businessmen on their way out of the room, he set the tankards down in front of the waiting merchants.

"Let me know if you need anything else." He nodded to them and then spun around to hurry across the room to greet the Bakers properly. "Mr. and Mrs. Baker, and Miss Baker, it's been too long since your last visit."

"Business is booming here. Well done." John shook Flint's hand with a pleased expression on his face. "Sorry I've not made it out here in a while. I've been very busy as well."

"Let me find you a table." Haley lifted a brow at Flint but remained silent. As he skimmed his gaze over the room to locate a table for the family, Flint pondered Haley's silent message. What had kept John so busy he couldn't make his usual visits? "There's one. Follow me."

He led them to the table by an open window at the rear of the building. The warm breeze didn't provide much cooling on such a hot summer afternoon but at least the air flowed. "How is this?"

"It will suffice." John helped Tabitha sit down and then sat beside her. "We'll have the usual, if you have it."

"I believe so." He motioned to Cassie to come help the Bakers with their order. "Cassie will take care of you."

Haley lifted that brow again and he hesitated to turn away. Was she warning him to keep Cassie away from John? Or something else? Uncertainty kept him rooted at the side of the table as Cassie strode toward him. Perhaps he should rethink his choice. When Cassie reached his side with a smile on her lips, he made his decision.

"Will you ask Mandy to take the Bakers' orders, please?" Flint smiled back at her, putting on an act for John's benefit. "I have something else I'd like for you to do."

"I'm here." She glanced at the family seated around the table. "Welcome back for dinner."

"Our pleasure." Tabitha folded her hands in her lap, the colorful gemstones in several rings flashing in the lamplight, her friendly green eyes lingering on Cassie. "You look well."

"Thank you." Cassie's soft smile drooped as she met the woman's assessing gaze. She tensed, her chin lifting. She glanced at Flint with concern flickering in her eyes. "What did you want me to do?"

He had no idea but he felt like she needed to keep her distance. He spotted Sterling Nelson hesitating in the dining room doorway, searching out a seat for himself and the gentleman beside him. Both men wore somber attire and refined top hats, frothy cravats beneath their dark frock coats. He indicated with his chin for Cassie to look behind her. "Can you help those gentlemen find seats and take their order?"

"Of course." She cast a quick glance at John and then back at Flint, acknowledging his reason with the mere hint of a smile. "I'll take care of them."

Abram stopped at the open door as Cassie approached to seat the other men. He nodded to Mandy as she cleared the table vacated by the merchants, mugs and plates clinking as she stacked them on the tray. When Cassie led the men to a table near the piano, he congratulated himself on removing her from a potentially dangerous situation. At least temporarily.

Flint turned his attention back to John and the ladies. "Let me get your drinks. I'm sure Mandy will be with you shortly."

"We're not in a hurry." John relaxed in his seat, contemplating Flint with a serious countenance.

Flint acknowledged his comment but didn't respond. The man had come to observe and report to Reggie as to the caliber of effort Flint put forth as well as the results. The list of suggestions Abram had thrown at him after the brawl with his brother would help to increase the business as well. The turnout tonight proved what he'd done to date had been successful. He scanned the busy scene, happy to see Sterling enjoying his dinner and conversation based on his contented expression. He'd become a more frequent guest as Flint had added new menu items and entertainment as well as updated the inn's general appearance. The realization helped him relax a tad but not much. He kept his guard up and his pistol at hand. The feeling of imminent if unspecified threat persisted. Barney's warnings about the number of murders in recent weeks echoed in his brain as he gazed on the family and the man in charge of them. If only he knew for certain whether the man actually was guilty of their suspicions.

Abram crossed the room, dodging around crowded tables of customers, to stand by Mandy as she finished clearing the table. Flirting with the waitress, the fop grinned and motioned with his manicured hand. But he'd left the fine coat off, wearing a more casual tan one instead of the tailored blue. In fact, he'd changed much about his attire. His new clothes, which had been fitted a few days ago and delivered earlier in the day, made quite a difference in his demeanor as well. Perhaps he wasn't a lost cause after all. Giles walked into the room, spied him observing Abram, and strode purposefully toward him. His gaze slid to encompass the Bakers, resting longest on Haley.

"Everything all right?" Giles stopped at his side. "You looked intrigued."

"I'll tell you later." Flint pasted a smile in place and included the Bakers in the conversation. "John was saying his business has picked up nearly as much as the inn's. I suppose as more people move to Alabama to enjoy the fertile soil and lucrative prospects we'll all prosper."

Haley coughed lightly. "You're looking fine this afternoon, Mr. Fairhope."

Giles inclined his head at the compliment, his hair brushing his cheeks. "Thank you but I thought we'd agreed to not act so formally with one another. Please, call me Giles."

John blinked as he gripped the knife handle resting on the table. "When did this occur?"

"Oh, Father, please don't be upset." Haley pressed a hand on the table, as if trying to placate him from across the expanse. "Mist…Giles has been kind enough to talk to me about what it's like in Mobile. I've been curious about life on the Gulf as it fascinates me so."

The fabrication surprised Flint as much as Giles, as evidenced by the jerk of his shoulders. The girl had quickly invented a plausible if not probable reason for their conversations of late. And her frequent visits. Did John have any clue about those? Flint could tell the couple had grown fond of each other even if the reason for her visits was not a pleasant one to contemplate. Surely Haley must find it difficult to walk the line between daughter and spy, to be in the middle between protecting her father and her kind.

"I had no idea you were so intrigued." John glanced at Tabitha for confirmation, receiving a light shrug in response. He addressed Giles once more. "Then thank you for satisfying my daughter's curiosity."

"Haley, I'll be around so whenever you're in the area, stop on by and we can have a cool beverage together and talk more." Giles smiled at her and then slid his gaze to John. "With your permission?"

Clever. Flint held his breath as he waited to hear what John would say. Asking the father's permission to talk or court? Sharing a drink or a meal constituted a private meeting, a courtship, did it not? Which request was really behind the question? Apparently, there were two budding relationships occurring under his supervision. Not counting the one he had with Cassie, of course.

"I have no objection as long as you are in public." John released the metal handle and rested his hand on the table as he pinned Flint with a demanding look. "And as long as Flint will vouch for you."

Hope shone on Giles' and Haley's faces. "Yes, sir. Giles is an honorable man and will look after your daughter with great care."

"You have my word." Giles bowed to John and then to

the ladies. "My greatest desire is to ensure your safety and well-being."

John sat silent for several moments. "See that you do."

John regarded Cassie's brother with a hint of suspicion in his eyes. Did he suspect that Giles possessed supernatural strength? Perhaps his concern stemmed not from the man's abilities but from his interest in Haley. A father's concern. But said father also seemed to fear and denounce those with powers or who performed witchcraft. Which put the entire Fairhope family in danger from him.

A sobering thought flitted about and then landed with a warning for him. Flint's ability to talk with ghosts also put him in the same proverbial hot water. He'd need to downplay the reality in order to not draw attention to it any more than he already had. The hot water might boil over otherwise. And then what?

"Come on, you almost had it." Cassie paced in front of the open window the next morning, avoiding the doll's house as she tread slowly around the parlor. "Try again."

"What was missing that time?" Abram asked, standing in the center of the painted floor.

"My hair is longer and lighter in color, and don't forget my teeth aren't even." Not after the tumble she'd taken as a girl.

She'd been far more of a tom boy as a girl. Always running around, climbing trees, catching tadpoles in the creek, and playing with a hoop and stick along the lane. That long ago day had been like any other except she'd tried to jump across a ditch while chasing after a butterfly. One foot twisted on a rock and she tumbled into the ditch face first. She was fortunate she hadn't lost the tooth but it had twisted slightly. Not enough to be a bother but enough to spoil her smile.

"I think of you as perfect, so I guess that's why the teeth won't cooperate." Abram smiled at her but shook his head. "I suppose if I'm to look exactly like you then I need to focus on how you really are."

"Try again." He thought of her in such a fine light it warmed her heart.

He closed his eyes, squeezing his lids tight as he concentrated. After a moment, Cassie stood in front of her instead of her brother. A gasp of delight escaped before she could stop herself. Abram/Cassie opened his eyes and smiled at her. It was like looking in a mirror although the "image" didn't match her movements.

"Well done." She strode closer to inspect every detail. "The dimple is right, too."

He looked down at his changed appearance and then grinned at her. "I did it."

"Now that you know how to shift into other beings, what will you use your talent for?" She winked at him as she walked around him, assessing his accomplishment from every angle. "You could start spying by becoming whom-ever you wanted to know more about."

"That's one possibility." He curtsied with a grin on his lips. "Or be someone they trust so I could ask questions."

"That could be a useful approach as well." Coming to a halt in front of him, she considered other uses for his ability.

He snapped his fingers. "I could be you and talk to Mandy, find out how she really feels about me."

"That's not fair." Cassie shook her head furiously. "Don't even think about using my appearance to spy on Mandy, you hear me?"

"Fine."

"Nice job, son." Mercy appeared a few feet away, hovering several inches from the floor.

"Ma." Cassie didn't jump this time, having fully expected

her mother would make an unexpected and uninvited appearance while Abram practiced. "I need to find some way to put a bell on you."

Mercy smirked at her and then smiled at Abram. "I knew you'd figure out how to manipulate your appearance to suit."

Flint strode into the parlor, a newspaper tucked under one arm. He came to an abrupt halt. "Wow."

"Abram's a very convincing me." Cassie hurried over to take hold of Flint's arm and pull him farther into the room. "Come look."

Flint dropped the paper on a nearby chair before scanning the other Cassie. "That's impressive and scary at the same time."

"Thanks, man." Abram blinked and shifted back into his own form. "I appreciate the compliment."

"Now you have full control over how you look." Mercy smiled softly at her son. "Something I know you've always dreamed of being able to do."

"We both know appearances matter most. You've always taught us to dress well and make the best impression." Abram gazed at his mother's ghost with a bemused expression. "The very reason why I gave you the looking glass."

"I didn't realize." Cassie tilted her head to regard her brother. "You took her advice to heart, didn't you?"

"It's served me well in my position." Abram glanced down at his casual outfit, tan jeans and dark green collared shirt with leather shoes. "But I am starting to understand I want to fit in where I am rather than being overdressed for the occasion."

Flint wrapped an arm around Cassie's waist. "I think it's important as well. I'm glad you decided to tone down the outfits."

Abram shrugged lightly with a wry smile. "It's because of Mandy, actually. She helped me to see how important it is to fit in with your surroundings, your peers. I'd forgotten."

His time spent with the other woman had been good for him. Cassie hadn't thought they'd make a good couple, but after seeing them together for only a few days she'd changed her mind. Mandy had become a friend, filling a void she'd been unaware existed. Another woman to talk to about girly things. Sewing patterns and trim, for one thing. They'd settled on the pattern for the new uniforms and Cassie would begin cutting the fabric as soon as she had time. She'd been caught up with helping Abram perfect his talents and with helping Mandy wait on the growing number of customers frequenting the inn. She'd come to rely on her help as much as Sheridan had grown dependent on Matt's help in the kitchen.

Flint squinted at Abram with a frown between his eyes. "Take care you don't hurt Mandy. She's not as sophisticated as you are."

"I have no intention of hurting her because I don't expect to stay." Abram glanced at his mother and then at Cassie. "Once I know Cassie's safe and settled here, then I have to go back to my job."

"Then you'll be here for a while yet." Relief and disappointment warred in Cassie's chest. She'd hoped he'd be like Giles and change his mind about leaving. "There's time for us to work on convincing you to consider living here."

"No, that's not an option." Abram crossed his arms over his chest and pursed his lips. "The senator needs me to return to assist him."

"Isn't someone helping him while you're away?" Flint retrieved his newspaper and folded it.

"Of course." Abram uncrossed his arms to slide his hands into his pockets. "Why?"

"Then they could continue doing so." Flint tucked the paper under his arm with a flourish.

"But...the senator..." Abram's objection died on his lips.

"Will get by." Flint nodded once to Abram and then gave Cassie a kiss on the cheek. "I have work to do in the office." He saluted the others and then headed toward the office door at the far end of the parlor.

Shock and sudden certainty filled her brother as he stood there gaping at Flint. The sad realization he could be replaced from a long list of others deflated the egotistical pride Abram had carried around like a bucket of rocks. Weighing him down but proof of his importance.

"I have some gardening to do, too." Cassie glanced at Abram and then her mother. "See you later."

"I think I'll take a ride and clear my head." Abram's features drooped into a frown as he turned to walk out of the room.

"I guess that's my cue to leave as well." Mercy smiled at Cassie and then shimmered and vanished.

Cassie stood in the parlor, alone and yet content. Her brother had achieved his aim of shifting to appear like her down to the uneven teeth in her mouth. Yet he'd also learned something about himself in the process. Appearances can shift and change, but it would be interesting to see how the ability to do so might change the man inside.

Chapter Seventeen

*L*ater that morning, Cassie led Sheridan out back to the garden so she could weed and snip the dead blossoms from the flower beds. She planned to use some of the flowers to make rose water and others to make tinctures and simples. Sheridan's insistence that he accompany her while Teddy helped in the kitchen seemed foolish. It had been bad enough to have the boy as her shadow, but having the older man do so felt worse. The whole idea, in fact, of needing somebody to stand guard proved disquieting and rather upsetting.

"I'll stand here." Sheridan held the gate open for her to slip past. "I want to talk to you anyway."

"About what?" But she knew and didn't want to have the discussion. She tugged her gardening gloves on and then pulled her snippers out of a pocket.

"I think I should go to Savannah."

A lead weight settled in her stomach, cold and heavy and immoveable. Exactly what she'd dreaded. "You do?"

He rested his large hands on top of the gate. "Your pa may need my help to convince her to come back with him."

"If he finds her." She dragged in a long breath and stared at the row of red and yellow rose bushes. Far easier to contemplate the flowers than his suggestion. The idea of him leaving.

"I would help him on that task as well."

"Is it safe for you to travel alone?" She grabbed hold of a dead blossom and snipped it off. "Isn't it risky?"

"As a black man, you mean?" His grip on the gate tightened, rattling the metal and wood structure. "I'll carry my papers."

His emancipation papers, evidence of his status as a freeman. Necessary for him, and yet something she and her family wouldn't need to make the same journey. What if he were mistaken for a runaway slave and they didn't believe the document to be valid? Her imagination flew with the many possible horrible results of such a situation. A shiver racked her back as she reached for another withered bloom. Such a long way for him to want to go.

"What about the senator's visit in a little while?" She raised her eyes to note the determination in his expression. "How will Flint manage without you?"

"Matt will stay and handle everything in the kitchen." A small smile curved his lips. "He's a fine cook, too."

"You're proud of him, aren't you?" Cassie moved down the row, snipping and discarding the dead flowers. After she pruned those, she'd go back and harvest fresh blossoms for her concoctions.

"He's turned out fine, Cassie." He paused until she reluctantly looked at him. "I have to go. I have to try to find my wife."

"But, Sheridan, we need you here. I need you." She stopped her work to address him. "You promised to help Flint. My pa promised to find Pansy. You don't need to go so far away."

The big man drew in a long breath and let it out on a sigh. "You're right, I did promise."

"Please don't go." What else could she say? Sheridan

164

had been her confidant for years. He helped her through the initial weeks after her ma's death. His quiet confidence and good humor had calmed her when she'd become upset at her ma's heavy-handed ways. "Pa will bring her home in a couple of months like he said. You can do more good here to prepare for that important visit in November."

"Your pa is counting on it to be a spectacular event, too." He sighed again as he rubbed a hand over his head. "I suppose you're right. I'll leave it to Mr. Fairhope to find her and bring her to me if he can."

Cassie hurried to stand in front of him, gripping her work basket with both hands. "Thank you. That means a lot to me, to Flint, and to Pa, I'm sure."

He rubbed his forehead with his fingertips. "I do what I can."

"Now, tell me what you think about Flint asking me to marry him?" Her heart soared with relief at Sheridan's change of mind. Now she could finally seek out his advice. She'd been wanting to ask him about Flint's proposal for some time but other events had intervened. "Do you think it's a good idea? Would Pa approve?"

"Well, now, when he first came here, I wasn't too sure about him. He's so young to be in charge of such a large place." He dropped his hands to his sides. "But he's proven to be resourceful, and caring, and kind."

"I love him, Sheridan. I can't help it."

"You could do far worse." He looked away, toward the mountains behind the inn. "You need to follow your heart, like I did with Pansy."

His attention drifted far away as he searched the foothills for several moments. She left him in peace for a span and then cleared her throat. "You'll see her again. I know it."

"I do hope so." He regarded her with a slight grin. "After all, I found my sons."

"Keep the faith, my friend." She smiled back at him,

pleased to sense him relaxed and hopeful. "Give me a few minutes and I'll be all done here."

"Take your time." He propped an elbow on the gate. "I'm enjoying being out here for a little bit."

She began gathering fresh flowers, laying them gently in her basket. Preserving some, cooking down others with herbs and spices, the resulting medicines would serve the residents of the inn over the cold winter months. When her pa and hopefully Sheridan's wife would also be in residence.

Could it be possible? He wasn't as necessary as he'd been led to believe. Abram seethed as he marched across the carriageway toward the stable. He'd taken enough time to change into breeches and tall boots before leaving the inn for his impulsive desire of taking his horse out. But he needed to get away and think. Away from his sister's knowing glances. Away from his ma's sudden and disturbing appearances. Away from the sudden doubt about his own future. But mostly away from the weight of new responsibilities and expectations.

He blinked as he crossed the threshold of the barn aisle, the sweet smell of hay and leather calming the anxious weight inside. He let his eyes grow accustomed to the dimmer light as he scanned the horses in several stalls. He strolled down the wide dirt aisle, toward his eager horse. Then he spied his brother with that woman again. At the far end of the aisle, close together. Kissing.

"A-hem." His annoyance with Flint's assessment of the future of his chosen career shifted into anger at his brother's clandestine relationship.

They sprung apart, Giles flashing a surprised and then guilty expression at him. Haley moistened her plump lips, glancing between him and his brother. A horse nickered behind him as an orange marmalade cat ran past and disappeared out the back of the barn.

"Hey, Abram." Giles turned to face him, the guilt sliding off his features. "Did you want something?"

Why, yes. He wanted many things. Certainty of his path to promotion. Nerve to escape the influence of his sister and brother, and even ghostly mother. Return to home and his normal life with all the cultural and epicurean delights he was accustomed to enjoying. Answers to whether his aunts actually posed a threat to Cassie or if something else was lurking. Even to know how Mandy had managed to infiltrate his defenses. Most of all, he wanted peace inside. Feeling upset and anxious as well as defensive proved unsettling.

"What the hell are you doing?" He glared at his brother then flicked a glance at the trembling girl. "What is this?"

"None of your business." Giles sidled closer to Haley, took her hand.

"You sneak about and disappear frequently. With everything else at stake, I think it is my business to know what my brother is up to."

"You needn't worry about me."

Abram cocked an eyebrow as his anger battled with the compulsion to hit something. Or someone. "You're out here thinking only about yourself and what you want. Like always."

Back when they were boys, Giles had acted all macho and important. He was the oldest brother, after all. He'd been on this earth longer and knew more, according to him. Routinely, he'd boss the younger boys around, directing them on how they should act and what they should do. Like he was some stage director instead of a brother. He apparently needed to be center stage and in charge. All the time. It was all about Giles.

Giles stiffened and released Haley's hand to take two steps toward Abram. "That's not true."

Pressure built in the center of Abram's chest at the challenge in his brother's glare. He raised his chin and stared down his nose at his brother. "I say it is and I should know given that I was frequently on the receiving end of your self-centeredness."

Giles balled his hands into fists at his sides. "What are you talking about?"

"Your needs and wants always came first." Abram shook his head once in growing annoyance at the lack of understanding. "Bossing me and the others around like you ran the place."

Giles blinked several times and then the glare on his face hardened. "We were kids, but you guys needed direction. I was there to give it to you."

"You bullied and bossed us and I won't let you continue to treat me that way."

"What do you intend to do about it?" Giles took another step closer, fists slowly lifting.

"Stop it!" Haley pushed between them, a palm on each man's chest. "This is ridiculous."

Abram pulled back, away from her hand. He squinted at his brother and then slid his gaze to meet hers. "Why do you two keep sneaking off?"

That was something else he wanted. Answers to his questions. For his brother to trust him and include him in his life. Discuss his options and decisions like pals instead of directing and insisting on how Abram should live and be.

Haley glanced at Giles as if silently asking for approval. Approval? That's not what these rendezvous were about. Didn't they know he could tell?

Abram bristled as he huffed out a breath. "Oh, for goodness sakes. Are you two in love?"

Haley swiveled her head to gape at him. "Love?"

"Wh-what?" Giles reared back his head with his mouth falling open.

Abram crossed his arms. "Sneaking off to kiss and fondle each other? You best be careful."

Haley blushed crimson, eyes wide as she slowly closed her mouth but kept her gaze on Giles. He studied her for several seconds and then nodded once to himself. He swallowed before taking her hands in his.

"Haley, I think he's right." Giles cradled her hands against his chest. "I do love you."

"Oh, Giles." Haley blinked and a lone tear trailed down her cheek. "I didn't mean for this to happen, but…"

Abram tensed on Giles' behalf at the hesitation in her voice and the searching look she gave the man hanging on her every word. Damn, he hadn't meant to embarrass his brother by his conjectures. Or put them on the spot. He'd merely come to the barn to saddle his horse and take a ride. Just look at the mess he'd made.

"But what?" Giles lowered her hands as he studied her serious expression.

"But…" A smile blossomed on her lips. "I'm glad it did happen. I love you, too."

Relief rushed through Abram's chest, washing away the earlier annoyance and anger. Still, something more was going on between them than simply falling in love. "I'm glad you've found each other. But why the secrecy?"

Haley pulled her hands free and pressed her lips together. "Giles, we should tell him."

"Are you sure?" Giles glanced at Abram and then back to her. "I think we can trust him."

"Thanks." The one word dripped with sarcasm Abram couldn't stop.

Arching a brow in response, Giles smirked at him. "Promise to keep this to yourself, all right?"

"Just tell me."

"Promise."

"Fine."

Haley cleared her throat and leveled an intense look at Abram. "You know I've been tracking my father's nighttime activities for some time. I'm very concerned about what he's doing in the wee hours of the night."

"You've said as much before."

"She's convinced he may be involved in something illegal, or immoral, or both." Giles draped an arm around her shoulders. "We think he's responsible for the murders."

"Whoa." John Baker seemed like a decent man, an upright citizen of the new state of Alabama. Obviously, Abram's father trusted the man since he entrusted him to oversee Flint. But... "Murder?"

"I don't know. Maybe?" She shook her head, biting her lips.

"But why? What would he gain?"

"Did you know most of the women who were killed are—" She stopped to inspect the barn, her gaze flashing around before coming back to rest on Abram. "Were witches?"

A chill crawled up his spine. "You're sure?"

"My mother and I knew them." She stared at him. "I believe Father doesn't like magic and witchcraft. He seems to think it's dangerous and corrupting."

"And reason enough for killing those who practice it, apparently." Giles grasped Haley's hand again. "He doesn't know, and do not tell him, his wife and daughter are witches. We don't know what he'd do to them if he learned the truth."

"What do we do now?" Abram's stomach roiled as he considered the dire and far-reaching implications of their revelations. "Our entire family are witches."

Chapter Eighteen

I need to know." Abram was wandering around after he returned from his ride, looking for something to occupy his flustered mind when he'd spotted Flint grooming his paint horse. He decided on the spur of the moment to ask him point blank the question niggling his brain.

Flint kept rubbing the curry comb over the horse's haunches. "Probably not."

"Would you look at me?" The man was infuriating, continuing to send dust and hair flying into the air. For once, the calming presence of horses munching on hay and swallows flitting above did nothing to settle him.

"That's what you need to know?" Flint paused, resting the toothed wooden oval on his horse's back as he glanced at Abram.

"No, that's not what I meant." Leave it to him to twist his words around like a pretzel. He frowned at the uppity attitude. Not a good look for the man. Nor an endearing quality. "I've seen you snuggling up to my sister and I need to know what your intentions are toward her."

"Oh, is that it." The dust cloud drifted toward the open window as Flint scrubbed harder. "I've asked her to marry me."

"And?" Getting information out of the man was worse than securing the senator's commitment to a proposed bill. "What did she say?"

"Yes." Flint turned to beat the clods of dirt and hair out of the grooves of the comb.

She agreed to marry this taciturn being? Without even discussing it with him let alone Giles. As the eldest brother, during their father's absence Giles was in charge. Which rankled but must be admitted. Flint glanced at him and then began to work on the paint's neck. Ignoring him.

"Did you ask Giles for his permission?" Crossing his arms, Abram drummed the fingers of one hand on his elbow.

"No."

He drew in a deep breath, striving for calm and patience but failing miserably. "Why not?"

"It's not his decision to make." Flint stroked the horse's nose as he moved around to the other side and continued currying. "Nor yours."

"You're not good enough for my sister."

"Like I said, it's her choice." Flint ran the comb over the withers and met Abram's glare. "She accepted my proposal but we're waiting until your father comes home before making plans for the wedding. Does that meet with your approval?"

"I think she doesn't know her own mind." He shook his head as he dropped his hands to rest on the half wall. "A young girl can't be trusted to choose...wisely when it comes to serious decisions such as marriage."

"I love her and she loves me." Flint huffed and strode toward Abram. "I intend to be at her side always, to care for her and to protect her." He stopped on the other side of the wall from Abram. "From any threat to her safety or happiness."

"I'm going to have a little talk with her about this unfortunate and unwise choice she's made."

"Back off, man." Laying the curry comb on top of the half wall, Flint gripped the wall on either side of Abram's hands. "It's not up to you. Cassandra knows what she wants and that's me as her husband."

"We'll see." Abram removed his hands from the wall, feeling threatened by the other man's intense stare and proximity. He wouldn't back down though. Not on such an important consideration with grim consequences.

"What's going on in here?" Giles sauntered down the wide dirt aisle and stopped beside Abram.

"Just having a chat." Flint sidled over to the stall doorway and ducked under the rope stretched across it. "Abram seems to think he's in charge of Cassie now."

"Well, she'd disagree with that." Giles chuckled as he met Abram's surprised look. "What?"

"Are you taking his side?" he asked, shocked. The very idea that the brothers couldn't stand together to oversee their sister's future irked deep inside.

Over the past days with Cassie spending more and more time coaching him he'd slowly come to realize how much he loved his sister. Her encouragement and guidance were what he needed as he learned how to work with his newly discovered talents. Everything she did demonstrated her caring, loving nature. She exuded concern and consideration for others and helped wherever help was needed.

"It's the wise thing to do, brother." Giles shrugged as a smirk grew on his lips. "Especially when he's right."

"Face it, Abram, the note you sent announcing your arrival also spoke volumes about how reluctant you were about coming to see her."

"How do you mean?" His brows weighed down in confusion. "I came, didn't I?"

"I think it said something like, and I'm not quoting exactly, you'd meant to stay home but the senator convinced you to fulfill your family duty." Flint pointed a finger at

Abram. "Otherwise you wouldn't even be here to worry about her choices."

He'd forgotten how irritated he'd been to receive her brief note, asking for him to come to the inn after their mother's death. To pay his respects and be there for her until their father returned. He had resented and resisted the idea he owed Mercy or Reggie anything after they'd chased him away from home. Let alone such a long, arduous journey away from the finer living in Washington in the Territory of Columbia. To come to the wilderness of north Alabama, with its snakes and dense forests and dangerous roads.

But once he arrived and learned about the changes in himself and the many family secrets haunting them all, he'd slowly changed inside. He'd come to see his tendency to always act as if everything was fine, even when it most definitely was not, had pushed people away. He'd raised an emotional pretense when he actually needed someone to recognize the fear and loneliness inside. Mandy had initiated the internal shifting sensations and emotions when she'd broken through the mask, and Cassie then encouraged and accelerated them merely by listening to him. She deserved to be happy and safe. Flint's desire to protect her mirrored his own growing determination to do whatever was necessary to ensure her happiness and well-being.

"I regret sending such a terse note but I'm here now. And I do care about her." Abram pressed his lips together as he glanced between the two men. "Look, I'm trying to be what she needs. If you think she's made the best decision, I will learn to live with it. And accept you, Flint. But that doesn't mean I'm convinced."

"It's a start." Giles brushed off his hands as he looked at Flint. "You ready?"

Flint inspected his dirty palms with a slight grimace. "Let me wash my hands and I'll meet you inside."

"What are you doing?" Abram felt adrift in the vague conversation. "Need any help?"

"We're going to set up the room next to Cassie's for the aunts when they arrive. Make sure all is comfortable for them." Giles tilted his head to one side and shrugged. "Although I doubt Cassie will be comfortable once they settle in."

"Let's get this over with." Flint gestured for Giles to lead the way down the aisle. He hesitated with a grin at Abram. "Come along if you'd like."

He nodded and fell into step with them. Striding out into the late morning sunlight, he noted storm clouds building above the foothills. With good fortune, it wouldn't be an omen.

"Sit right there, Teddy." Cassie mounted the few steps into the shade of the gazebo, pointing to the right-hand bench. "Are you enjoying the story?"

"Mostly." The thin boy settled onto the hard bench and opened the book he'd carried out. "I don't like the idea of being trapped on an island."

She sat on the center bench and inhaled the scent of roses from the vines clinging to the roof and columns of the gazebo. "I bet Robinson Crusoe didn't much cotton to the idea either."

A ripple of something undefinable made her look out across the expanse between her and the stable. She noted the normal level of activity, of carriages and men on horseback coming and going. The chickens pecking along the grassy edge of the drive. Inhaled the sweet aroma of flowers and approaching rain. Dark gray clouds boiled up behind the mountains, effectively limiting the length of time she'd have to find inner calm and quiet her mind.

"At least he had Friday to help him." Teddy flipped to a page and then peered at her. "Are you okay?"

"I'm fine." Simply feeling like something was coming, something she couldn't quite sense entirely but it wasn't good. "Let's sit quietly and read for a bit, until we get chased back inside."

He nodded and lowered his eyes to scan the page. The boy had adapted well to the life at the inn. Pitching in without being asked most of the time. Though of course he had moments when being a boy was more important than the chores assigned to him. Then she'd find him out with the dogs, running around the backyard with a stick to throw for one or the other to retrieve. Since Flint insisted someone—namely, Teddy—be with her, she started making sure he received some education along the way. Thus the reading of one of her favorite stories.

She looked down at the book in her hands. Abram had let her borrow his copy of Sir Walter Scott's novel, *Waverly*. Apparently, he had easy access to many books in the cosmopolitan world he lived in. He'd recommended it to her as a distraction and a great romantic tale. She opened the cover and noted it had been out for seven years, but it was entirely new to her. The story of an idealistic young man who fought for the Jacobites in 1745 Scotland seemed like a good way to not think about what was happening around her. To not think about what might happen when her aunts arrived. To not think about what other family secrets lurked in the shadows. Turning to the first page of the story, she ignored everything else.

Or tried. The rattle of wheels and thump of hooves tempted her to see who was coming and going. The smell of cake baking in the bread oven wafted past, teasing her nose. Her stomach rumbled, making her wish it was closer to dinner time. Another tweak to her empathic senses made her glance up, seeking the cause. Inwardly she shrugged. She wouldn't actually see what caused the sensation. She returned her wayward eyes to the page and tried to absorb its contents, the reasons for why Scott had chosen the title name for the main character. She read the passage again but finally gave up with a sigh and let her gaze wander as she closed the book. So much for losing herself in an enchanting tale.

A grand coach-and-four suddenly materialized in front of the inn. She blinked in astonishment as her senses reeled with new emotions assaulting them. The shiny black paint on the coach was relieved by gold trim and appurtenances. Four pristine white horses stamped their hooves impatiently. The liveried driver hustled to dismount from the high front seat and drop to the ground. He smartly opened the door to the coach and offered a hand to someone inside. She sniffed rosemary and sensed magic in the air, her hands tensing on the cover of the book.

A cold wave of determination crashed through her. She pressed a hand to the center of her chest to calm the riot of emotion inside. Whoever was in the vehicle had very mixed feelings, very strong ones. She shivered when a second wave followed, one of curiosity and uncertainty. She pressed harder, physically quelling the turmoil inside with an iron will of her own. She concentrated on erecting the barrier she'd learned to employ to shield herself from such intense emotions.

A woman in a black traveling cloak and bonnet emerged from the coach and stepped down to the crushed stone drive. The source of the strong determination she'd sensed. When the unfamiliar woman spun in place to survey her surroundings, Cassie espied her pale yellow dress peeking from beneath the cloak. Even from where Cassie sat she could tell the woman was used to being in charge.

She was followed by another woman in a red traveling cloak and black bonnet over her long black hair falling to between her shoulders. As the second woman mimicked the first woman's actions, Cassie noted she wore a boring medium gray dress. But the curiosity stemmed from the second woman. One thing was certain.

Her aunts had arrived.

"Come on, Teddy. Time to go inside." She rose, hoping the shadowy gazebo would mask her presence from the unwelcome guests. Delay the inevitable first meeting with them. "I need to find Giles and Abram."

Teddy stood and snapped the book closed. "But I didn't finish the chapter…"

"Later." She eased down the steps of the gazebo, keeping an eye on her aunts. "Let's go around back and see if the guys are out there."

"I would doubt that, but if you want to." Teddy trailed after her. "I thought they were in the barn."

Anything to avoid going in the front door where her aunts headed. They strode briskly through the open front doors and disappeared inside. What did they really want? Maybe her ma was right and they wanted her to join with them. Given the strong determination she'd sensed, she could only hope she had the fortitude to stand up for herself and her druthers.

I hunkered out of sight, watching the young witch with the boy sitting in the shadows of the gazebo. I kept to my own shadows until deciding it was time to move on. I started to retreat but then froze in horror when an impressive coach-and-four materialized in front of the inn. It shone in the intermittent sunlight, spotless. Impossible, unless the two cloaked women handed down by the driver were also witches and used their evil magic to transport themselves. I squinted at them, memorizing their features so I'd recognize them again. I added them to my mental list of women to keep an eye on, to find a way to remove them if they didn't depart of their own accord. I don't need even more witches working their mischief. Enough was enough.

Chapter Nineteen

$\mathcal{F}$ lint hesitated as he crossed the entrance hall toward the dining room. He and the other guys had put the finishing touches on the spare bedroom for the aunts to use while they stayed for a spell. He grimaced at his own pun and tapped a rolled newspaper on one palm. How long would they be at the inn? Too long for Mercy's comfort, surely. Probably Cassie's as well. Footsteps on the porch alerted him to guests arriving. A moment later two women strode into view, pausing when they saw him. Their traveling cloaks and bonnets were so clean they practically sparkled. How had they managed to travel without becoming dusty and soiled? Tucking the newspaper under his arm, he approached them with a cautious smile on his lips.

"Ladies, welcome to the Fury Falls Inn." He stopped in front of them, hoping his assumption was incorrect. "Do you have reservations or are you here for an early dinner?"

The woman in black smiled sweetly at him, her green eyes hard as ice. "I am Hope Hopkins, and this is my sister Faith Covington. I believe our niece Cassandra Fairhope is expecting us."

So much for not being correct. If he remembered rightly

from Giles' stories, Hope's son drowned as a young boy and she blamed Giles for his death. A wave of concern swept through him. What if she hadn't forgiven him? First things first, though. "Yes, we have been expecting you."

Abram and Giles pushed through the door from the covered passage. Giles swept his gaze over the trio and then hastened to join the group. Abram hesitated, a slight frown weighing on his brows, then walked slowly over to stand by his brother.

"You're just in time to greet your aunts." Motioning to the two men, Flint addressed the aunts. "These are Cassie's brothers, Giles and Abram."

Hope assessed the two young men with a haughty smile and sharp eyes. Her gaze lingered on Giles for several beats. "You must be Giles."

Flint stiffened at her austere tone combined with the dislike in her pinched features. Apparently, Hope had not forgotten nor forgiven the elder brother for his role in her son's drowning.

"Yes, I am." Giles didn't move, didn't offer to shake her hand or give her a hug in greeting. "I trust your trip went smoothly."

Faith nodded briskly, her hair dancing around her shoulders. "We ensured we had no major delays or obstacles."

One of the benefits of being a witch, smoothing their way with a flick of their wand or a blink of their eyes. Perhaps that explained their clean clothing. Would they use magic during their stay? A thought he'd avoided. He resisted the futile urge to draw his pistol from its holster to ward off the implied threat. A bullet held no sway over supernatural powers.

"We prepared your room in the residence. I'll show you to it so you can freshen up after your sojourn." Flint forced a welcoming smile back on his lips.

"We want to see Cassandra. Where is she?" Hope untied her bonnet strings and slid it off.

Faith also removed her bonnet, holding it by the scalloped edges. "We've come a great distance to see her."

"She was outside, reading." Giles indicated the open door with his chin. "She enjoys the outdoors."

"Would you mind fetching her?" Hope leveled her glittering eyes on Flint. "I want her to show us to our room so we can get to know her better as soon as possible."

"There's no need." Cassie eased into the entrance hall through the still open side door. "I'm here."

Her usual smile nowhere in sight, she warily strolled closer until she stood at his side. He could feel her tension practically humming inside her. She moistened her lips and then held out a hand to Hope, who glanced at it and then clasped it with her own.

"Which aunt are you?" Cassie blinked at the older woman.

"I'm Aunt Hope, dear. You're quite grown up, Cassandra." Hope released her hand and glanced at her sister. "This is your Aunt Faith. Would you take us up to our room, dear? We'd like to change and chat with you." She smiled gently at Cassie.

Something in the woman's demeanor set Flint's teeth on edge. She acted like a sweet, doting aunt. All gentle smiles and polite affection toward her niece, though definitely not her oldest nephew. He detected a steeliness to her personality and a strength of character to accomplish her own aims. She likely managed to achieve her goals despite any and all obstacles put in her way. Faith had a similar if more gentle personality. She'd specifically stated they'd removed the obstacles on their journey north. They'd be formidable foes if challenged.

Cassie swallowed and pasted a weak smile on her face. "If you'd like."

Betty Bolté

Abram eased over to Cassie's side. "I'd be happy to bring up your luggage, Aunt Hope."

Hope pinned Abram with a look and then smiled secretively. "No need to trouble yourself. I shall take care of it."

Flint's stomach tightened. She wanted his girl alone, at her mercy. Should he permit it? Insist on accompanying them? Cassie glanced at him with concern but nodded once, submitting to the request albeit with reluctance. She turned to face her aunts, squaring her shoulders and lifting her chin. Pride swept through him at her confident bravery.

Giles moved to Cassie's side, silently supporting her with his presence. "Are you okay?"

"I'll be fine." She laid a hand on his upper arm for a moment. "Don't worry."

Giles met Hope and Faith's steady gazes with defiance in his eyes. "If you have a problem with me, you talk to me about it. Don't blame Cassie for my past mistakes."

"Trust me, Giles Fairhope." Hope held her bonnet with both hands, calmly addressing the large man bristling in front of her. "I would never do anything to harm my niece. You have nothing to fear."

Behind the two aunts, Flint saw a flash of light and then Mercy shimmered into view. She hovered there only long enough for Flint to see her panic at the presence of her sisters. Then she shimmered again and disappeared. He understood her panic. The aunts had an agenda. But what exactly?

Giles lifted one brow, doubt and suspicion evident in his glowering expression. "That's for me to decide."

"Giles, that's enough." Cassie tapped his shoulder lightly, a hesitant smile on her mouth. "I'll be fine."

The big man inspected her open features for several moments before letting out a slow breath. "Very well, but let me know if you need me. For anything. Clear?"

"I will." She drew in a breath and met Hope's smirk. "Are you ready?"

Unease swept through Abram at his sister's question. She might be fine but he surely was not. He needed answers to several burning questions. "Before you go, may I ask how long you plan to stay?"

"Abram…" Cassie shot him a disapproving look.

"For…for planning purposes." Abram darted a glance at Flint, seeking confirmation.

"That would be helpful to know." Flint rushed to fill the silence. "A few days or…?

"That depends on Cassandra." Faith smiled at Cassie. "Which is why we need to have a chat."

"Where is Reginald?" Hope pursed her lips as she looked at each person in the group. "I want to talk with him as well."

"I'm sorry but he's away on business." Cassie's voice emerged breathless and unsure. "He won't be back for a while yet."

"What?" Hope's surprise echoed in her harsh tone. "My, oh my, it's a good thing we came. You poor dear. Alone, unmarried. Stranded out here with no parents to rely on." She tsked several times as she grabbed Cassie's shoulders and pulled her close. "We're here now. We'll take care of you."

"She may be unwed but she's not alone." Flint bristled with indignity and outrage. "I've been here all along as well as the staff."

"She has us, too." Abram studied his aunts' expressions and soon realized they were false fronts of empathy and understanding. He glanced at Cassie. Her face, too, was a careful mask. "We came as soon as we could after hearing about Ma's death."

He grimaced inwardly at his white lie. He did come as soon as he decided to make the trip. Which admittedly he'd wrestled with for a few days. But he was here and stepping up to defend and protect his sister with everything he possessed.

"Two of you, but where are the other two?" Faith arched a questioning brow. "Why aren't they here as well?"

"I haven't heard from them but I expect to every day." Cassie stepped away from Hope's embrace. "I'm sure they will come as I requested."

"Well, it seems to me if they cared about their sister, let alone their dear departed mother, they would have dropped everything to do their duty to their family." Hope shook her head. "After all, that is what Faith and I did."

Appearances mattered to Abram, so much that he could easily tell when people tried to hide who they were and their true intentions. He didn't have Cassie's empathic abilities but he didn't need them to see that Hope and Faith hid their real reason for making the long trip north. Turned out Ma had good reason to worry about those two women. Which meant they all needed to stay on guard.

A movement off to his right drew his attention to where Mandy hurried from the dining room. Her reflexive grin in his direction faded when she noticed the tense group by the open front doors. He turned back when he heard Flint speak.

"I could show you up to your rooms since I'm sure Cassie must have things to tend to at this time of day." Flint studied Cassie's controlled expression. "If you want me to."

"I appreciate the offer but I believe my aunts would prefer my company for a few minutes."

"All right, but I expect to have you help in the dining room this afternoon." Flint glanced at Hope and Faith and then back to Cassie, his eyes boring into her with unspoken meaning. "Mandy can't expect to handle the dinner rush alone."

"I'll be back by then." Cassie winked at him and then addressed the aunts. "Ready?"

Without a word, the three strode toward the side door and through to disappear into the residence. Abram held himself back from following them with an effort, his concern escalating the longer he stood there staring at the closed door. He couldn't insert himself into that situation. Not yet. No direct threat existed. In the meantime, he needed air.

"Well, let's get back to work then." Flint ran his fingers through his loose hair. "Keep an ear out just in case."

Giles sighed heavily and fisted his hands. "The owl is back as a warning. I don't like it."

"Me either." Abram crossed his arms over his tense stomach. "But what can we do?"

Abram looked out the open front doors as he contemplated his own question. The black coach-and-four gleamed in the late morning sunlight. He glanced back to Flint but a flash of light drew his gaze back to the coach. Only the coach and horses had disappeared. When did it pull away? Why didn't he hear the harness or hoof beats? Then he understood. The witches had conjured the conveyance until it was no longer needed. He drew in a sobering breath as he realized the threat their powers posed.

Abram turned to face Flint, unsure whether to point out what he'd just learned.

"What do we do? The only thing we can." Flint pulled the paper from under his arm to roll and unroll repeatedly. "Try to stay close to her as much as possible."

Abram heard light footsteps and spun about to see who approached. Mandy. Just who he wanted to see. To be with. Something about her drew him in, intrigued and enthralled him. He liked everything about her. Her tender smile. Her trim figure. Her intellect and curiosity about life.

She paused beside him with a smile to the other two men as they departed. "Are you okay?"

He wasn't certain, if he were to be honest. "I'm fine."

"Who were they?" She searched his expression with her lovely eyes. "You seem tense."

"My aunts." He raked his fingers through his hair and shook his head. "Hey, would you meet me at the gazebo before your shift? I need to get some fresh air and I'd like to talk with you if you're willing."

Her smile widened. "I'd be pleased. Let me make sure it's okay and then I'll come out."

"Wonderful." He returned her smile, his heart gladdened by her ready acceptance of his attentions. "I will wait for you there."

She gave a small wave in farewell as she sashayed toward the kitchen. The sway of her slim hips and swish of long skirts drew his gaze and his admiration until the door swung shut behind her. On a sigh, he moved to the open front door, intent on finding a way to center and balance between protecting his sister and his heart.

Disconcerted by the eyes boring into her back, Cassie crossed the parlor and climbed the stairs to the bedrooms. She reached out to attempt to read their emotions since she couldn't tell anything from their expressions other than they were pretending they cared. Her probe ran smack into a fog bank of resistance. Not surprising that they would take defensive measures against others knowing their inner lives. Their secrets and intentions. She quickened her pace, wanting nothing more than to be able to face them. She felt utterly defenseless with them behind her.

Reaching the top landing, she hurried to the room next to hers and flung the door open. "Here we are."

She crossed the threshold into the cheery room, surveying its contents to ensure it had been properly prepared. A gusty breeze scented with rain rippled the curtains hanging at the open window. The four-post bed boasted a down mattress and pillows covered with fine cotton sheets and a lightweight spread. The necessary ewer of water and basin rested on a small square table beside the wardrobe. A pair of carved wood chairs flanked a round chintz covered table in front of the window. Small oval braided rugs provided a spot of warmth and color on either side of the large bed. All seemed in order.

"I hope you'll be comfortable."

Hope swung into the room with a slow judgmental sweep of her gaze. She pulled a gnarled wood wand from an inner compartment of her cloak and gave it a flick. A rushing sound filled the room as a light blue fog rose and fell away. "That's better."

Cassie gasped and blinked in surprise. A wide bed with a step up to its thick mattress stood where the four-post bed had been. Thick blankets and an array of pillows decorated it, while a plush rug spread across the floor. A miniature waterfall flowed on a large table, magically not spilling onto the floor but seeming to refill the ewer to pour into the basin over and over. Fine wood chairs flanked a low table with a shining silver tea service and porcelain cups and saucers. A tiered set of plates offered an array of cakes and fruit to one side.

"Sister, be nice." Faith pulled her black gloves from her hands and slid them into her cloak pocket. "You shouldn't rearrange things without permission."

"You're right, Faith." Hope shrugged, a wry smile aimed at Cassie. "My apologies."

"Pa is away with the intent to improve what the inn has to offer."

"When is he planning to return?" Hope untied her cloak and eased it from her shoulders.

"By Allhallows Eve." Cassie crossed the room to open the doors on the wardrobe. "You can hang your things in here."

Faith tugged on the ties of her cloak and removed the heavy garment. "That seems a long time."

Indeed. Yet he'd made it clear to her that he had to oversee the work to ensure it met his high standards and expectations. "Perhaps, but Flint is here and doing a fine job of improving the operation and appearance of the inn." She stepped away from the wardrobe as her aunts started toward it.

Hope hung her cloak on a peg at the back of the cupboard, glancing at Cassie as she emerged from its depths. "So tell me, my dear, what magical powers do you possess?"

Taken aback by the abrupt question, Cassie froze in place. "Powers?"

"Don't be shy." Faith finished hanging her cloak and then shut the doors. "We know you and your brothers have them even if your parents wouldn't tell us what they are. What are yours?"

Cassie swallowed the uncertainty racing through her. "I—"

"Don't say anything." Mercy shimmered into sight beside Cassie. She glared at Hope and then Faith. "It's none of your business."

Hope and Faith gasped and fell back several steps, mouths gaping and eyes blinking rapidly.

Cassie put a hand to her throat but relief flooded through her. "Ma…"

"Ah, our dearly departed sister." Hope recovered first from the shock of seeing her sister's ghost. "I didn't realize you were still around. I'd hoped you'd be resting peacefully."

Mercy drifted nearer to Cassie, between her and the powerful witches. "You stay away from my daughter. You can't have her."

Hope cackled, eyes hard and glittering. "You're a ghost. What can you do to stop us?"

Stop them from what? Cassie stared at the trans-formation in her aunt from a seeming gentle woman to an adversary. Her loving smile turned to a sneer. Her tender caress she'd bestowed earlier now felt sinister and invasive.

"You don't want to find out." Mercy stayed in front of Cassie, hovering a few inches from the floor. "You've come here for nothing."

"We'll see about that." Faith eased a step or two toward Cassie. "It's her choice, not yours."

"No!" The ghost seemed to solidify then shimmered back into a translucent entity. "Leave her alone."

Chortling, Hope splayed her hands into a welcoming gesture. "Come here, my dear. Let's have a nice little talk while your mother's ghost goes back to where she came from. We have much to discuss and decide, plans to make."

Cassie gaped at her aunt for several moments before snapping her mouth closed. What did the witch expect of her? She willed herself to not tremble in front of her aunts. Her ma had said several times they wanted her, whatever that meant. She stiffened her resolve to be her own person. They couldn't make her do anything she didn't want to do after all was said and done. Even if they were powerful.

"Heed my warning, sisters." Mercy shimmered and drifted from side to side. "I will not let you take my daughter."

"She'll come with us willingly." Faith smiled at Cassie, motioning for her to join her. "Just wait and see. Once we talk with her and explain things, she'll want to come."

Anger, swift and hot, combined with fear flashed through Cassie. "Would you stop talking about me as if I'm not here?"

"Oh, my dear, we're simply trying to help you see your potential." Faith summoned Cassie with a curled forefinger. "We can help you hone your abilities once we know what they are. So come, let us have a conversation."

"No, Cassie, don't trust them." Mercy pivoted to aim her troubled eyes at Cassie. "You mustn't."

Hope laughed at Mercy's plea. "Oh please, sister, you have no say in what your daughter does any longer."

Faith smiled at Cassie and summoned her again. "Come."

A sense of inevitability washed into her core. She may as well have the conversation and see what they had to say. It was going to happen whether her ma wanted it to or not. She could see it in her aunts' expressions. Cassie glanced at her mother's ghost with a grimace and a shrug, then walked toward Faith, Hope gleeful at her side. Tears smarted Cassie's eyes. Every single one of them thought they should control her life. Not her.

"Oh, Cassie..." Mercy shifted side to side again until Cassie reached Faith. "Don't let them..."

"There, there, my dear." Faith drew Cassie into a hug, patting her on the back. "You've made a wise decision."

The salty tears flowed down her cheeks but she couldn't determine the root reason for them. She succumbed to the delicious temptation of the comfort offered from her estranged aunt. She would never receive another hug from her ma. The painful realization made the tears flow more freely. Sniffling, she held on to her aunt's waist.

A low growl erupted from across the room, startling Cassie out of her aunt's embrace. The next thing she knew her ma's ghost whooshed at Faith, knocking her to the floor, before lifting higher and spinning about. The specter hesitated and then started for Hope, who ducked to one side as it whizzed past her. When did Ma figure out she could do...that?

"Ma! Stop." Cassie waved her arms to attract the attention of her incensed mother. "I will make my own decisions about what I will and won't do."

The ghost hovered for a moment and then Mercy lowered to the floor and assumed a rigid stance. She glowered at Hope and Faith, shaking a finger at them. "I'm warning you one last time to leave my daughter be. Stay away from her. Go home." With a last shake of her finger, Mercy shimmered and vanished.

Cassie huffed and dried the wet tracks from her face as Faith scrabbled to her feet. "I'm sorry about Ma. She can be intense at times."

Faith smoothed her gray dress into place and then pulled her long hair over one shoulder. "She's always been a bit touchy."

"I'll leave you to finish settling in. Do you want me to get your bags?" Cassie scanned the room, checking one last time that all was in order and giving herself time to quell the anger still stirring her gut.

Hope waved a hand in the air with a few words. Two strapped suitcases appeared on the floor by the bed. "No need."

"Right, well…" She shouldn't be surprised at the magic. Her ma had said they were powerful witches. Yet witnessing the ease with which they flourished it about was a different matter entirely. "Come down to the dining room in a while and I'll bring you some refreshments."

"Perhaps you'll join us for that chat." Hope smirked at her for a moment, then replaced it with a gentle smile. "We need to get to know each other better after all this time."

"Perhaps. I'll see you later." Cassie kept mum regarding her preferences as she strode out of the bedroom, impatient to find Flint and tell him about what her mother had done now.

Chapter Twenty

$\mathcal{T}$he entrance to the inn was uncharacteristically quiet for the first time since Abram had arrived. He relaxed in the shade of the gazebo, enjoying the stillness even if only for a few minutes. Coming to the inn had proven far more complicated than he'd ever thought possible. He'd been right in one way about not wanting to make the journey. Reconnecting with the family did what he anticipated by adding both new and old memories to contend with. On the other hand, he also realized how much he cared for his sister and brothers. He hoped Daniel and Silas would arrive before he had to return to his real life.

He fingered the side seam of the tan jeans covering his muscular thighs. Changing out of the more refined garments allowed him to blend in with the family and the customers. Doing so also enabled his relaxed state until the confrontation with his aunts. What were they really here to achieve?

Standing, he paced to lean against a post, shoving his hands into his pockets. Mandy's shift would begin soon as the flow of guests increased throughout the morning. She was a surprise complication in his visit. She stayed in his mind in a way no other woman ever had. Her quiet confidence and gentle smile appealed to him. The example she set ended up being more influential than all the etiquette and protocol books he'd pored over when he first tried to improve himself to qualify to be an aide. The ground rules were simple. Be kind, patient, caring, and helpful. Nothing in them suggested how he should dress or pretend to be someone other than himself.

The real test came from determining what being himself entailed. He'd worked hard to make himself into a polished and sophisticated aide to a senator. Well dressed and with impeccable taste and manners, partaking of the finest foods and liquor, frequenting the trendiest exhibits and plays. He'd dated beautiful women wearing elegant clothes and jewelry, the envy of the other men in the room. But now looking back on everything he'd accomplished, he felt hollow inside.

The quaint setting of the inn fell far short of what he was accustomed to and yet the longer he stayed the more like home it felt. The dogs and chickens. The cows and horses. His family, too. He'd been adrift and on his own for so many years he'd forgotten how it felt to have family involved in his life. Pushy perhaps but also concerned and caring about his decisions and actions.

Mandy appeared at the top of the porch steps, wiping her hands on her apron. She spotted him and smiled, trotting down the steps to stride toward him. The graceful sway of her slim hips enticed him. Her eager smile and happy eyes lightened his soul. If he could pull her inside and carry her spirit with him always, then mayhap he'd be a much better and definitely happier man.

"Hey there." He pushed away from the pole and held out a hand to her.

"I only have a few minutes before I'll need to go back." Placing her fingers on his palm, she joined him inside the gazebo. "What did you want to talk to me about?"

"Are you glad to be staying at the inn?" Abram's relief was great that Flint insisted it was not safe for her to be walking about while a killer stalked women and thus required her to live at the inn. "Are you getting along with Cassie well enough?"

"Yes, it's fine." Mandy shrugged as she smoothed her apron. "I think she appreciates having me with her since your aunts have arrived as well. But you know I can't live here forever, right?"

"We'll see. Thanks for coming out here to talk." He clasped both of her hands and urged her to move closer, to stand in front of him while he gazed at her tempting mouth. "I've been waiting for you."

Her eyes twinkled as she smiled up at him. "Why did you want me to meet you?"

It had been a spur of the moment desire when he'd seen her hesitating at the edge of the entrance hall. An undefined urge which now crystallized as he searched her eyes. "May I kiss you?"

Those eyes widened as her brows arched. "I don't know you well enough."

Now he had hope she would let him sometime later. After they knew each other better. "So ask me anything and I'll answer."

"With the truth?" She pulled her hands free and went to perch on the center bench.

"Of course." He moved to sit beside her, taking one hand in his again as he peered at her. "Ask away."

"All right." She tilted her head to one side, tapping a finger on her chin. She inspected him from head to toe and then grinned. "I know. When you first came here you were dressed like some kind of dandy. I think you even had on a girdle to define your waist. Why would you want to wear such attire?"

On the positive side of her question, it proved she'd

noticed him right away. On the negative side, she apparently found his choices unacceptable. He took a moment to frame his response so she'd understand. "Those clothes were very much appropriate and expected among the people with whom I work. I studied the tailoring of my peers and ensured that I wore equally fine garments."

She laid her free hand on top of their clasped ones. "I'm glad you decided to wear simpler clothes. It makes you seem more open and easy to talk to. It suits you."

"While I'm here, these work fine. But if I go back to Washington my career demands something more refined." His fellow aides would laugh at him if he were to appear in work jeans and loose hunting shirt like he wore at the moment. "I enjoy working for the senator and hope my time with him will pave the way for me to move up the ladder to bigger opportunities."

Only the opportunities he once thought exciting and beneficial had somehow lost their appeal since he'd been in Alabama. What had changed?

"I'm sure you will find a way to make all of your dreams come true, when you go back." She patted his hand and then laid her free one on her lap. "With or without fancy clothes."

The clothes. He stared at the coarse fabric covering his legs. While not as fine, the jeans were comfortable and practical for life in the wilderness. Likewise the sturdy boots and durable cotton shirt he'd adopted after observing what the other men wore. More to the point, what his older brother wore. Appearances did indeed matter but comfort and the right kind of clothes for the activities performed also must be factored into the decision. As long as he was staying, he needed to adapt.

Cassie emerged from the inn, hurried down the steps and across the carriageway toward the barn. She marched inside the barn, every motion and angle of her body shouting her distress. Looking for Flint most likely. She'd naturally turn to her beau when upset. A rumble above warned of an approaching summer storm. Abram would seek her out later and discover the source of her agitation. While he was at the inn, he meant to ensure her happiness and contentment as well as her safety.

Which raised a question that lingered in his mind for several beats of his heart. How long was he staying? Measuring his visit couldn't be done with days or even weeks. No, the length of his visit depended on his sister's safety and well-being. Surprise flowed through him as he nodded to himself.

"What?" Mandy peered closer at him.

"I guess I'm going to be here longer than I first thought." He couldn't very well abandon Cassie's care to others when he'd just discovered how much he needed his family. She needed family, too. Which also gave him more time to explore his feelings about the young woman holding his hand. "Would that be all right with you?"

She stared at their joined hands and then slowly raised her eyes to meet his. "I'd enjoy being able to see you more often." She moistened her lips. "To get to know you."

The urge to plant a relieved and delighted kiss on her mouth overwhelmed him for a second but he reined in the errant desire. "Then I'm glad I decided to stay for an indefinite period because I really want to get to know you, too."

Another revelation to add to the many others. How many more might there be?

Dipping a rag into the can of pungent saddle soap, Flint prepared to rub away the water marks from the last ride into town. He'd been caught in a sudden shower on the way home but hadn't had a chance to properly clean and treat the leather. During the lull between rushes, he'd slipped out to the barn to take care of his favorite tack so it would last as long as possible. A barn swallow flitted past and out the rear door. A normal day working in the calm of the barn.

This part of his routine always managed to steady him no matter what else might transpire. The gentle quiet within the stable brought peace along with the sweet smell of hay and manure. The crunching of horses as they ate the mound of hay provided a soothing background while he worked with Buck or cleaning his tack. Moments like these made him glad he'd changed his plans about moving on to bigger and supposedly better opportunities at more magnificent hotels.

Buck nickered from his stall drawing Flint's attention away from the saddle to see Cassie marching toward him. A roll of thunder in the heavens alerted him to a change in the weather. The scowl on Cassie's face alerted him to her changed mood. He braced for the storms rolling his way.

"Flint?" She swiped at the tears on her cheeks as she reached his side, her long skirts swirling about her legs when she came to a sudden stop. "I am so angry I could spit."

Her flushed cheeks and glittering eyes enhanced her usual lovely features. If he stared too long, though, she'd grow more distraught, but with him. Better to keep working and let her vent. Then he would comfort her, give her a kiss or two and hold her in his arms for a few wonderful moments.

"What's wrong, sweetheart?" He rubbed the cleaning cloth over the brown leather, slowly removing the small dark spots.

"They think they can run my life." She folded her arms across her waist and sniffled.

"Who?" He kept his attention on his task with an effort. The quick glimpse of her beautiful anger haunted his memory. Another spot on the side needed removal so he leaned closer to rub on it more effectively.

"Ma and my aunts." She tapped one foot on the dirt floor, the strident thud revealing her agitation with each puff of dust. "Would you look at me, please?"

One last inspection of the job and then he snapped closed the lid on the soap can and dropped the cloth on top. Meeting her gaze, he strived to remain calm and in control when all he wanted to do was kiss her into silence. "I'm done. Now tell me what's going on?"

She drew in a deep breath and let it out with a rush of words. "Aunt Hope and Aunt Faith want me to have a conversation with them about going with them when they leave."

A frown crashed down on his brows. Not at all what he anticipated. "You can't."

"I'm not." She hugged herself harder. "Ma got so mad she literally knocked down Aunt Faith and then tried to do the same to Aunt Hope. I've never seen anything like it."

"She knocked them down?" Flint peered at her, not following. "What does that mean?"

Cassie shrugged but didn't let go of her waist. "She became solid enough to actually move objects, in this case my aunt."

"Were you scared?" Mind reeling, he stepped closer and gently grasped her upper arms. His imagination created a vision that worried him on her behalf. "Come here, sweetheart."

He enfolded her in his embrace, deep concern for her safety warring with anger at the violent scene she witnessed between the three sisters. The very idea her aunts would suggest taking her back to Montgomery with them sent pain through his gut and heart. He couldn't live without her at his side.

"Scared, yes, and angry. Oh, so angry, that they'd think

they could decide my future for me." She wrapped her arms around him and clung. "I'll make my own decisions. Not them nor anyone else."

"They didn't hurt you, did they?"

"I'm not hurt. Just outraged."

The two women had only been on the property for minutes before they'd managed to disrupt and dismay his woman. Threatening to remove her when they left. They'd traveled a long way to recruit her to their side. For what purpose had yet to be determined. But ultimately it didn't matter why they wanted to take her away. He wouldn't allow such an event to happen.

"We'll make this better." He held her close, trying to warm her and still her trembling. "I promise." He spied Abram briskly striding into the barn and down the aisle toward them.

"What's wrong, sis? I could tell you were upset when you came out here."

Cassie squeezed Flint's waist and then eased away. "It was quite a scene, let me tell you."

Abram stopped beside her. "Should I be worried?"

Flint picked up the can of saddle soap and rag. "We all should be."

"Tell me what happened." Abram braced his feet apart and crossed his arms. "Then we'll make a plan."

"Tell him, sweetheart, while I put this stuff away."

"I doubt he'll believe me, but I'll try." She turned so she could address her brother face to face.

"Go on, sis. Tell me."

Flint carried the cleaning supplies to the tack room and put them on a shelf while Cassie explained to Abram what she'd just told him. Hard to believe. Mercy had the ability to materialize in such a way as to knock someone down. Probably best he didn't inquire too much into how or why she learned such an ability. Leaving the tack room, he rejoined Cassie and Abram as she finished her surprising tale.

"Then I left to come out here and find Flint." Cassie shuddered and folded her arms around herself again. "It's all so disconcerting."

"We can't plan a response if we don't know what they're plotting." Abram drummed the fingers of one hand in a slow repetitive pattern on his other arm. He stilled and arched a brow. "Want me to see what I can find out?"

Cassie tilted her head and frowned at him. "How?"

"I think you know how." He aimed a conspiratorial grin at her. "Right?"

When Cassie hugged her brother, Flint wasn't certain what Abram meant but he was certain he probably wouldn't approve.

Chapter Twenty-one

*G*o for it." Cassie winked at Abram.

"Go for what?" Flint looked confused, glancing from Cassie back to Abram.

Abram drew in a deep breath and fisted his hand, chanting the protection spell. Then he closed his eyes, focusing on centering and envisioning his sister in detail. The tingling and prickling began, slowly encompassing his entire body. When it stopped, he opened his eyes and inspected his hands and then grinned at Cassie. Flint stood open mouthed, eyes wide, as he compared Abram's version of Cassie with the real woman.

"How do I look?" Abram pirouetted in front of Flint, pulling the long skirt of the dress out as he came to a halt and curtseyed.

"That's still incredible to see." Flint ran his fingers through his hair, shaking his head slowly. "If I hadn't seen it, I'd never believe you weren't the genuine person."

"Good. Now, Cassie, where was this conversation supposed to take place?" Abram smoothed the skirts of the dress, getting into character.

"In the dining room. I invited them to come for refreshments after they settled in." Cassie made a face as she studied Abram. "I guess you should go and I'll stay here in the barn. We can't both be seen at the same time."

"Good point." The undergarments she must wear all the time proved confining and uncomfortable to him. He wriggled his shoulders trying to settle the corset into place. "Tell me again what the argument was about in detail before I go."

He listened intently as she repeated the contentious discussion between the three sisters and Cassie. In case either of their aunts brought up some aspect of it, he wanted to be prepared to respond appropriately. While she talked he studied her mannerisms, the angle of her head, the way she gestured with her hands. Being a person was far more complicated than a barn cat.

"Offer them something to drink and a plate of biscuits or whatever Sheridan and Matt have prepared." She paused, patting a hand on her upper thigh. Finally, she crossed her arms and shrugged. "I think that's everything. I'll wait here until you come back to tell me what you find out."

"Right. I guess I'll be going…" Abram inhaled deeply as he turned around to walk slowly down the dirt aisle, getting accustomed to the heeled shoes he copied from her outfit.

He had never considered how difficult it was to work in a dress with all the confining garments hidden beneath the outer layer. He'd have far more appreciation for the ladies as they went about their chores as a result. He tugged on the bodice, trying to make it more comfortable but failing. He'd need to stop fidgeting though or it would be obvious he wasn't the real Cassie.

"Wait, Ab—I mean, Cassie."

Abram looked over his shoulder to see Flint striding toward him. "What?"

"I'll go with you. It would look odd for me to stay out here when Cassie came out to talk to me especially now that it's time I should be inside for the next rush."

Abram fell into step with Flint as they crossed the carriageway and entered the inn without speaking. He concentrated on being his sister. The weight of her long blonde hair bouncing around his shoulders and tugging on his head took some getting used to but made it easier to pretend to be female. Or what he thought it would feel like to be an actual woman.

He scanned the dining room as they entered, spotting Hope and Faith seated near the square piano in the front corner of the room. He glanced at Flint and smiled like Cassie would have to her beau. Flint hesitated and then grinned back.

"I'll go see what they want." Abram squared his shoulders, bracing for a difficult exchange.

"Let me know what they want to drink." Flint sauntered over to the bar as usual when he reported for duty in the dining room.

Abram hurried as fast as he could in the unfamiliar shoes to talk with the aunts. "All settled?"

Hope looked him over with the hint of a frown on her face. "Are you all right, dear?"

"Yes. Why?" He held his breath for fear the powerful witch could detect the counterfeit of her niece.

She studied him for two heart-stopping seconds before shaking her head. "Nothing. Come join us, won't you?"

"I will right after I take your orders." The close call had his pulse racing and his palms sweating. "What would you like to drink? Cider? Ale?"

Faith smiled at the second option. "I'd appreciate the ale, please."

"Same here." Hope laid a hand on the cloth-covered table. "You'd suggested some refreshments and I find that I am hungry. Could you bring us something to ease the pangs?"

"Of course. I'll be right back." Abram breathed easier as

he adopted Cassie's swaying stride over to the bar to tell Flint the drink orders, and then escaped to the kitchen. As he pushed through the door, he smiled at the sight of Matt preparing some rolls to put in the oven. "Look at you."

"What?" Matt glanced at him and went back to shaping the bread dough. "This is nothing new. You've seen me make these many times."

Caught, Abram realized his mistake. He'd forgotten he looked like Cassie. "I know but it's always nice to see you hard at work. But I don't have time to chat. My aunts are hungry. What do you have?"

"A few fried meat pies are keeping warm by the fire." Matt pointed with his chin at the covered plate on a metal stool near the cook fire.

"That's perfect." Abram soon had plates of pies on a tray. "Thanks. I'll talk to you later."

"Most likely…" Matt chuckled as Abram pushed through the door.

Adjusting his stride to mimic Cassie's, he hurried back to the dining room and handed out the plated pies and cloth napkins to his aunts. "They're still warm and Matt promises they're delicious."

Faith lifted a mug of ale Flint had delivered to her and sipped, dabbing the foam from her lips as she set the mug on the table. "They look fine."

"Please sit with us, my dear." Hope bit into her pie, the aroma of spiced pork with onions and garlic filling the air as she laid it back on the plate. She swallowed as she pointed to a chair between them. "We have much to discuss."

Taking the seat his aunt indicated, Abram yet again felt trapped in a bad situation. Stuck between the two witches on a mission of unknown dimensions. The hard chair made it difficult for him to settle. He perched on the edge of the seat like a student waiting to be chided by the teacher.

"Apparently, we need to help you more than we realized." Faith studied Abram as she slowly smiled at him.

"What kind of help do you believe I need?" Abram had the feeling his aunts decided what they'd say long before they arrived. "I have my brothers and Flint to help me with everything I need."

"Oh no, honey. That's where you're misinformed." Faith gingerly lifted the pie to take a small bite.

Abram stilled his hands from fidgeting with the hem of the tablecloth. "What do you mean?"

Hope aimed a smirk laced with determination at him. "You have newly discovered abilities I dare say you do not know how to control or take full advantage of. We're here to help you learn to do both."

Abram forced himself to sit back in the chair, putting as much polite distance between them as he could manage. How to respond to such an offer from Cassie's standpoint? He opened his mouth to reply then shut it again when Faith started speaking.

"You'll come home with us and we'll teach you everything you need to know." Faith took another bite and chewed, her lips in a smug smirk.

"Why do I need to go with you?" Abram struggled to find the right way to dig for more information without revealing his true self and the depth of his distrust. "You could teach me here."

Hope lifted her mug. "That would never do, my dear. That's entirely out of the question."

Unease flooded Abram at the certainty and resolve in his aunts' expressions. He swallowed the fear on behalf of his sister as he contemplated what they might have in mind. But he couldn't imagine what it might be. "Why is it out of the question?"

Hope laid a hand on Abram's where it gripped the edge

of the covered table. "Because, my dear, we need you to join with us."

Faith also laid a hand on top of the other two. "To enable us to benefit from our heritage. Our combined powers into a trinity will make us invincible and fulfill our destiny."

"It's a grand vision, one your grandfather worked to achieve after your mother was born." Hope's eyes turned hard as she gripped Abram's hand. "She refused. But you won't, will you?"

Abram opened his mouth to say something but no words came. He scanned the room, noting Flint studying him from behind the mahogany bar where he polished the gleaming surface. Then he spotted his mother's ghost near the fireplace, glowering at the three of them. She shook her head, her long braid whipping her shoulders. She shook her finger at Abram, obviously thinking he was her daughter, and then she shimmered and vanished.

He moistened dry lips and met his aunt's steady regard. "I—I need to think about it." He dragged his hand free from the pile and pushed back his chair. "I have to go."

Hope clasped his wrist as he started to turn away from the table. "We'll talk more later. You'll see. It is for the best."

"Yes, the best for all of us." Faith steepled her hands, tapping the tips in a slow, mesmerizing pattern. "We've come to bring you home where you belong."

He doubted Cassie belonged with them but he didn't dare say anything definitive.

"I must go." He spun on his heel and marched out of the room, a tilt of his head toward Flint asking him to follow.

Hesitating in the hall, he spotted Giles coming in from the covered passage as Flint stopped beside him. Abram motioned to Giles to come with them as they headed for the barn to tell Cassie what he'd learned. Cassie had demanded to make her own decisions, and what their aunts proposed counted as a major decision he refused to make for her. Though he knew what he hoped she would choose, would she?

The aroma of sweet timothy hay combined with the earthy tones of leather and manure filled her nostrils, bringing soothing comfort while Cassie waited for Abram's report. Thunder continued to warn of the storm looming outside. She'd laid a horse blanket on a bale and fiddled with a piece of hay, glancing at the empty barn doorway at the far end of the dirt aisle. Without a watch and unable to see the sun's position, she had no idea how long she'd hidden away in the barn, hoping the stable boys didn't come in to clean stalls or feed the horses. She planned to hide behind the few bales of hay stacked around her if they did show, but so far she'd been alone.

She stood and stretched, dropping the wisp of hay to float to the floor. With luck, Abram's charade would yield the truth behind their aunts' presence. Whether she liked what he learned or not remained the big open question. Perhaps she should have found out for herself instead of enduring the torture of suspense. When her brother proposed his idea, she'd been relieved to not have to face them. Now she just wanted the anticipation to end.

"Cassie!"

She shot a look to the doorway and jolted when she saw herself leading Giles and Flint toward her. She'd never grow accustomed to such a sight. Though it did give her an opportunity to assess her appearance from a unique perspective. She rather liked what she saw, but perhaps she should wear her hair differently and definitely sew a new dress. The one he was wearing looked worn and tired indeed.

The trio halted in front of her and she arched her brows at Abram. "You can stop being me now."

"Oh…yes." Abram closed his eyes and shifted back to his true form. He shuddered and rocked his shoulders as he opened his eyes again. "That feels better."

"That was strange." Giles stared at Abram. "I didn't know you could do that."

"It's a new thing I perfected recently." Abram smirked at his brother. "I'll try you next."

Giles held up both hands, palms out. "Not if you value your life."

Abram chuckled. "We'll see."

Flint crossed his arms over his chest and peered at Abram. "So what did you find out?"

"Yes, I'm curious." She was glad Flint had asked, not wanting to appear overly anxious even though she felt like gnawing on her fingernails. "What did they say?"

The smile on Abram's face vanished. "They want you, Cassie."

Ice formed in the pit of her stomach. "What do you mean?"

Her imagination spun out of control, creating images of bondage and torture floating past her inner eye. Her ma's fears became her own without even knowing exactly what her aunts had in mind. Knowing they leaned toward magic with insidious and mysterious purposes only heightened her anxiety as she stared at Abram's strained expression.

"They want you to join with them to become a trinity, to combine your powers into something far stronger. It's what our grandfather had tried to create before his death." Abram glanced at Giles and then Flint before meeting her gaze. "Ma refused to join them. Now they are resolved to take you with them when they leave."

"No." Her knees gave out and she flopped down on the hay bale. "Why would they want me?"

Abram shrugged. "I assume having a trinity of witches increases their power in some way. This is all new to me, too."

"What do I do? I don't think I have the strength to stand up to them." Grabbing her knees through her skirt, she chewed on her lower lip. "They frighten me."

A clap of thunder heralded the onslaught of rain lashing the side of the barn. A horse neighed as the orange barn cat ran for cover.

"We're here for you." Giles gave her a reassuring smile. "We'll keep you from harm."

"I don't want to go with them." She hugged her waist, chilled through despite the summer heat. "They can't make me. Right?"

Flint sat down beside her, wrapping an arm around her shoulders. "Of course not. We won't let them force you to do anything. Right, guys?"

Giles turned fierce, puffing up his mighty chest and bracing his feet as if for battle. "They cannot make you go or do anything, sis. I shall see to it."

"I don't want anyone to get hurt, Giles. Not on my account." Concern spiraled inside as to what her brother might do with his superhuman strength. And whether or not strength could even defeat magic from two very powerful witches. "After all, they are family."

"Maybe there's a way to convince them to leave without taking you or hurting anyone..." Abram looked away, rubbing his fingers on his jaw. When he looked at her, he grinned. "I think it might work."

"Tell us." She clasped Flint's free hand with cold fingers.

"I know you don't want to defy them yourself, so..." He hesitated, pinning her with a long serious look. "So what if I, acting as you, convince them you'll join them but only after Pa comes home. They'll need to wait a little while longer but you won't go until you talk to your father."

"But I don't want to join them." She frowned at him and shook her head. "That's a lie."

"It's a delaying tactic." A slow smile grew on Giles' face. "When Pa gets home he could have a better plan on how to refuse their offer without causing hard feelings or worse."

"Either way, if Abram can convince them of your sincerity, it buys us time and avoids unpleasantness." Flint squeezed her shoulders and kissed the top of her head. "I think it really could be a temporary solution."

"I don't know…" She leaned her head against Flint's shoulder, her gaze flitting between Giles and Abram. "I do want to see Pa so that much is true. What if you tell them…I appreciate the offer but I can't make such an important decision until he comes home? Then I'll give them my answer."

Abram nodded as a smirk grew on his lips. "I should think that would appease them and we can figure out what happens next."

"Only don't do so until after tomorrow's competition." Cassie sat up straight and glanced at Flint. "Just in case they don't take to the idea very well. I don't want anything to interfere with the event tomorrow afternoon."

"Yes, please don't let anything stop that." Flint stood and pulled her up to stand beside him. "The two battling chefs would never forgive us. And I want to earn back the money spent on all those fancy fixings."

"We have a plan then." Abram stepped aside as Flint led Cassie past him.

"Now that we're all ourselves again," Cassie said, "let's go back inside."

"We'll need to make a run for it through the cloudburst. Ready?" Flint asked.

"As I'll ever be." She grabbed his hand and they all raced across the carriageway.

She simply had to get through another couple of days with her aunts watching her every move. Probably plotting ways to recruit her to their cause. Then everything would be fine.

Chapter Twenty-two

Something called her to her ma's attic. She only had a short span of time until the afternoon rush would begin, but she had to find out what whispered her name in such compelling tones. She unlocked the door with the attacking owl adorned key and hefted the flickering oil lamp as she pushed inside. Setting the lamp on the table by the window, she surveyed the quiet, dusty space. What called to her so? She'd experienced this sensation before, when she and Giles had first unlocked this room. She'd felt some kind of beast inside her unfurling, stretching and clawing to gain her attention. Something in one of those closed trunks whispered her name, yet she hesitated to seek out the source. She'd not experienced this urgent summons in weeks, so why now?

Instead of answering the command, she moved to the afghan draped chair by the table and fingered the crocheted blanket. She lifted the soft material to press to her cheek for a moment. Tried to imagine her mother sitting at the table, reading or writing...spells? The blanket laid across her legs as she worked. Possibly an ostrich quill pen and ink stand at hand. She dropped the blanket back on the chair and then pivoted to stare up at the shelves of books on the wall, perusing ornately lettered, unfamiliar titles on the leather spines of the tomes.

"There you are, my dear." The quiet voice rattled around in the silent space.

Cassie startled and glanced to the doorway as Aunt Hope paced into the room. "Oh…"

She shouldn't be in her mother's private room. Among her most treasured possessions without her mother there to intercede. Or her father to lay claim to them. The family heirlooms seemed to tremble in their hiding places, or she imagined they would. Not knowing what her aunt might do with the valuable and powerful artifacts made *her* tremble, at least. For once, Cassie wished for her ma to appear and handle the unpleasant and unwarranted intrusion.

"What is this place?" Hope asked, surveying the small room with eager eyes. She paused in her inspection when her gaze landed on the blond wood trunk near the window. "I recognize that ash trunk."

Cassie strode over to stand in front of the trunk, the keys safely hidden in her skirt pocket. "Ma wouldn't want you in here, Aunt Hope. I must ask you to leave."

"Oh, Cassandra, dear, it's fine." Her eyes sparkled with glee as she advanced toward Cassie. "Mercy shouldn't have hidden these things away like they're dangerous or something. They are far too valuable."

"You know what's in the trunks?" She swallowed the rising fear in her throat with each determined step her aunt took.

"Of course, my dear. Well, the ash trunk anyway. The magical items in that trunk belong to the family, not just to my sister." Her emerald eyes glittered in the dim light when she stopped in front of Cassie. "She never should have removed them to a place so remote as to be inconvenient for Faith and I to access as well."

"I-I didn't even know about them until after she was killed." The array of secrets she'd unearthed after her mother's death threatened to overwhelm her. Too many to count. Yet, it seemed like there were more to be discovered. "What can you tell me about them?"

Hope sidestepped around Cassie and tugged on the locked lid. She arched a brow at Cassie. "I assume you possess the key?"

Slipping her right hand into her pocket, she fingered the set of keys. Hesitated to unlock the trunk because she didn't trust her aunt to tell her the truth. Then again, her mother had withheld the truth for years. Who should she believe? Hope had offered more information about her mother and her past without expecting anything from her. Not yet, anyway. What more could she learn without committing to anything? She needed to know more about her family and one member of said family stood in front of her offering to fill that desire. She pulled the keys into the light and selected the appropriate one.

She met her aunt's expectant gaze, searching her eyes for some kind of reassurance but found only anticipation and delight. "You must promise not to remove anything without my permission."

"Yours, my dear?" Haughty surprise swept across Hope's face. "Why would you presume to insist on such a thing?"

"Because my father isn't here to formally take possession. Only I am and I can't let you have them." She put the keys back in her pocket, out of sight and hopefully out of her aunt's reach. "I'll only unlock it if you agree to my terms."

"Well, well, you are a feisty little witch, aren't you?" She nodded as she stepped to one side. "I like that you're standing up for yourself. Fine. I shall accept your terms. Now unlock it and let me show you what's waiting for you."

"Waiting for me?" The curiosity beast purred and swirled inside her core at the prospect of learning what had been calling her.

Hope gestured to the trunk. "You. I think you'll be pleasantly surprised, too."

She yanked the keys from her pocket before she could change her mind. Soon the lid was up and the array of jewelry boxes, old books, and keepsakes were exposed. Hope leaned over the open trunk, reaching in to lift first one then another of the heirlooms to inspect. Thankfully, replacing each as she sifted and sorted through the collection.

"Aha!" Hope rummaged deeper into the trunk, and then held up a twisted piece of reddish-brown wood. "I found it."

"What is it?" Surely that thing wasn't for her. Something else must have been calling to her.

"Why, your wand, of course." Hope handed it to her, handle first, a scowl descending on her features. "My sister didn't even let you keep the wand you made as a girl?"

"I didn't find out I was a witch until a few weeks ago." She tentatively accepted the tapered wand. The smooth wood warmed to her touch, humming softly, much like a kitten purring in its sleep. "I don't recall making it."

"I was there the day you found the fallen limb of a tree and held it up with such joy on your face." Hope shifted to aim a bemused expression at her. "Your father shaped the handle into that slow twist and then let you sand it smooth with your little hands. I think you were two or so at the time so it's quite understandable you don't recall doing so."

Gripping the handle of the wand, she gave a tentative flick of the blunt tip in the air. Nothing happened. "How does it work?"

Hope chuckled and shook her head slowly. "Not like that. You must have a purpose and intent in mind when you use it to direct your will."

She waved the wand in a slow arc in the air and then held it up in front of her. "Like that?"

Hope pulled her own wand from her skirt pocket. She looked around the room and then smiled at the quill pen in its stand on the table. "Choose what you wish to do, focus on it, and then aim your wand or give it a flick to conjure what you want. Like this."

A quick flick of her wand and Hope levitated the quill out of its stand and made it swish to and fro in the air. Then another flick of her wrist and it returned to its home.

"Now you try." Hope pointed her wand to the floor as she encouraged Cassie with a rolling hand.

Nodding to her aunt as much as herself, Cassie peered at the quill and envisioned it repeating its floating performance. She raised her hand and aimed her wand at it, then gave her wrist a jerk. The quill quivered but didn't rise. She swallowed and focused more, recalling her own advice to Abram when he was striving to learn how to use his shifting ability. With a smooth flick of her wand, the quill sedately rose and rocked back and forth for a moment. Smiling, Cassie flicked her wrist again and the long feathered pen wrote her name in midair. Another flick, and it returned to the little stand where it belonged.

Hope clapped her hands lightly together. "Well done, my dear. Very nice."

"Thank you, Aunt Hope." Cassie studied her wand for a moment before addressing her aunt. "What more do I need to know?"

"Where to begin? Let's start with the basics. You must understand the type of wand you have in your hand. It's made from cherry wood, black cherry to be specific."

"Why does it matter what kind of wood it's made from?" She inspected the grain of wood, trying to understand how its composition might impact its utility.

"If you'll stop interrupting me, I'll tell you." Hope huffed out a breath of annoyance. "Each kind of wood brings different properties and meanings with it."

"I don't understand how that matters." She frowned at her aunt, struggling to grasp the logic behind her statement.

"You do have a lot to learn, don't you?" Hope asked, with a sigh of frustration. "Mercy has failed you, my dear. I could teach you but not here. Not in this oppressive environment."

She had to agree with Aunt Hope about the tyranny she'd endured from her mother throughout her life. She'd longed to escape and now she had the perfect opportunity with a sound reason for accepting it. Cassie didn't want to remain ignorant of her potential but someone had to instruct her. Her aunts had offered. Her mother had not. She had no choice but to agree to her aunt's terms like her aunt had agreed to hers. "Please, Aunt Hope. Won't you teach me? I need to know."

"Yes, you do." Hope regarded her for several seconds before nodding. "Of course I'll teach you. As soon as you come join with us. We'll teach you everything you need to know."

She hesitated before saying anything more. The prospect of becoming a full-fledged witch tempted her like nothing else. How else would she grow into her potential unless someone, like her aunts, taught her the methods and approaches and techniques she needed to know? Someone to teach her about her family and heritage. Obviously, her own mother had refused to help her and had mischaracterized her sisters and their helpful intent. From her new perspective, Cassie didn't view her aunts as a threat at all. They could be her mentors, her teachers, and help her secure her true and proper future working with magic. Her destiny awaited.

"Thank you." She drew in a breath, realized she needed to inform her brothers and Flint of her new intention, and let it out in a rush as Hope smiled. "But I must inform my family and beau before I can go with you."

"You can't possibly mean that." Abram stared at Cassie later that afternoon as he paced the parlor floor with agitated strides. "Tell me you didn't promise to leave with them."

"I have to in order to learn to be a proper witch." She glared at him from where she sat on a cushioned chair by the fireplace. "Ma has not been forthcoming and I apparently have much to learn."

"But, Cassie, what about us?" Flint asked, as he tapped one hand on the mantel. "You said you wouldn't leave me and now you're anxious to do so."

Giles occupied another cushioned chair across from Cassie, leaning forward to lend urgency to his next words. "If you go, then I'll have to go in order to protect you."

"No, you don't." Cassie shook her head and grinned at him. "They can teach me to protect myself. With magic."

"Who's going to protect you from them?" Abram halted his pacing, looking down on Cassie's upturned face. "That's what I'm afraid of."

"What's going on?" Mercy asked, shimmering into sight. "What are you afraid of, Abram?"

Abram inhaled sharply but managed to not flinch at his mother's sudden appearance. "Cassie has agreed to go with your sisters."

Mercy blinked and then shimmered with agitation as she rounded on her daughter. "No. That's impossible."

Cassie jumped to her feet, marching to her mother's ghost. "No, it's not. I am going because they haven't hidden my abilities nor kept secrets from me. They promise to teach me what I need to know, unlike you."

"Cassie, don't be angry at Ma." Abram strode over to his sister, a placating hand on her arm.

She shook off his hand and glared at him. "You haven't had to live with all of her warnings and chidings so don't tell me not to be angry with her. All she's ever done is tell me what I can't do, what I shouldn't do. Never has she told me of what all I *can* do! I'm sick of it."

"See, this is what I was afraid of all along. They've turned you to their side and now you can't see reason." Mercy drifted side to side, shimmering with dismay. "You can't see what they're doing to you."

"What? Educating me? I see that clearly." Cassie paced away from her mother to stand behind the chair she'd vacated, gripping the back until her knuckles gleamed. "Why didn't you teach me?"

Mercy looked down and away and then slowly raised her eyes to meet Cassie's demanding glare. "I was afraid for you. For all of us if my sisters learned of what each of you can do. They'd want to gather you into their fold and make you part of the darker side of magic. I couldn't let that happen. Not to my precious children."

Abram rocked back on his heels at her statement. "Precious children? Since when?"

"Always." Mercy turned quizzical eyes at him. "I've always loved each and every one of you."

"You had a strange and hurtful way of showing it," Giles said, rising from his seat to confront Mercy. "You made me leave and never come back home. Never even contacted me unless I wrote to you, and even then it was terse and unfriendly."

Mercy stared at the floor for several seconds then lifted her gaze to look at each of her children. "For your protection. To keep you out of reach of my sisters. You must understand and believe me. I've missed you."

"You didn't even tell me about my wand when we were

going through the trunks." Cassie nodded to the cherry wand on the table even as she gripped the chair so tightly it tapped against the carpeted floor. "How do you expect me to trust you now when you've done everything you could to keep us separate, keep us apart and in the dark about who we are and what we can do? Tell me that, Ma."

"I'll make it all up to you, I promise. Now that you know your true nature and heritage, I'll answer any questions you have. Teach you everything I can."

"I think it's too late for that. I've already promised Aunt Hope to let her teach me everything. You're too late, Ma." Cassie released the wooden chair and turned away, pressing one hand to her forehead as she bowed her head.

Abram tread over to peek at her lowered head, pulling the curtain of blonde hair back so he could see her face. "Cassie, you don't need to go with them to learn how to use your powers and your wand. Ma said she can tell you. Won't you let her?"

"Don't go, Cassie. Please?" Flint added, shifting his weight to stand straight.

"None of us want you to do this, sis," Giles added.

Abram nodded to the other men and then shook his head at his mother's ghost. She may not have wanted to hurt her children, but she'd done some definite emotional damage to each of them in various ways. By far, the worst thing they could imagine had happened. Apparently, his aunts had managed to persuade his sister to do something she'd not wanted to do until that day. Surely, he could find some way to change her mind, change the outcome before someone—namely his sister—got hurt in one way or another.

Chapter Twenty-three

$\mathcal{S}$ trolling into the dining room the next afternoon, Abram gaped at the crowd milling around the tables. The air hummed with anticipation and the murmur of approximately fifty people. His mouth watered at the delicious aromas assailing his nostrils. Skimming the crowd with his gaze, he finally espied his aunts observing the gathering from the far side of the room. Cassie moved from group to group, checking on their needs, but casting furtive glances at her aunts. Then Mandy appeared at the doorway, surveying the people and arrangement of tables, before she sashayed toward him.

"Quite a crush." Her twinkling eyes made him smile in return. "I hope you're hungry."

"Starving." His heart skipped a beat when she moistened her mouth with a swipe of a pink tongue. He forced himself to meet her eyes instead of search for the tempting tongue to reappear. "What should I do if I want to try these new dishes they've concocted?"

"You'll get to sample everything and then we'll do a hand vote in a while about which of the dishes should be included on the menu." She tapped her thigh, apparently anxious to continue with her work. "We'll bring out plated meals in a few minutes so go ahead and find a seat."

"I'll let you get back to work then." He longed to kiss her luscious mouth but even if she'd given him permission to indulge his desire the dining room was not the proper place. "See you later?"

"Of course. I'll be here." She spun around and headed toward the kitchen.

He watched her wiggle her way out of sight and then saw John Baker and his family come through the door. The three hesitated before entering the dining room, John's sharp gaze sliding across the crowd of people until stopping. A frown drew his brows together. Abram followed the direction of his gaze to his aunts. His own frown formed on his brow at the inquiring look John aimed at the two women. They gave no evidence of their witchy ways from their attire or even their expressions. They appeared as normal women, so why the frown? Even if John held grievances against witches like they suspected, did he sense something unique about them from across the room? Perhaps he was merely reacting to seeing women he didn't recognize. That would explain his expression, too.

Flint appeared in the doorway and hurried to join him by the bar. He had to fight through the crush of bodies. "Whew. What a turnout."

Cassie made her way towards Abram, curiosity in her expression.

"That's a good thing." Abram acknowledged her questioning gaze and then saw a distinguished gentlemen at the door with a lovely woman on his arm. "Who is that just arrived?"

Flint turned around to see whom Abram referred to. "Ah, the Nelsons are here. Just in time, too. Let's begin."

Giles appeared at Sterling's side, smiling and nodding as he shook hands with him. Then he ushered the Nelsons to a table at the front of the room and close to two smaller empty tables set apart from those for dining. Sterling pointed to a chair and Giles nodded as he pulled it out and sat down, facing the rest of the dining tables. The Guardian had arranged to be where he could see the entire crowd. Nicely done.

"Everything all right?" Cassie asked, drawing to a halt at his side.

"So far." Abram scanned the people milling about but didn't see anything amiss.

"Now that everyone is here, let's kick this competition off." Flint hung the ubiquitous towel over the rail and then moved into the center of the room. He clapped his hands loudly, then raised them to silence the chatter. "Ladies and gentlemen, thank you all for coming to the cookery competition. If you'll take your seats, I'll have our two wonderful cooks present their meals for your sampling and commentary."

"I guess that means me, too." Abram winked at Cassie and then scanned the available seats. Haley waved at him and indicated an empty seat at her family's table. Not a bad idea. "I'll go sit with the Bakers."

"All right. I have to help with the displays and such. Be honest in your judgements." Cassie smiled at him as he strode away from her. Haley indicated a concern regarding her father with a slight tilt of her head in his direction. Perhaps she'd also noticed his surprising interest in Hope and Faith. He braced for an uncomfortable conversation as he pulled out the chair across the table from John and Tabitha. "Are you ready for the tasting?"

"I brought my appetite." John met Abram's gaze before glancing at the Nelsons' table and then to where Hope and Faith settled onto chairs at a table in the corner. "An interesting mix of people here today. I don't know those ladies."

"They're my aunts from Montgomery."

"Ah, I see." John drummed his fingers on the table for a moment. "When did they arrive?"

"Yesterday for a short visit." He hoped, anyway. "They were fortunate to time their arrival to enable them to attend this fun event."

"Yes, it is quite a coincidence, isn't it?" John said.

"It's a unique opportunity to have a free lunch and share one's opinion of it." His aunts were oblivious to the scrutiny aimed their way. Abram dragged his attention from the two innocuous looking women, dressed in typical day dresses of linen and calico. Nothing about them announced their predilection for witchcraft and spells. "It will be interesting to see who wins the challenge."

"All right, ladies and gentlemen." Flint gained every-one's attention with his commanding voice, bringing silence to the room once again. Sheridan stood at his side, with Mandy joining them carrying a tray with a variety of dishes upon it. Flint motioned to her to place the tray on a nearby empty table reserved for Sheridan's prepared meal. Then he addressed the crowd. "First, Sheridan Drake, our esteemed cook, will tell you what he has created for your pleasure this afternoon. So, what do you have for us?"

Sheridan stepped over to the table to pick up a steaming plate. "I've used ingredients that represent what this area is known for and which come from the surrounding hills and fields. Here I have pan roasted duck breasts with huckleberry sauce." He set down the plate and pointed to a trio of bowls. "With a watercress salad topped with berries and nuts and a light vinaigrette, then some hot creamed corn, and a tasty polenta with cheese."

Murmurs accompanied enthusiastic applause when he bowed and then stood behind the table, a huge grin on his face at their encouragement.

"Thank you, Sheridan. Now, for the challenger." Flint gestured at the young man who strode quickly to stand by the second empty table as Myrtle placed a tray of various sizes of bowls on it. "Matthew Simmons came to us recently and we're very glad he did for more than one reason. What do you have, Mr. Simmons?"

"I went farther afield for my choices, bringing a taste of other countries to your beautiful state." He lifted the largest of the bowls and angled it slightly to let people see the gleaming yellow mixture sending a fragrant spicy aroma into the air. "East Indian Curry containing a blend of spices and aromatic herbs over white rice. You can garnish it with peanuts, fried bananas, and chutney as you like." He grinned at the pleased smiles and bobbing heads as he replaced the bowl and pointed to a pair of smaller ones flanking it. "With a Salmagundi salad containing an array of fruits and vegetables, hard cooked eggs, almonds, and gherkin pickles, with a delicate French green pea soup seasoned with herbs and butter." He bowed and positioned himself behind the table like Sheridan, glancing at his father's arch expression with a twinkle in his eyes.

The gauntlet had been thrown. The crowd applauded again with anticipation in their expressions. Abram joined in the clapping, anxious to taste the spicy concoction and the duck breasts. He enjoyed excellent cuisine and hoped the two delivered on the promise of the menu choices.

"We'll be serving portions of each to you so if you'll remain in your seats, Cassie and Mandy will be bringing your meals shortly."

Abram kept his eyes open, observing the interactions between the staff and the guests. Cassie served their aunts with efficient movements, then hurried back to the kitchen to retrieve more plates and bowls. Mandy brought a laden tray to the Bakers' table and Abram quickly rose to help her hold the heavy tray while she handed out the dishes of hot and aromatic delights. Cassie returned and delivered meals to the Nelsons and others around them.

"Thank you, Abram." Mandy batted her lashes at him as a smile bloomed. "That was sweet of you." She pivoted and hurried away before he could reply.

A flutter in his gut preceded warmth in the vicinity of his heart at her flirtatious behavior. The sprite had performed her own kind of magic on him during the time he'd been at the inn. Finding her way straight into his heart and softening his hard resolve to present the best appearance possible. His definition of a good appearance underwent a huge transformation as a result of her comments and suggestions.

"Oh, this is delicious." Tabitha Baker poked at the curry with her fork, lifting another bite of the spicy mixture of chicken, chutney, fried bananas, rice, and sour cream. "If they include this on their menu, I'll be happy to visit even more often."

Abram surveyed the samples of each of the items prepared by the cooks arrayed on his plate. He sliced into the portion of duck and sniffed to determine the seasonings Sheridan used. He could see the huckleberries in the buttery sauce. Inhaling deeply, he detected thyme and port wine. "Let's see how it tastes."

He chewed the bite slowly, savoring the delectable blend of flavors. Haley sat watching him, a small amused smile on her lips. Behind her, he spotted Faith staring at Cassie as she moved about the room, delivering meals and picking up empty plates. When Hope leaned over to murmur something to Faith, he swallowed with difficulty. They were plotting some kind of mischief.

"Well, how is it?" Haley asked.

Dragging his attention back to the samples, he nodded. "Delicious. But I would expect that of everything Sheridan creates. He's an excellent cook."

"Agreed." John stabbed a bite of the Salmagundi on his plate, selecting a stack of beet, egg, and spring onion, and slipped it into his mouth. "The salad is very fine as well."

"Have you tried the soup?" Abram stirred the small cup of green pea and spinach soup, spotting diced onions and basil leaves in the aromatic creation. Tentatively, he spooned some into his mouth. "Very nice."

"Everything is so well done I don't believe I can choose between them." Tabitha inspected the remaining portions of watercress salad and polenta on her plate. "The creamed corn was fabulous and you can't go wrong with salad greens, blackberries, and goat cheese. The dressing was light and flavorful though I can't say what it was made of."

"I tasted a hint of molasses." Haley glanced at Abram and then frowned lightly at the dressing pooled on her plate. "Some kind of berry flavor as well. Whatever the mysterious ingredient, the combination proved very tasty."

"Ladies and gentleman, may I have your attention please?" Flint stood by the two front tables positioned near the bar. "It's time to vote on your favorites. I'll name a dish and you raise your hand if you believe we should add it to the inn's menu. Ready?"

Abram turned in his chair so he could see more clearly. Flint called out each dish and hands went up all around the room for each one. Abram let a small smile onto his lips. Flint would have a job deciding which ones were most popular with so many votes for every dish. Sheridan and Matt stood by their creations, beaming as the crowd showed their enthusiasm for their efforts. The fatherly pride in Sheridan's expression when Matt's curry received cheers warmed Abram's heart but also made him long for his own father to approve of something he'd accomplished.

"All right. Thanks for your honest appraisal of Sheridan and Matt's dishes, folks." Flint motioned for the cheering and clapping to quiet. As the room settled, he surveyed the customers with a slow shake of his head, then pivoted to address the two cooks. "The judges have spoken, gentlemen. So the winner of this cooking competition is…"

Flint paused, dragging out the suspense like pulling taffy on a cold winter morning. Abram darted a glance around the room, smiling at the open-mouthed anticipation on every face. He didn't envy Flint the decision in front of so many but especially between the father and son cooks.

"Get on with it!" Giles called from his seat near Flint, motioning for him to continue. "We're dying to know."

"Okay, okay." Flint shrugged. "I wanted to build some anticipation but if you insist."

"I do." Giles splayed his hands in encouragement. "So?"

Flint drew in a deep breath. "The winner is all of these wonderful dishes. We'll add all of them to the menu from now on."

Applause erupted across the room as Flint strode to Sheridan to shake his hand and then did the same with Matt. Mandy smiled at Abram from where she stood beside the bar. Her beautiful features called to him, stirring desires he'd never felt before. Not physical ones that were easily satisfied, but a longing and need to be with her. Perhaps always. The woman he once thought of as mousy was in fact one of the most beautiful women, inside and out, he'd ever had the pleasure to know. He returned the smile and crooked his forefinger in invitation for her to come to him. She started toward his table, gracefully dodging between the other customers until she'd reached his side. He rose and took her hand, leading her out of the room and into the hall.

"Did you want something?" Mandy studied him while he held her hand.

"Yes, I wanted to ask you if you'd be my girl." Abram searched her eyes for any hints of rejection or worse revulsion. He saw only happiness and friendship. "I want to court you, Mandy. Will you receive me?"

"I would love that, Abram." She pivoted and took hold of his other hand, squeezing both of them. "But won't you be leaving?"

He'd planned to all along. Now? "I've found more reasons to stay than to go back. Including my feelings for you."

She peered up at him. "You're staying? Really?"

He nodded slowly, the realization spreading through him that he'd decided to stay after confirming valid threats against his family. "My family needs me here. And I hope maybe one day you'll be included in my family, too."

She smiled at him, his very own angel of light and love. "I think that might be arranged."

Her lips tempted him. He had to know if she tasted as good as she looked. "May I kiss you?"

"Please."

At her slight nod, he focused on those sweet lips and lowered his head. She closed her eyes as his lips met hers. He wrapped his arms around her and pulled her close, mashing her firm breasts against his chest. The longing inside changed to a need, one he wanted to assuage but would not. Yet. He ended the kiss and leaned his forehead against hers for several moments. He drew in a breath and let it out slowly as he lifted her chin with one finger.

"Thank you." He pecked her lips once more. "I should let you get back to work, right?"

She tilted her head with a light shrug. "Flint would appreciate it."

"I'll talk to you later but know one thing, sweetheart." He smiled down at her upturned face. "I'm not going anywhere."

"Glad to hear it." She waved the fingers of one hand as she spun around and hurried back into the dining room.

He stood rooted to the spot, aware his life had just changed in dramatic and unexpected ways.

The situation is growing desperate. I am appalled at the increasing number of magical beings—I can't call them people—taking up residence in the area. Watching them interact with regular, upstanding people as if they belong infuriates me. The cookery competition had drawn out a good crowd, but so many I already know use magic and spells and who knows what other evil effects? The two witches who appeared suddenly have a keen interest in the young Fairhope witch. Why might that be? Is she more powerful than I thought? What about her brothers? And the innkeeper himself whom I know has been rumored to be able to confer with ghosts. They are all in this diabolical plot against the populace, I'm certain of it. I'll need to do something about it, and soon.

As the crowd of diners flowed out of the room, Cassie stacked the remaining dishes onto a tray. Her aunts departed along with the others, bringing a guilty sense of relief to her chest. She carried the tray of dishes to the kitchen to be cleaned. Wiping her hands on her apron, she excused herself and headed for her room. After all the excitement and exertion of serving the large crowd, she needed to lie down for a few minutes and rest before the supper rush in a few hours. She went into the parlor on the residence side, prepared to cross the room and go upstairs.

"Cassie, my dear. Come join us." Hope sat in a chair by the fireplace, a suspicious smirk on her lips, with Faith sitting in the opposing chair regarding her.

Her heart sank. What did they want and how long would it take? She glanced at the mantel clock. Time was not on her side. "I was going to…"

"Whatever it was will have to wait." Hope indicated an empty chair with a flick of her hand. "Sit. We need to talk."

Perhaps if she did as requested it would be a short conversation and then she could have a nap. Refraining from rolling her eyes, she took the seat and clasped her hands together in her lap.

"Now, my dear, tell me about your powers." Hope settled back in her chair, resting her palms on the armrests like a queen ruling from her throne. "What are they exactly?"

She blinked at the blunt demand made in such a commanding tone. "Why do you want to know so badly?"

"So we can help you learn to control and manipulate them, naturally." Faith kept her serious eyes on Cassie while slowly tapping each fingertip on the armrest of her chair in a steady rhythm. "We don't want you to make the same mistakes our sister did, after all."

Cassie frowned at her aunts. "What mistakes?"

"She didn't tell you. How like her to not take responsibility." Hope pursed her lips for a moment and then shook her head sadly. "She killed our mother."

Icy shock reverberated through Cassie as she clutched her hands together. "What?"

"She was tinkering with a new spell and wouldn't listen to us. Said she knew what she was doing." Faith studied Cassie, her expression grim. "But she obviously did not. We don't want you to make the same tragic mistake."

"How did she...?" She couldn't say the words.

Hope pressed her lips together as she gripped the chair. Anger flashed in her hard eyes. "She combined the ingredients incorrectly and caused an explosion. She wasn't in the room, of course, when the pressure built to such an extreme, but our mother was. She died instantly."

The anger and hate seething inside the two women staring at her made her nauseous. Her stomach roiled from the overwhelming emotions. Their hatred proved so great it breeched their own defenses so that Cassie could detect it. She pressed a hand to her midriff to try to quell the surging and tumbling inside. Swallowing back the rising bile, she raised her inner barrier to protect herself.

"We've come to convince you of your destiny, my dear." Hope relaxed her death grip on the chair but not the intense scrutiny aimed at Cassie. "Since our sister refused and now cannot fill the roll our father intended, you must and will."

She had agreed to join them, to accept her destiny, but now she hesitated. Too much information had been thrown at her. She had many questions, but feared to ask them since they would think she was interested instead of realizing she had renewed doubts. She wished Flint were at her side to steady her. Or Giles to stand between her and the two powerful witches confronting her with new revelations and secrets.

"What destiny do you envision?" The biggest question couldn't be stopped from slipping past her tense lips.

"Why, to join us and create the most powerful trio of witches in the southeast or perhaps all of the country." Faith stopped tapping her fingers to lean forward and peer at her. "Like your grandfather always wanted. Your mother refused to cooperate but you do not have that option."

"If she had joined her powers with ours, then she would have learned the proper techniques and not murdered our mother." Hope's grip on the armrest threatened to break the wood. "So what is your power?"

Having someone train her in how to use her powers would be useful. She'd figured out some things on her own, but what more might she be able to do? And she still needed to know how to wield her wand. They were offering to help her sort all of that out. Perhaps she should stick with her revised plan and let them. What harm could come from revealing her gifts? It couldn't hurt to find out.

"I'm an empath and can influence others with my voice." She swallowed the fear. Knowing more might help her in ways she couldn't imagine. Not yet. "Is that what you wanted to know?"

"An empath." Hope sighed with envy dripping from her words. "That is the perfect complement to our gifts. You can persuade people to do things we need them to do. But only if the three of us are together will we be able to achieve our utmost strength. It is good that you've chosen to come with us so we can teach you everything you need to use your gifts to the maximum benefit."

"To the benefit of your nefarious endeavors, you mean." Mercy shimmered into view beside Cassie, floating a few inches from the floor as she aimed angry eyes at her sisters. "Always concerned about yourselves and your underhanded ways. Don't listen to them, Cassandra."

Hope and Faith cringed and flinched away from the agitated spirit. They recovered quickly, however, and sat up to defend themselves against their sister. Hope pulled her wand out, holding it at the ready.

"But they said they could teach me, Ma." She'd grown accustomed to having her mother spring into sight without warning. Confusion swept through her before she was blasted with a wave of disappointment mixed with concern from her mother. "What's wrong with that?"

"They'll teach you to depend on them and hold you in bondage to their wants and desires." Mercy spun around to face her sisters. "You can't have my daughter. She's not like you."

"But, Ma, if they can help—"

"I will teach you what you need to know." Mercy rounded on her and floated close, deep concern in her eyes. "Listen to me. They'll use you and your abilities to trick and hurt other people. You must not trust them. I did once but they lied to me and the results killed our mother."

Cassie blinked and frowned at her mother. "They said you killed her."

"Because Hope told me not to add in a key ingredient until later than the spell called for. Only, the spell was written correctly and she knew it. She wanted me to be blamed so that Father would…"

"Now, who's lying?" Hope stood and took two strides toward Mercy. "Don't blame me for your mistakes."

"I'm not lying." Mercy spun around in place, glanced at Faith's angry expression, and then crossed her arms. "I see you've convinced Faith I'm guilty as well. You don't want to take the blame but I know the truth."

Hope glanced at Cassie, a question in her eyes, before she looked at Faith. "Don't believe a word she says, sister. I told you she'd try to point the finger at someone else."

Mercy chuckled mirthlessly and shook her finger at Hope. "You lying witch."

"Stop it." Cassie sprung from her chair and glared at the three sisters. "I make my own decisions about my own life. I'm not going anywhere with anyone who can't be honest with me. The deal is off."

Trembling with anger, Cassie fled to her room.

Chapter Twenty-four

*T*he display of glassware behind the bar sparkled beneath the glow of many oil lamps around the dining room. Flint inspected the bar's surface, leaning to look at it from the side, and then polishing away a smear with a clean white cloth. His quick ride into town earlier that morning to pick up the mail had put him behind schedule. With the dinner rush looming, he must hurry to prepare for the next onslaught of customers. After word got around of the huge success of the cookery competition the day before, surely more people would want to sample the fare. He returned the cloth to the small rail it called home and tugged his vest down into place. The letter for Cassie in his inside pocket crinkled as if reminding him of its presence. Another brother coming most likely.

He shouldn't resent her brothers answering her summons. Seriously, he shouldn't. He sighed as he moved behind the bar to check supplies. Every time one arrived, however, he had to defend himself against their suspicions and disbelief that she would have anything to do with him. Giles accepted him but Abram still had reservations. He peered at the colored bottles, rearranging them so he could more easily take inventory. He heard footsteps approaching and straightened.

Cassie entered the room, carrying a large basket piled with table linens. The new uniform with the hem just above her ankles was attractive and fit perfectly, the dark blue fabric of the skirt hugging her slender hips as gently as one would hold a fresh egg. He hoped the customers would approve of the new look, because he found it flattering. She wore a white collared blouse beneath her pale yellow apron. She'd fashioned her hair into a chignon and added ear bobs to sparkle at her ear lobes. A rush of pride and love swept through him. She looked mature and capable in addition to being the most beautiful woman he'd ever seen.

"Cassie, I have a letter for you." He pulled the missive from his pocket and held up the tan envelope with a boldly scrawled address on the front. "When you have a moment."

"I hope it's one of my brothers." She placed the basket on the floor near the bar and took the letter from him. She perused the handwriting and then grinned as she opened it. "Daniel. I hope he's coming."

"I know you do." He braced his hands on the edge of the counter. "The new uniform looks nice on you. You did a fine job."

She paused in unfolding the sheet of paper to smile at him. "Thank you. Mandy said she liked having a nicer outfit to wear as well." She skimmed the letter and then nodded. "He's coming soon."

"Who's coming soon?" Abram crossed the dining room in several long strides, his brown boots thudding across the hardwood floor. "Silas?"

Cassie shook her head and handed him the letter. "Daniel."

Abram huffed and scanned the page in his fingers. "Sorry for the delay, sure he is. He probably overcommitted his time yet again like he's always done so he couldn't, you know, *possibly* get away."

"At least he's coming." Cassie snatched the paper out of

236

Abram's hand as Mandy appeared in the doorway with a basket of white tapers to put in the candlestick holders on the tables.

"Somebody coming?" Mandy sashayed toward the group at the bar with the flower basket hung over one arm. She wore her new uniform and had pulled her hair back with a pair of silver combs on either side of her head. She set the basket on one of the small tables in front of the bar and peered at Abram. "You sound like you don't want whoever it is to do so. What's the problem?"

"You don't know Dan like I do." Abram shook his head and then shrugged. "Or did. I haven't seen him in years."

"So he may have changed." Putting a hand on Abram's upper arm to fix his attention on her, Mandy gave him a patient grin. "Don't judge when you don't know."

"You don't like your brother?" Flint asked. There was no mistaking the doubt in Abram's eyes. "Am I missing something?"

"What are you guys talking about over there?"

Giles sauntered into the room, his dark trousers and red hunting shirt declaring he'd been out patrolling the grounds. Again. His casual gait suggested he hadn't discovered anything to raise an alarm. Cassie glanced sharply at Flint and winked. She'd apparently sensed his relief knowing the Guardian was on duty.

"Abram thinks your brother Daniel overcommits." Flint grabbed a mug and filled it with ale and handed it to Giles. "Here's something to wet your whistle."

"He does and thanks." Giles gulped several swallows and set the half-empty mug on the counter. "He wrote me last year to brag about all he's doing as a professor in Knoxville, the beautiful woman he'd been seeing, and all his volunteer work doing good for so many. Blech."

"He's a professor?" Cassie aimed a quizzical look at her oldest brother. "Of what?"

"I don't remember. I ignored most of what he said in the letter." Giles quaffed another mouthful of ale. "With all he's got going on, I wouldn't expect him to commit to help like we are."

"Don't make light of your brother's accomplishments." Mercy shimmered into sight next to Abram.

Abram took an involuntary step back, away from the ghost, then grimaced and returned to where he'd been standing. "Why not? He makes it sound like he had to fit us into his oh-so-busy schedule."

Mandy frowned and stared at Mercy. "Who is that? And where did she come from?"

"I'm his mother, that's who, and I abide here." Mercy gave Abram her haughtiest glare. "Where were we? Oh. Didn't you do the very same thing? In fact, your boss had to make you answer your sister's plea."

"Wait." Flint held up a finger to pause the conversation, a slow realization dawning inside. "Mandy, you can see Mercy?"

Mandy cautiously nodded, her eyes darting to each person in the group. "Why?"

Flint shook his head as the consequences of Mercy's visibility to those outside of family and friends ricocheted through his gut. "That's not good."

"We have a new problem, don't we?" Cassie folded her arms and firmed her lips.

"But how?" Flint angled his head, a frown on his face.

Cassie tapped a finger on her chin and then snapped her fingers. "She materialized earlier. Could that make her visible to everyone?"

"I guess so." Flint captured Mercy's attention with a finger pointing at her. "Which means you need to be circumspect as to when you pop in and out so you don't frighten away your husband's business."

Mercy smirked at him for a minute but then agreed with

a quick nod. "All right. I will try to behave for Reggie's sake, but no promises when it comes to my sisters."

"What are you talking about?" Mandy asked, confusion and dismay lacing her words.

Abram met Mandy's raised brows with a grimace. "I'll explain later. Right now, we need to sort this out before Dan arrives." Guilt flashed across Abram's features as he pressed his lips together and addressed his mother's ghost. "My reluctance to answer my sister's request stemmed from different reasons. I actually had people counting on the work I do." He shrugged at her. "Or did. I gave my notice."

"Is that what that letter was about?" Abram had shoved it into Flint's hands as he prepared to ride out earlier. "I wondered."

A blush crept up Abram's neck. "I figured it was time to let the senator know I wasn't coming back."

Mandy grabbed his arm and stared at him. "You quit your job? You're really and truly staying?"

"I really am." He kissed Mandy on the lips. "We can seriously explore a relationship. A future."

Mandy smiled at Abram, and Flint felt the familiar wash of quiet joy at another's happiness. The look they shared reminded him of how he felt with Cassie in his arms. Or merely standing beside him. Her very presence made him strive to be a better man.

Cassie crossed to her brother, as Mandy moved a little to one side, and hugged him. "Thank you, Abram." She pivoted to smile at Giles. "You too. I appreciate both of you staying and all you've done already."

"You both have made me proud." Mercy smiled at each of the brothers in turn. "I expect Daniel will, too."

Giles and Abram exchanged looks laden with disbelief and doubt. Daniel apparently left a different impression on different people. Helpful and yet not available when needed. Bragging and yet doing some wonderful things.

"In his own way and his own good time, maybe. I guess we'll see when he arrives." Abram took Mandy's hand in his. "Will you walk with me for a few minutes? I mean, before you have to serve this afternoon. I need to be honest with you about everything…" He glanced at Mercy and raised both brows.

"I guess that's my cue. Be nice, son." Mercy shimmered and vanished.

"Where did she go?" Mandy looked around the room and then back to Abram.

"I'll explain if you'll walk with me for a few minutes."

Mandy glanced at Cassie and then Flint. "What do you say, boss?"

"A few minutes." He shooed them toward the door. "But only a few. The rush will begin soon."

"Then I'll put out the cloths and napkins." Cassie lifted a pale green folded tablecloth from the basket. "Hey Mandy, I'll take care of the candles, too. That will give you a few more minutes."

"Oh, thanks." Mandy flashed a grin and waved as she and Abram left the room.

The young couple warmed Flint's heart. Mandy deserved a decent man like Abram. In fact, Abram had changed since meeting her. More relaxed, less of a dandy. Even his vocabulary had become friendlier and not so uppity sounding. A jolt of surprise made him grin. Flint actually liked him now.

"What are you smiling about?" Cassie stopped on the other side of the bar from Flint.

"Young love." He pointed to the mug in front of Giles. "Another?"

"No, thanks. I'm going to go take a nap or something until dinner." He indicated his sister with a tilt of his head. "Take care of her while I'm gone."

"Always." Flint retrieved the empty mug and put it on a tray with other used glasses. "As long as she'll let me."

Cassie tilted her head to one side, a mischievous grin on her lips, then sidled around behind the bar to wrap her arms around his neck and kissed him. Flint tensed from the sudden action but quickly relaxed into the experience. She closed her eyes and pressed her lips against his for several moments until Giles exaggeratedly cleared his throat.

Then she broke off the kiss and smirked at her brother. "What?"

Flint loved her and the way she and her brothers loved each other. Their presence and determination to see to her best interests augmented the few things he could do. Their special abilities would do even more. With yet another brother on the way, the question remained as to what other special skills would arrive with him.

Some tales are difficult to tell. Abram strolled up the hill toward the falls, Mandy at his side. He didn't know where to start the story he needed to tell. He held out his hand as they walked and she slowly placed hers in it. The warmth of her hand spread into his heart. It was only fair for her to know what exactly she faced if they were to have any hope of a relationship.

"You know the reason I came here in the first place was to pay my respects to my dead mother and to see how my sister fared." He waited for her nod and then continued. "What I discovered the day I arrived is that after she died, she didn't rest in peace. She haunts the inn."

Mandy squeezed his hand and pulled him to a stop. "Why? How?"

"I believe the 'why' is because she still needs to teach us about…" He shrugged and rolled his eyes. "It's so hard to say this to you, sweetheart."

She took his other hand and squeezed both of them. "I'm listening."

Such a normal morning with the sun shining above, a gentle breeze cooling his cheek. The surrounding countryside lay peaceful and serene. Yet inside of him turmoil and concern ruled the day. How would she react to what he was about to reveal not only about his family but about himself?

"I guess the best way to tell you is straight out." He searched her eyes and saw only patient curiosity in their depths. "My family...we're all witches. With special abilities that Ma is helping us learn about."

She clutched his hands as she blinked rapidly. "Witches."

"We didn't know because our parents kept it a secret from us."

"But your abilities? You didn't know about those either?"

"Ma bound our powers before they sent us out into the world to find our own way." He couldn't help the bitter sound his statement carried. "Only after she died did the spell break. Coming here is the only way I learned that I'm a shapeshifter."

"This is a lot to take in." She studied him, moistening her lips with a quick swipe of her tongue. "Should I be frightened by this information?"

"Not at all, my love. We are here to protect Cassie from threats we're still trying to understand." He squeezed her hands and then kissed her lightly. "And I'm still learning how to control my power. But you're not in any danger."

She frowned at him. "But you wanted me to move to the inn for my protection. From what?"

"Whoever is behind the killings of those poor women." If anything happened to Mandy he'd not be responsible for his reaction. Every moment he spent with her only served to deepen his affection. "It's safer for you to stay with us for a time."

He wrapped his arms around her. She nestled her head against his shoulder with a sigh. He held her for several moments, his heart swelling along with his determination to protect and defend his family. Including the woman close to his soul.

"One thing, sweetheart. You can't tell anybody about Mercy, nor about us being witches. Not everyone is so understanding."

She nodded against his shirt. "Does that mean your aunts are also witches?"

"Yes, and not very nice ones according to Ma. They are one of the threats to Cassie as well."

Mandy pushed away from Abram far enough to look into his eyes. "How many witches are there around here?"

"I'm not sure, honestly. Other than my immediate family, I know my aunts are. I presume others in my extended family may be. And then there's the Bakers, Haley and Tabitha."

Mandy widened her eyes to blink at him slowly. "My friend?"

"You didn't know." Maybe he shouldn't have said anything. Dang. That wasn't his secret to tell. "Keep it to yourself. Mr. Baker isn't a fan of witches from what Haley told me."

She tilted her head to peer at him for a long moment. "Is he one of the threats, then?"

"We don't know. Maybe." She was a sharp lady picking up on that thread so quickly. "I'm relieved you're not put off about all of this."

She shrugged and started walking back down the hill. "I've always believed there is more to the world than meets the eye. Why not ghosts and magic, too?"

"Very philosophical of you, sweetheart." He tucked her hand into the crook of his arm. "Just remember to keep our secrets, please."

"I would never do anything to harm any of you." She snuggled closer as they continued their descent. "Besides, who would I tell who doesn't know already?"

"Sweetheart, please." Concern swept through him at her flip comment. "I am very serious. I'm trusting you."

Many what-ifs flashed through his brain as the inn came into view below them. What if she let something slip when John Baker could overhear? What if she unintentionally raised awareness of the haunting of the inn? Or what if she decided she couldn't keep secrets and told a gossip? Flint would have his hide if anything happened to mar the inn's reputation and thus viability as a prosperous business.

"I won't let you down." She pressed against his arm. "I promise."

She'd promised and he felt he could take her at her word. But promises were often made to be broken.

Chapter Twenty-five

$\mathcal{T}$empting aromas drifted through the kitchen door to tease his nose and make his stomach rumble. Flint strolled into the kitchen, letting the door swing shut behind him. He inhaled appreciatively, bacon, fried potatoes, and baking bread combined to assail his senses. Even mid-morning the kitchen proved busy. He crossed to the work table as Matt briskly nodded a greeting while kneading bread dough on the floured surface, punching down the elastic white mound and then folding it over to repeat the process. Meg and Myrtle busily sliced and chopped various fruits at a side table to add to an immense bowl between them. Sheridan laid down the butcher knife and wiped his hands on his apron.

"Do you need something?" Sheridan pressed his palms on the table, leaning forward to gaze at Flint.

"Whatever you have for breakfast." Flint swiped a hand through the air. "It smells wonderful."

"Sure thing." He spun around and snared a plate from a stack on the sideboard. Then handed the plate to Flint and gestured to a ladle hanging by the fireplace. "Help yourself."

Flint accepted the plate and strode over to the simmering pots and pans positioned at different heights and distances from the cook fire. He mounded potatoes and bacon on the plate before spotting a pot of scrambled eggs keeping warm on a metal pedestal. Adding some of the fluffy yellow mixture to his breakfast, his mouth watered in anticipation.

"May I have a word with you, Flint?" Sheridan leaned against the table, arms crossed tightly. "In private?"

Flint looked up from inspecting the seasoning on the sliced potatoes to see the older man's serious expression. Sheridan had never looked so stern and determined. After the success of the cookery competition, he should be happy not solemn and brooding. In fact, the overwhelming response led Flint to consider making it an annual event. The sense of community and togetherness infused everyone with a happy glow. Except for Sheridan.

"In my office?" Flint moved to the sideboard to select a fork from a basket of clean utensils.

Sheridan removed his apron and laid it over a chair back. "After you."

Without a word, Flint started for the door, grabbing a clean napkin off the stack by the door as he passed. His thoughts spun as to the issue Sheridan wanted to discuss. Somehow they made it to the office and he set his plate on the desk with a longing look. Sheridan closed the office door with a soft thump and then turned to face him.

"Have a seat and tell me what's on your mind." Flint waved at one of the chairs in front of the desk.

Sheridan hesitated and then took the offered seat, perching on the edge of the wood surface. "I've been thinking hard about what Cassie told me about my wife."

Leaning back in his chair, Flint regarded the sober man. "What have you been thinking?"

"I've wondered about her and my boys for years. Now that my boys have found me, I need to find my wife. Their mother." Sheridan leaned forward, hands on his knees. "I want my family reunited."

"You want to go to Savannah?" Surprise and then dismay swamped his chest. "What about your job here?"

"Matt is a fine cook as he just proved. He'll manage in my place while Zander and I make the trip." Sheridan inspected Flint's expression. "I've saved my money all these years and now I have hope of freeing her and bringing her home."

"I'm glad to hear you don't intend to go alone." Flint raked his fingers through his loose hair and pressed his lips together to prevent the oath of worry escaping. Sheridan had every right to search for his wife now that he had an inkling of her whereabouts. He tried to imagine for a moment the anguish the man had felt for so many years without his wife. Tried to imagine not seeing Cassie or knowing her whereabouts for so long. Tried, but ultimately failed. How could he know? But he could support Sheridan in his quest. "I understand. We will, of course, miss you but I'd do the same if I were in your shoes. Go and good fortune."

"Thank you. We'll only be gone long enough to find her and bring her back with us." Sheridan cast a look around the office, out the window, and then back to Flint. "This is my home. I want my family to be here with me."

"I'll write Reggie and let him know you're coming and why." Flint stared at Sheridan for a long moment, envisioning his boss' surprise when he received the note in several days. "I'll give you the address of where he's staying before you leave so you can look him up when you arrive."

Sheridan pushed to his feet and Flint rose to his as well. "You're a good man, Flint. Take care of Cassie in my stead. She's vulnerable right now with all that's going on."

How much did he truly understand of the troubles surrounding Cassie and the inn? Flint had avoided sharing much with anyone except her brothers in hopes of controlling the situation. Sheridan, as her closest and staunchest friend, knew her best of any of them. A sudden thought drew concern to his brow. She'd not react well to having Sheridan absent for so long.

"She's my primary concern, so don't fret about her." Flint moved around the desk to address Sheridan more directly. "We'll all be looking out for her."

The big man nodded and turned to leave. He hesitated at the door to glance back. "I will find Pansy and bring her home. You've my word."

"I believe you. When will you leave?"

"Tomorrow morning." Sheridan's half smile apologized for the short notice. "We're traveling light and fast so not too much to pack."

"Then I'll take a letter to the post office this afternoon so Reggie is waiting for you." Two trips to the post office in one day but it was necessary. Flint rested the tips of his fingers on the desk, stabilizing his body as well as his concern over the rough and dangerous journey ahead of the two men. "Maybe he'll even have good news for you by the time you get there."

Sheridan grinned broadly and nodded. "From your lips to God's ear."

With that, Sheridan opened the door and strode away to pack his things. Flint stood still for several seconds rehashing the conversation filled with hope and risk. Moving slowly, he returned to his chair and sank down on it. He needed to write an urgent letter to Reggie and let him know he was soon to have company. That his premier cook was leaving the inn to risk life and limb and possibly even his freedom to locate his wife and bring her back. How long would he be gone? Would Reggie come back with him? Would he and Zander make it there and back safely? Reggie may react badly to Sheridan's self-proclaimed mission, of him abandoning his job for an unknown span of time. But he was his own person and could do as he pleased.

Flint had no reason to stop him or even ask him to delay, given how much the man had suffered by not knowing where his wife and children were for so many years. Matt would have to pick up the slack until his father returned.

His breakfast plate sat in the center of his desk, the eggs cold and hard. Shoving it aside, his hunger vanished, he pulled a sheet of stationery out of a drawer and grabbed up a pen. No point putting off the obligatory task. He quickly scratched the tip across the page then laid down the pen and dried the ink with a bit of sand. Folding it and putting it into an envelope, he addressed it with a slight tremor in his fingers. He held the letter between his hands and stared at it for several moments. Dragging in a breath, he pushed back his chair and hurried to the stable to saddle Buck and take the letter to the post office. He could only hope he still had a job after his boss received the letter.

"Do you enjoy working here, sweetheart?" Abram perused Mandy's lovely features, memorizing them so he could envision them when she wasn't around. "It's a lot of hard work."

"I do. I've met some very interesting people." She smiled gently at him as she squeezed his hand.

"Same here." He scanned the carriageway from where they sat together in the gazebo enjoying the morning coolness in the summer air. Before long, autumn would begin, but not for a few weeks yet. With good fortune, the dangers to his sister would be long over. If they could figure a way to ferret them out and end them. Preferably without anyone getting hurt. He met her happy gaze. "I'm glad I met you in particular."

The front door to the inn slammed shut. Startled by the incongruous sound, he glanced at the front porch. Cassie barreled down the steps and marched toward the gazebo, a book in one hand and a frown on her face. When she was within a few feet of the steps, she spotted them and hesitated.

"It's okay." Abram motioned for her to join them. "What's wrong?"

She huffed and flounced onto a hard bench. "Aunt trouble."

He swallowed the chuckle when she pinned him with her angry eyes. "Now what have they done?"

"They're pressing me to go with them when I've tried to make it clear I don't want to. Not after the three sisters accused each other of lying." She laid the book beside her on the bench. "I can't seem to make them understand."

"Want me to try?" Abram glanced at Mandy, gauging how much she followed the underlying meaning of his offer. She gave him a brief smile. He met Cassie's querying expression with one of his own. "We talked about what to suggest earlier."

"It may be the only way to stop this." She sank back against the seat. "Would you? I just can't face them again."

"If it will help you, then of course." Abram gripped Mandy's hand and then released it. "If you'll excuse me for a few minutes, you two can have a nice girl talk while I see what I can do."

He left the two women to chat as he strode back to the inn. In the entrance hall, he met Giles coming from the residence. He looked frustrated and worried.

Abram waved him to a halt. "Where are the aunts?"

"In their room, I believe." Giles scrutinized Abram's careful mask. "Why?"

"Cassie…" Abram ensured they were alone before continuing. "*She* needs to talk to them, if you get my meaning."

Giles raised his brows but merely nodded. "Be careful."

"I'll see if Flint will let me use his office for a moment."

The small quiet space so close to the aunts' room would give him a place to shift without startling or frightening anyone. And the location would ensure not only his privacy but also that nobody else would see him as Cassie.

"He's ridden into town so you have it all to yourself."

"Perfect." Abram left Giles staring after him as he quickly strode to the empty office.

He could hear his aunts talking in their room on the second floor, their voices rising and falling with heat and conspiracy. Or so he imagined. Soon, he'd put an end to their conniving and pressure long enough to devise a plan to end their interference once and for all.

Emerging a few moments later as Cassie, Abram adopted her rhythmic gait and mounted the stairs to confront his aunts. He paused outside the closed bedchamber door to suck in a calming breath and release it slowly. Then he recalled how angry Cassie had been when she joined him at the gazebo minutes before. Some anger would linger in her voice. He rapped on the door twice, sudden silence following on the other side.

The door opened slowly and Hope smirked at him. "Have you reconsidered?"

He lifted his chin a tad and glared at her. "Not entirely. May I come in so we can discuss this in private?"

Hope opened the door wider and ushered him inside. "Are you coming with us willingly or must we resort to force? That's the question."

Faith stood by the open window, her long gray dress swaying in time with her slight rocking from one foot to the other. He needed to convince them not only that he was his sister but that they needed to leave without her. Time and distance would give them a chance to work out an effective strategy and plan.

"As I've said repeatedly, I don't want to go with you. At least, not yet."

Hope crossed her arms and stared down her nose at him. "Because?"

"I need to speak with my father about several important topics." He glanced at Faith to gauge her reaction, and went on alert at the simmering ire in her eyes. He addressed Hope instead of thinking about the emotions behind her glowering expression. "And my other brothers are anticipated to arrive shortly. I must see them. You must trust me...to come later."

"How much later are you suggesting?" Faith sauntered across the room, one measured step at a time.

Thank goodness he was not an empath like his sister. Faith's regard evoked enough of a tremor inside without knowing exactly what she was feeling. Or what she intended to do to him if he refused on his sister's behalf. He swallowed the rising fear. "He's due by Allhallows Eve. Less than two months until I can talk with him about everything that has been happening. I need that time and opportunity before I can even think about leaving."

The two women exchanged a suspicious look before standing side by side in front of him, arms folded over their chests and glittering eyes searching his face for any sign of deception. They had intimidation down to a science. He focused on keeping a calm and sincere expression on Cassie's face instead of considering what they'd do if they uncovered the depth of ruse at play.

"And...and like I said, I asked my brothers to come pay their respects and Daniel and Silas haven't arrived yet." He swallowed nervously, role playing as best he could how his sister would behave. "I can't leave until after they do."

He prayed they'd hurry, too. What abilities did they possess which may assist in removing the pressures on his sister and the family in general? Only after they made their way to the inn could the brothers find out who could do what and how they could use that ability for their benefit.

His father, too, possessed powers they were unaware of and wouldn't discover until he did in fact return.

"I see." Hope continued to study him, her brows sinking into a frown. "You're saying you will join us in Montgomery, become part of a trinity of witches to perform powerful magic. But not yet. Is that right?"

"Yes. I can't go yet." Something in the glance Hope gave Faith had his stomach churning.

"Will you swear on the Book of Shadows you'll join with us?" Faith's intense stare slowly became a challenge. "Make the ultimate promise that if broken has dire and often deadly consequences?"

Another threat, but what else could he do? He swallowed again, buying time before he responded. "Deadly?"

"As long as you keep your word, my dear, you have nothing to fear." Hope arched a haughty brow at him as she waved a hand and evoked the mysterious Book of Shadows, holding the large black bound tome out in front of him. "Will you swear on the Book you will join our trinity after your father and brothers have returned to the inn?"

They'd cornered him. If he swore as Cassie, would the consequences apply to her? Or to him? He had no way of knowing how the spell would play out if he broke his promise. But he'd already sworn to protect her, which he'd do any and every way at his disposal. Since he was being forced to decide immediately, he had to assume he'd bear the burden of the oath.

He took a deep breath and laid his hand on the book. "I will."

Faith cackled with delight and smirked at him.

A flash of light preceded Mercy's ghost careering into sight and flying toward Hope. Dodging to one side, Hope barely escaped being knocked down. Faith backed close to the wardrobe and glared at the enraged ghost darting around the room.

"For pity sake, Mercy, stop acting like a child." Hope straightened her skirts and smoothed her hair. "The deed is done."

"I warned you to stay away from my daughter." Mercy vibrated with anger as she hovered near Abram. "You witches have no right."

"We have every right and you know it." Hope glanced between Mercy and Abram, a pleased look on her face. "Our work is done here, Faith. We shall pack and go home to prepare for Cassandra's arrival."

"Yes, there's much to do to be ready for her real training to begin." Faith peered at Abram through half-closed eyes, glee on her lips. "Write to us, my dear, and keep us informed of happenings here. I want to know the minute we can expect you at your new home."

Hope waved her hand again, the Book disappearing, the suitcases standing by the four-post bed, and the sound of harness and horses' hooves drifting through the window. The room had been turned back to its original mediocre appearance. "And please let our driver know we'll be down shortly." Hope speared Abram with the most autocratic gaze he'd seen.

Abram could only nod, mute in the face of what he'd promised and the power evinced by Hope's simple flick of a wrist as Mercy shimmered and vanished. Oh, how he longed to do the same. But first he had to confess what he'd done to the real Cassie.

Chapter Twenty-six

*A*bram waited for Cassie to meet him in the gazebo. The heat of the day had started to relent. The last of the supper rush had departed, taking their chatter and jangling harness with them. Quiet settled over the property, the chickens in their fenced coop, the dogs dozing on the porch, the pigs in their sty, the cows in their field, and the horses in their stalls. When he'd ventured toward Alabama and his sister, he'd never anticipated such a peaceful feeling. He didn't even miss the hustle and bustle of the city. Preferring to search for and slowly spot emerging stars in the cobalt sky.

"You're very at ease this evening." Cassie sauntered up the few steps and took a seat beside him. "All warm and gooey inside, hm?"

He scanned the pastoral scene before him once more. Delaying the difficult conversation as long as possible. "Surprised?"

"Somewhat, but this place seems to work its magic on those who visit." She perched on the edge of the seat, angling her body so she could look directly at him. "What did you want to talk about?"

So much for delaying the inevitable. He tensed and pushed back to sit up straight. "I told you about why our aunts left so precipitously."

"Yes, they're waiting for me to join them…" She widened her eyes as she studied him. "You're suddenly very much on edge. What did you do?"

"I promised to protect you any way I could, right?" Her slow nod encouraged him to continue posthaste. "That's what I did."

"What aren't you telling me, Abram?"

Confessing to her what had transpired proved much more difficult than he'd thought. So much uncertainty rattled around in his brain as to what the ramifications might be and who would pay the price if the vow were broken. On the other hand, what might the benefits be if the vow were kept? By him or Cassie. A certain amount of temptation to discover what more they didn't know niggled in the back of his mind. His mother's warnings tempered the desire but it remained.

"They wouldn't leave until I swore an oath on the Book of Shadows." He searched her eyes, hoping for understanding. "That I—you will join them to form the trio they proposed."

"Oh, Abram…" A tear appeared and clung to her lashes. "If I don't go?"

He pressed his lips together and then swallowed. "I don't know exactly. Aunt Hope only said there are 'dire and deadly consequences' if the vow is broken."

She clutched her hands together and studied him for several moments. "What exactly did you promise?"

"I will join them after Pa and our other brothers arrive here." Abram bit his lip as her dismay claimed her features, her mouth fell open and her eyes clouded. "I bought us time but there's more."

"Such as?"

"I don't know if the vow is mine or yours. So if you go instead of me, does that break the vow and put you in danger when they discover the ruse?"

"They are expecting me. They want me." She shook her head slowly as she tried to sort out the ins and outs of the promise. "I wouldn't think they'd harm you if I go. As long as they have me they should be satisfied."

"But the spell… It doesn't care about that. It only cares that I made the vow and I must keep it." He dragged in a long breath. "So I will go as promised which will keep you safe from them."

"What a mess. If I go, you may be hurt or punished for breaking the vow. If I don't go, they're not going to stop coming after me and may still hurt you." She stilled, her eyes turning inward for a several beats before pinning him with shock. "What if the consequence is death? I can't lose you now."

He gulped back the rising bitter bile at her words. "I wouldn't put it past them to resort to such drastic measures."

A rustle in the grass drew his attention to where his sweetheart approached the gazebo, a bemused expression on her face.

"Another deep conversation I'm interrupting." Mandy halted at the base of the steps. "May I join you?"

"If it's okay with Cassie, I think it would be a very good idea for you to know what's going on."

Cassie let out a small sigh and nodded. "Come on up."

Mandy walked slowly up the few steps and hesitated before moving to sit on the bench to one side. "What were you talking about?"

Abram summarized their previous conversation and the dangerous situation they faced. She listened, hands clasped, eyes wide, as he talked, Cassie filling in details here and there.

"So, we need to figure out what we do now to keep

everyone safe." Abram stood and went to sit beside Mandy, taking her cold hand in his. "I know we've talked about being together and I want that more than anything. But I'd understand if, now that you know everything, you changed your mind."

She sat quietly for a minute, staring at their hands. Then she looked at Cassie until she shrugged. "That's really everything?"

Cassie nodded. "As far as we know anyway."

Mandy met Abram's worried gaze. "Haley had told me the Fairhopes are special." She laid her other hand on top of their joined ones. "I didn't know how special until I met you."

What a remarkable young lady. Not only lovely and hardworking, but smart and brave as well. The two most important women in his life waited for him to say something. All he could think about, though, was finding some way out of the quandary he'd created with his rash promise. He needed to consult with someone who knew more about spells and curses than they did. His mother had not been much help with details and he was reluctant to trust her reaction when it came to her sisters. She'd already proven she would rather fight than argue with them. Which meant waiting for his father to come home like he'd already promised to do.

"I love you both and promise to do my utmost to keep both of you unharmed. Will you trust me to do so?"

Both women agreed with a nod as Mandy squeezed his hand again. One thing he couldn't deny. Coming to the Fury Falls Inn had changed not only his life but also his heart. He'd realized how superficial his life had been and taken the necessary strides to be more real and personable. Came down off his high horse to become grounded in who he wanted to be. He didn't even bother to glam away his little scar anymore. It was part of who he was and would always be. A reminder of his humanity and imperfections. But most importantly, he'd found the woman he wanted to spend the rest of his life with and rediscovered the love he'd always felt for his sister.

The dreaded moment arrived. Cassie stood on the front porch, staring at the barn door. In mere moments Sheridan and Zander would lead their mounts out and soon be on their way. He'd forgiven her for withholding the information about Pansy, understanding her reasons at long last. Tears smarted at her eyes but she blinked them away. She wouldn't let her dear friend know how upset she was by his departure. His understanding ear would be sorely missed. For how long though?

"Hey, sweetheart." Flint slipped an arm around her waist and pulled her close. "Are you all right with this?"

"I have to be." She spotted Matt easing through the inn's door and coming toward where they stood. "Do you wish you were going, too, Matt?"

Matt stopped beside her and shrugged. "Yes and no. I would dearly love to see my mother but we can't all go and leave the inn without a proper cook."

"They'll bring her home." They would find the woman, free her any way possible, and return with her father. She had to believe as much. More than ever, she needed to have a conversation with her pa about her future. So much was at stake she didn't know how to address. Her heart said one thing but her head debated every option.

Giles and Abram appeared around the corner of the inn, strolling together in deep conversation as they neared the steps. Her heart sang at having her brothers home with her. She respected their privacy by not attempting to reach out to read their emotions. Besides, she knew they were content with their choices and unwavering in their resolve to keep her safe. She hadn't understood how much they cared about her prior to their aunts coming for a visit and then attempting to recruit her, using her own curiosity against her, to their nefarious intentions. Thankfully, she'd seen through the ruse and hadn't gone with them. But that didn't mean they'd given up.

"Hey guys, what's up?" Flint called to the two men as they paused at the base of the steps.

Abram darted a look at Giles and then started up the steps. "Just discussing possibilities."

"We need to strategize and plan for what might happen in the coming weeks." Giles reached the top of the steps and moved to lean against the column, regarding Cassie with kind yet serious eyes.

She lowered the barrier and absorbed the love and concern wafting from her brothers. The steely determination in her oldest brother and the hint of regret mixed with hope from her other one. Her Guardian and her stand-in when she needed one. Knowing the other two brothers, with unknown powers, would likely come gave her hope as well for a successful end to the threats aimed her way.

"I know I messed up, but at least the immediate danger from Aunt Hope and Aunt Faith has been mitigated." Abram crossed his arms and scanned the faces of the group. "Right?"

Giles shook his head slowly, his gaze drawn to the barn and then back. "But there's still a killer on the loose and our aunts have certain expectations that will need to be met one way or another. We can't let our guard down."

"I think Barney may have a lead on the killer but he wouldn't share details with me when I was in town the other day." Flint hugged Cassie's waist, pulling her close in a protective gesture.

"I can't imagine I'm in danger from a random killer." Cassie stared at Giles for several seconds. Perhaps he could explain why they all seemed to think her at risk of being killed in her own home with so many others around. "Can you?"

"Until we know the motivation behind the killings, every woman is in danger." Giles straightened away from the column.

Movement in front of the barn drew Cassie's attention away from Giles to see the two men leading their horses across the circular drive. Actually, the two chestnut geldings belonged to Zander and Matt, but Matt had let his dad use his for the auspicious journey. The time really had come, finally ending the suspense building inside. Sheridan wore a crisp red collared shirt, blue jeans, and brown leather boots, a wide-brimmed hat on his head. Zander had copied Giles' look with dark jeans and a loose red hunting shirt hanging about his hips. Black cowboy boots and a matching wide-brimmed hat completed his outfit. Both horses had saddlebags and bed rolls in place, further indicating the length of the trip ahead of them. Cassie swallowed the tears threatening, unwilling to have them on her face as the last thing Sheridan saw before riding away.

Tying the reins to the hitching rail, the two men climbed up the steps to join the growing group of friends. Mandy emerged from the inn and stood with Abram, a question in her eyes as she surveyed the tense expressions. Cassie drew in a breath and hurried over to Sheridan.

"I hope you have a safe trip, my friend." She hesitated in front of him and then couldn't stop the impulse to hug him. She may never see him again. "I'll miss you."

He briefly returned the embrace and then gently set her away from him, his expression somber. "Do not worry. I'll be back, and with good fortune have my wife with me."

"We're going to find my ma and your pa, Cassie." Zander slipped his hat from his head and held it in one hand beside his leg. "Then bring them both home where they belong."

"The sooner the better." Flint eased over to stand with Cassie, taking her hand. "But we'll all miss you both. Especially Matt, I'd imagine, as he takes over running the kitchen."

"My kitchen." Sheridan glared at his son for a long moment and then smirked. "When I get back. Take care of it, will you, son?"

"Yes, sir." Matt nodded once, eyes shining, and then held up his index finger. "Speaking of which, I need to get to work or we won't have enough food ready for the dinner rush this afternoon."

Sheridan quickly crossed to Matt and gave him a brief hug. "You're a good man. I'm proud of you."

Matt's eyes glittered with unshed tears as he nodded silently and then went inside. Sheridan watched until he'd moved out of sight and then turned back to face the group. "Well, I guess we should be off."

She wanted to cry out against him leaving but she quelled the childish desire to throw a tantrum. He had to go. Hope burned inside him, obliterating all other emotions except for the immense love of his family. His wife. Cassie could not and would not stand in the way of his search for his missing Pansy.

Before he returned, her other brothers would surely arrive. Then her pa would come back and her family would all be reunited as well as Sheridan's. It would be quite a homecoming when that day arrived. But it couldn't occur without the sad departure about to happen.

She lifted her chin and forced a smile to stiff lips. "It's time you go find your woman, Sheridan." She glanced at Zander's gentle expression and then met Sheridan's twinkling eyes. "You both be safe and write when you can. Let me know what you find when you get to Savannah."

"I will find a way to send word, Cassie. Don't you fret." Sheridan turned and addressed the group. "Take care of her while I'm gone. Like I know you will. She's very precious to all of us."

"We will, don't you worry." Flint drew Cassie close again, wrapping an arm around her shoulders and holding one hand. "I'll make sure of it."

She snuggled against his shoulder, surrounded by friends and family all working to secure her safety. The love flowing around her warmed her heart and soul. "Bye, my friend."

Sheridan motioned to Zander and the two men traipsed down the steps and took up the reins of the horses. They swung into the saddles and reined away from the porch, trotting down the lane without looking back.

"I hope he finds Pa and they can indeed find Pansy." Cassie stared after the retreating figures, a small cloud of dust drifting up behind them. "Do you think Pa will be surprised to see them?"

"Not if my note gets there first." Flint squeezed her shoulders. "They'll be fine, you know. They're grown men, and Zander is used to traveling."

"He is." Giles cleared his throat of emotion from the touching farewells. "I'll miss my friend, too, sis."

After the two men rode out of sight, Cassie sighed. "Well, there's nothing for it but to get back to work. Shall we?"

Flint pulled her into a full hug and spun her around to face him. "Before we do that, let me say one thing."

"Okay..." The mirth in his eyes drew a wary smile to her mouth.

"We are all a family here." He scanned the others, intense Giles and fervent Abram and optimistic Mandy, then aimed his twinkling eyes at her. "No matter who comes and goes, you have us and we have you. More importantly, I have you in my life and I want you to always stay there."

"I hope that's where I'll stay." Her smile sobered. "But we can't predict the future."

"No, but we can plan for it." His gaze encompassed the entire group huddled on the front porch. "Together."

Her brothers regarded her without a word, though she sensed their commitment and their love for her. Abram took Mandy's hand and tugged her closer, his growing feelings for her evident in his tender look. Both he and Giles had met someone dear since coming home. Their destiny come to pass? Would Daniel and Silas discover their true destinies by answering her request? Only time could provide the answer to such a question. But she had the answer to another important one.

She reached up to lightly kiss Flint's lips. "Together we're stronger and smarter."

"We'll find out how much stronger and smarter after Dan gets here." Abram surveyed the group with a solemn look. "And Silas, of course." He hesitated and then continued. "It will be good to see them, see how they've grown and matured."

Giles nodded slowly as he met Abram's eyes. "You turned out all right in the end. Let's hope they did, too."

"I'm not sure I can handle two more of you guys." Flint grinned impishly at the two men. "You're going to have to help me."

Cassie chuckled as the tension in the air dissipated. "We'll help each other. That's what we do. That's what a family does. Together we can handle anything. You'll see."

Flint searched her eyes for a moment and then kissed her. "Yes, I guess we will."

She snuggled close, embracing her beau as well as her future, uncertain and unknowable, but hers.

The End

Thanks so much for reading *Desperate Reflections*! The adventure continues, so stay tuned for more to come in this six-book series.

To find out about new releases and upcoming appearances, please sign up for my newsletter via my website at www.bettybolte.com. I send out a monthly newsletter with book news to share with my readers, upcoming events and signings, and even a few favorite recipes, puzzles, and other doings!

I'd love to hear from you! Feel free to send me an email at betty@bettybolte.com, find me on Facebook at www.facebook.com/AuthorBettyBolte, follow me on BookBub, or connect with me on Twitter @BettyBolte.

You can always find an updated list of the titles in this series, as well as all of my other books, at www.bettybolte.com.

Thanks again for reading!

Made in the USA
Middletown, DE
03 August 2021